JUDGE DREDD
ECLIPSE

His ribs singing with pain, Dredd tried to scramble to his feet as the leader jetted across the distance between them. His STUP-gun had fallen out of arm's reach when he'd been thrown, and now unarmed and injured, he saw the blocky shape of the armoured suit coming at him like a guided missile.

Dredd's suited fingers closed around something by his side, and by reflex he pulled it from the moondust to brandish it like a spear. Unable to stop in time, the leader impaled herself on the spike, and Dredd rammed it home through her faceplate, turning it into a window of red ruin. She slumped backward into a heap, and only then did Dredd realise what he'd used as a makeshift weapon. Lanced through the suit's helmet was a steel rod that ended in a metallic flag of Stars and Stripes.

Judge Dredd from Black Flame

#1: DREDD vs DEATH
Gordon Rennie

#2: BAD MOON RISING
David Bishop

#3: BLACK ATLANTIC
Simon Jowett & Peter J Evans

More 2000 AD action

ABC Warriors

#1: THE MEDUSA WAR
Pat Mills & Alan Mitchell

Strontium Dog

#1: BAD TIMING
Rebecca Levene

Judge Dredd created by **John Wagner & Carlos Ezquerra**.

Chief Judge Hershey created by **John Wagner & Brian Bolland**.

Judge-Marshal Tex, Judge-Marshal Che, Arthur Goodworthy Jr. and Mister Moonie created by **John Wagner & Ian Gibson**.

Judge Kessler created by **John Smith & Paul Marshall**.

JUDGE DREDD

ECLIPSE

JAMES SWALLOW

For Adam, Ashley, Jael, Jim, Scott, Mark and Luffy, John, Nick, Toby, Andy and the Big Finish crew, all of you laws unto yourselves.

Acknowledgements:
With thanks to John Wagner, Ian Gibson, Mike McMahon, Brian Bolland, John Smith, Paul Marshall, Rob Williams and Pete Dougherty for their portrayals of Judge Dredd and Luna-1 throughout the history of 2000AD.

A Black Flame Publication
www.blackflame.com

First published in 2004 by BL Publishing, Games Workshop Ltd., Willow Road, Nottingham NG7 2WS, UK.

Distributed in the US by Simon & Schuster, 1230 Avenue of the Americas, New York, NY 10020, USA.

10 9 8 7 6 5 4 3 2 1

Cover illustration by Colin Wilson.

ISBN 1 84416 122 6

A CIP record for this book is available from the British Library.

Printed in the UK by Bookmarque, Surrey, UK.

LUNA-1, 2126

1. MOONFALL

Calvin Spinker hated the Moon. Hated it. Hated, hated, mother-drokking, spugging, snecking hated the big airless ball of dirt with every fibre of his being. He hated the way that you'd bounce like a low-rent Boing freak if you forgot to wear gravity boots or stepped clear of a street with g-plates. He hated the stupid mock seasons they had inside the Luna-1 domes, with synthi-snow, sprinkler rains and holographic rainbows. He hated how every damn thing imported from Earthside cost ten per cent more than the drab local produce, and some days he swore he'd wreck the next servo-bot that offered him a "Moon Pie" at the Eat-O-Mat.

But above all, the thing Calvin Spinker hated the most about the Moon was the air.

It had this sickly smell to it, see, this kinda plastic tang that reminded him a little bit of burning insulation or melting plasteen. It was everywhere. He couldn't take a breath without the stink being right there in his nostrils. He'd tried nose filters, strong cologne, even breathing through his mouth for weeks on end, but nothing could make the smell go away. If Calvin thought hard enough about it, he would start to feel sick. He knew that out there in the airless wilderness of the lunar plains there were domes half-buried in moondust where the stale, used breath from millions of Luna-cit lungs was being sucked in and reprocessed. Then they pumped it back out, used it to supplement the raw oxygen that was flown in by astro-tankers, and channelled it back down to where Calvin could breathe it again. Back down to here, to Kepler Dome on the outer rim of Luna-1's conurbation. The top-level domes, places like Kennedy, Armstrong and Lovell, of course they would get the pure new air straight away. Not the reused gases he was breathing – no sir, those rich fat cats with their thick stacks of credits, they got the fresh air. Spinker hated them too, now that he considered it.

Sometimes Calvin would get giddy thinking about how many times the breath he was taking in right now had been recycled, scrubbed and sent around the system. How many lungs had it already gone through? What sort of people had tainted it before he got it? How the hell was anyone going to stay sane when all they had to live on was second-hand air?

For what must have been the millionth time in his life, Calvin thought about going home, getting back to Earth and starting over somewhere where you didn't have to pay to breathe in and out. Okay, maybe the air wouldn't be that clean, but at least it would be free. You see, he hadn't chosen to live in Kepler. He'd been on the Moon reluctantly clearing up a divorce settlement with his stupid ex-wife when Judgement Day had happened. Spinker had been trapped here, stuck without a place to stay or anywhere to go. He didn't know the ins and outs of it, but Calvin understood in his vaguely moronic way that back on Earth, some weirdo from the future – this guy called Sabbat or something – this dingus had made the dead rise from their graves and start tearing up stuff. He still remembered the day he walked into the Luna-1 starport only to be told that all flights to Earth had been cancelled "due to zombie infestation". When he asked the robo-clerk when the next shuttle to Mega-City Two would be leaving, the machine told him simply: "That destination no longer exists."

It wasn't until a day later he found out what that actually meant. MC-2, his home, a massive city-state that covered most of North America's Western Seaboard, was gone, nuked out, vaporised. Overnight, he was a refugee. So Calvin was forced to stay in Luna-1 and eventually the city council found him a one-pod hab in Kepler. And there he sat, day after day, nursing his hatred and breathing in this repellent, germ-laden air.

But today, Spinker looked up from his cup of cold synthi-caff and something like confusion crossed his greasy knot of a face. Confusion, because he couldn't detect the stinky stale smell any more. Confusion, because the oxymeter in the ceiling of his hab that rattled around the clock had gone silent. Calvin stood on a chair and held his hand underneath the air vent, feeling for the telltale trickle of cool breathing gas that forever cycled through it.

Nothing. Not a single breath.

Then Calvin Spinker started to panic, and as his vision started to fog as carbon dioxide filled the cramped little bed-sitting room, he found himself desperately wishing, praying, pleading for just one more lungful of that hated, loathsome air.

While Calvin and his neighbours choked to death, a different kind of panic was rising in a frenzied tide on the streets outside the apartment block. Ernesto Diaz did his best to hide beneath the counter in his corner café and not wet his pants.

The morning had begun like any other. Ernesto had climbed down from his Komfy-Koffin capsule bed in the roof space and rolled open the shutters to declare Diaz's Hotties open for business. He'd had the usual thin crowd of early risers and a few grey-faced workers on their way to the zoom terminal that would take them into the city proper, off to toil in the mines or the oxy cracking yards. By mid-morning, he had the mock-meat sausages on the grill sizzling up a treat, and he was filling the dispensers with synthi-mustard and thinking about the lunchtime rush; it started then. He happened to look out the window, noting with studied disinterest a lone Judge outside the vacant store near the pawn shop – she'd rousted a couple of go-gangers and had them cuffed to a holding post. Ernesto frowned. He didn't like those punks, but he had to admit they'd done him a big favour by setting fire to the local branch of Luney Lunch.

Across the street from Diaz's store was a holographic billboard that was forever on the fritz. This week it had been running a recruitment advertisement for one of the ice mining concerns down in Clavius, but the braying voice of the announcer choked off in mid-sentence and the screen disintegrated into a storm of flickering pixels. Ernesto caught it out of the corner of his eye and looked up. A new image appeared on the billboard screen, a computer-generated cartoon character with a stylised moon for a head. It winked – right at him, so it seemed – and spoke in a chatty, conspiratorial manner. Every word the 'toon spoke was repeated in a ticker-tape stream along the bottom of the screen.

"Hey friend," it began, and now Diaz was sure it was talking to him. "Where do U go if U want 2 know what's up, up, up? Lemme tell U. Right here! Right now! Listen up, up, up! Moon-U has all U need to know, no matter what the Big Helmets say!" The little figure now sported a T-shirt with the words "Moon-U" emblazoned on it, and he struck a comic pose as a bumbling parody of a Luna City Judge ambled on screen. For a second, Ernesto looked around and saw that everyone on the street had stopped what they were doing to watch the billboard. From his vantage point at the café counter, he could see the Moon-U cartoon appearing on another public screen up at the Sagan Street crosswalk, and repeated here and there in the windows of the discount electrical store and on the back of some juve's telly-jacket.

"Shuddup!" drawled the caricature Judge in a thick Texas City accent, listing back and forth as if he was drunk. "Ya little runt! I ain't lettin' you flap yo lips–"

Moon-U gave Diaz a broad wink and out of nowhere produced a massive hammer that had the words "ten tons" written on it. Unbidden, hysterical laughter bubbled up out of Ernesto as the moon-faced figure used it to flatten the comic Judge into a bloody pulp. Someone chortled. "Yeah! Right on! Smash those Judges!"

Diaz saw the female Judge on the street corner speaking urgently into her belt mic.

"Quick! I gotta tell U before they get me!" Moon-U hissed urgently. "The Judges never did a thing for U, did they? And now they're gonna cut off the air!"

A ripple of anger and fear spread through the audience, and Diaz felt his heart tighten. Suddenly, strident voices were shouting.

"They can't do that! Stinkin' Judges!"

"They never liked Kepler, just 'cos we ain't a rich dome–"

"If those sneckers come down here, we'll bust 'em in the head–"

"They always pick on us! We gotta show them!"

"Ooh no!" cried Moon-U, and he pointed up at the dome ceiling hundreds of metres above them. "Look out!"

Like everyone else on the street, Diaz had looked up, and there he had seen something that made his blood run cold. At the very crest of the transparent glasseen dome, just as there was in every Luna conurb, a disc-shaped oxygen processor managed the airflow for Kepler, a train of green indicator lights forever marching around its base to signify its safe operation. The green lights winked out one by one and turned red. A muffled klaxon hooted: the air-warning siren.

Ernesto suddenly felt sick with fear. He stumbled back into the café, the mustard jar falling forgotten from his nerveless fingers. His mind was racing, caught in a whirl of emotions. Just seconds ago, he'd been laughing inanely at the cartoon without a care, but now he felt like his world was coming to an end. His head swam with nausea and anxiety.

He gripped one of the counter stools for support and dared to take another look out into the street.

Ernesto had a ringside view.

A cluster of citizens had surrounded the Judge. They were jeering at her and waving their fists; even one of the cuffed punks on the holding pole dared to lash out at her with a swift kick. Diaz couldn't make out what they were saying, but the meaning was clear. The Judge drew her daystick in a single fluid movement and brandished it in a wide arc, stabbing at the air with her free hand. Whatever she said appeared to have no effect; some of the people grabbed pieces of garbage and threw them.

The Judge blurred; Ernesto heard the high-pitched crack of the stick as it broke bone, and one of the citizens spun away trailing blood, hands pressed to a ruined face.

"Gee, that was a nasty thing 2 do," said the billboard.

With a roar, the crowd surged forward and the blue-black of the Judge's uniform vanished under a dozen kicking, punching, yelling bodies. Ernesto had to choke back bile when he saw something ragged and bloody – a limb, maybe? – go arcing up into the air to land on the pedway.

The screen began to show pictures, images from street cameras in different parts of Kepler, places that Diaz recognised like the zoom terminal, the shoplex on Clarke Avenue, the free clinic. There were people brawling everywhere, not just picking on Judges, but each other, fights breaking out all over as buried rivalries and petty disputes were given sudden, bloody purpose. He watched as the guy from the used droid place on the corner strangled some ugly kid with his bare hands, slamming the boy's face into the road over and over even after it was clear he was dead. Ernesto threw up and stumbled behind the counter to conceal himself, trying not to choke on the sickly cooked smell of the frying hotties.

He lost track of time; all he could hear was the rolling murmur of the mob outside, incoherent shouts and snarls melding into a landscape of violent noise. Glass broke and people screamed. Once, a brick shot over his head and smashed the bio-lume sign over the counter, showering him with flecks of plastic. Then there was a new sound that joined the rioting: the staccato popping of gunfire.

Diaz knew that sound all too well. He'd grown up in Banana City where the law of the spit gun had been the only law there was, but he had got out, gone to the Moon and found a life that, while not exactly better, was just a little less lethal. But now that sound brought it all flooding back to him, and Ernesto's gut knotted.

He took a careful look over the top of the counter and saw someone brandishing a pistol, cracking off shots at random, shooting out what windows were still intact or putting rounds into fleeing figures. The street, which before had been a decrepit permacrete avenue lined with dull little shops and limp moon-palm trees, was now a war zone. Cars were burning, sending palls of sooty smoke up to cluster in a thick disc at the apex of the dome, consuming vital draughts of oxygen. Plasteen lay in drifts around the yawning shop fronts and here and there dead bodies were lying like knots of discarded rags.

Ernesto flicked a glance up at the billboard, where images of the rioting continued to cycle, over and over. The only constant was the Moon-U logo, a laughing lunar face, in the bottom right corner. The man with the gun paused and fiddled with the weapon, and Diaz felt a sneer forming on his face. The half-witted idiot couldn't even work a snecking spit gun! What kind of moron was he? Without realising it, Ernesto drew up from behind the counter and moved to the door of the café to get a better view. The acrid smoke from the flaming cars tickled his nostrils with the scent of burning battery chemicals. His jaw hardened and a new bloom of hatred blossomed in his chest, hot and fierce. Clearly this jerk-o with the gun had no idea how stupid he was! Firing a gun inside a sealed dome, how idiotic was that? Sure, it would be a million to one chance that a bullet might penetrate a weak spot and cause a blow-out, but who would be Munce-brained enough to risk it?

Diaz's fear melted away and in its place was anger, pure and simple. His hands closed around the hilt of the knife he used for chopping up the hotties and he strode out into the street, spitting in fury. "Hey! Stupido! You wanna get us all killed?"

The gunman glanced up at him. "Get lost," he snarled back, and then he noticed the name of Ernesto's café on the cook's apron. "Diaz's Hotties? You're Diaz?"

"Yeah!" Ernesto brandished the knife, feeling potent and deadly. "What you gonna do about it, pendejo? I'm gonna cut you up and cook you!"

The other guy laughed nastily. "You know what? Your hotties suck, man. I liked Luney Lunch much better."

The gunman's comments made Diaz see red and he launched himself at him, swearing and stabbing. The cook plunged the knife into the other man's chest, his face splitting with a savage grin as blood spurted. All that Ernesto wanted now was to tear this fool apart and paint the street with his innards.

There was a crack of sound and Diaz reeled away and fell on his backside. He felt like a robo-horse had kicked him, and his right shoulder sang with burning hot pain.

The cook looked down to see a crimson patch growing around a blackened entry wound.

The gunman took a shaky step toward him, one hand clutching at the hottie knife still in his ribs, the other holding the smoking gun. "Y-you... You types. You think you're better than me, just 'cos you got a job." Blood trickled from his lips. "You ain't gonna look down on me no more. Not now I got me this." He nodded at the spit gun.

Ernesto tried to get to his feet. The flat of his hand fell on something angular and metallic – a pistol. Without hesitation, Diaz gripped the weapon and brought it up, pointing it at the gunman in a shaky, inaccurate grip.

"You dumb spug!" spat the gunman. "Lookit what you got there. That's a Judge's rod. You can't fire that!"

The cook never took his eyes off his target, but he could see the bulky shape of the weapon in the periphery of his vision. The gun must have been tossed aside when the mob was busy taking that lady Judge to pieces. A small flicker of memory tickled at the back of Ernesto's mind, something important, something about a Judge's gun, but he shook it away. Angry thoughts crawled around the inside of his brain like a troop of ants, scratching for a way out, blanking out everything else. "Shut it! You can't tell me what to do, jerk-o!"

The gunman grimaced and pulled the trigger. The spit gun's hammer fell on an empty chamber with a hollow click. "Ah, sneck–"

Ernesto growled, teeth flaring in a feral grin, and fired as well. In the instant his finger tightened on the electronic trigger mechanism, his mind threw up the thing that had been nagging at him. All Judges' guns had a key characteristic in common: a tiny computer-scanner combination that checked the palm print of any person attempting to fire it. If someone other than the designated Judge pulled the trigger, a countermeasure was activated. In some models, this was a simple safety catch or an electro-stunner, but like the pistols used by Mega-City Judges, firearms issued by the Luna-1 Justice Department had a self-destruct charge fitted to them, equivalent in power to a hand grenade. The gun's detonation killed both men instantly, leaving two more shredded corpses to litter Kepler Dome's streets.

On the electronic billboard overhead, Moon-U broadcast a replay of the moment across the whole complex, repeating it on any screen that the pirate signal could infiltrate.

Judge Spring cursed inwardly as the low battery buzzer sounded on his sonic rifle, just as a smoke-blackened rioter vaulted over the plastiform barricade. Without wasting a moment to swap out the power pack, Spring flipped the weapon over and used the heavy butt to crack the lawbreaker across the face. "Get back, meathead!" he snapped and the rioter fell away, unconscious.

Spring reloaded by touch alone, scanning the open plaza in front of the Kepler precinct house for any sign of a new rush towards the barriers – but no, the citizens seemed happy enough to continue tearing into one another or smashing up property. The Brit-Cit Judge frowned. This wasn't like any typical confront or Block War, there was just no direction to it. It was nothing but wanton destruction; violence for the sake of violence.

He spotted movement close to the flickering panels of a cracked wall-screen and called out to his deputy on the line, a female Judge from the Sydney-Melbourne Conurb. "Kenzy! Watch for any group movement."

She nodded. "On it. Where's that electro-cordon?"

He opened his mouth to answer, but a new voice interrupted him. "Spring! Where are you?" The Brit-Judge stepped back from the barricade as Senior Judge Koenig approached, emerging from drifts of grey smoke with a group of men in riot gear. Koenig was Sector Chief for Kepler Dome and Spring's direct superior. Spring had grown to respect the elder Luna-City officer during his secondment to the Moon and knew him well enough to read the grim set of his chin.

"Judge Koenig. Glad to see you brought reinforcements, sir. I hope they're not all you've got."

"Save it, Spring," Koenig snapped irritably. "What are you still doing here? We can't just hold the plaza, we need to move in and pacify."

"With respect, sir, we're spread too thin. Ten patrol Judges dead or incapacitated out in the field, a dozen more in med-bay. The citizens outnumber the rest of us fifteen-to-one and we can't chance using riot foam or stumm gas until the oxygen supply is reactivated. I put in a call for cordons and Mantas from the main dome, but–"

"But they're not going to get here for another four hours, at least," Koenig broke in, seeing the Brit-Judge's jaw drop. "I've just come from the zoom terminal. Rioters sabotaged the track, the train has blocked the tunnel and we've had a blow-out in the zipstrip to Luna-1. We're on our own."

"Grud," mumbled Kenzy.

"We need to crush this, before it gets out of control," Koenig added.

Spring felt his annoyance flare. "Look around!" he grated. "It already is out of control!" He took a step closer to the senior Judge. "We've got the lowest manpower and hardware capability of any outer dome on Luna and we're coming apart just holding these crazies in place!"

"Then maybe you should have been aware of this before it even happened! You're my sector deputy! Where are your street skills?"

"Maybe if you got out of your office once in a whi–"

Kenzy shouted, her voice mingling with the sound of a high-powered spit carbine: "Sniper!"

With a keening ricochet, a bullet deflected off the crown of Koenig's helmet and the elder Judge cursed. "Drokk!" In a swift movement, Koenig's pulse gun was in his hand and he cracked off a trio of well-aimed shots. On the far side of the plaza, a man clutching a rifle fell out of a tree and lay still. Koenig looked back at Spring, the sudden anger that had been building between them dissipated for the moment. "Where are they getting these weapons from? This doesn't make sense. I'd expect panic from an oxygen outage, but not a full-blown street war."

"Surveillance has had absolutely no indicators of any serious tensions for the past three weeks. It's like someone just pushed a button and got a riot, sir."

Koenig paused for a moment, considering. "All right, Spring, we'll do it your way. Bottle them up and let it burn itself out."

"Incoming!" called another Judge from further up the barricade.

"How many?" said Spring.

"Uh… All of them."

Koenig and Spring turned together to see a wall of figures boiling out of the entryways and into the plaza. Spring raised the sonic rifle and took careful aim, searching for obvious ringleaders.

"Form up!" Koenig shouted, his voice carrying over the line. "Set your STUP-guns to maximum stun. Knock them down!" The Judge flicked a glance down at his own pulse pistol and checked the charge. "Hold the line!"

Chief Judge-Marshal Tex flicked off the comm-screen with a grimace and pushed back the hat on his head, rubbing the furrows on his brow. From his office at the pinnacle of the Luna-1 Hall of Justice, the entirety of the Moon's largest city-dome was visible as a vast network of lights. Thousands of towers, bridges and sub-spheres all clustered beneath a huge silver-grey roof. From this height, Luna-1 looked like some intricately worked piece of jewellery, set in a cratered stone landscape. Kepler Dome was just barely visible, to the south west beyond the Armstrong Monument and the skyscrapers of Von Braun Territory. From such a vantage point it was hard to imagine that Kepler's streets were alive with violence and flame.

"We could consider a Class One contingency," Tex's second-in-command, Judge-Marshal Che spoke quietly, his soft Mexican accent carrying across the room.

Tex removed his hat and shook his head. "A domewide lockdown? I reckon that'd be a death sentence for anyone still in Kepler."

"We have to keep it contained, Chief Judge," Che insisted. "This is the worst incident yet. If word spreads that we can't keep a lid on our own citizens–"

"What?!" Tex snapped. "You think the Triumvirate will come in here and fire us? Send us to Titan?" He shook his head wearily. "The day we took these badges we swore an oath to protect this colony." Tex tapped the star-and-crescent-moon shield on his chest. "I'm not gonna put myself before that. Not ever."

"So what do you propose?"

"We're fallin' apart up here and we know it, Che. We need help to get to the heart of this and I know just the man to ask."

Che's eyes widened. "With all due respect, sir, I must protest–"

"Protest all you want, amigo. But just get me a secured line to Chief Judge Hershey at the Mega-City One Grand Hall o'Justice."

2. THE DAY SHIFT

The deck of cards unfolded into a fan before the young woman's face and she found her attention fixed on their glittering, shiny surfaces.

"Watch and be amazed!" intoned the magician, his eyes flashing darkly from under his top hat. "Choose a card, my dear, but don't show it to me."

The woman did as she was asked, ignoring the sneer on the face of her boyfriend. She took a careful look at the card. "Okay!" she chirped.

She was a little excited to be getting involved with the street performer's act. It was nice to be the centre of attention for a change, as all the other people gathered around stopped to watch what was happening. Foot traffic across the Barry Waffle Plaza was slowing as more and more citizens drifted over. With nearly ninety per cent unemployment among the six hundred million-strong population of Mega-City One, anything that broke up the boredom was a big draw – even something as simple as a person doing card tricks.

The magician made a deep murmur in his chest and extended a hand toward the concealed card. "You chose… the three of diamonds."

"Ohmygosh! Yes! Yes, I did!" She held up the card and showed it to the audience, who clapped and smiled. All of them except her boyfriend.

"Is that it?" he griped. "That's the best you can do?"

The magician fixed him with a practiced glare. There was always one who wanted to make trouble. "Would you like to see something else then, sir? Another demonstration of the incredible powers *of the mind*?" He gave the last words an echoed emphasis, thanks to the hidden sub-dermal resonator taped to his larynx. "So be it."

That gave the guy pause, but he quickly overcame it and snatched the deck of cards from the magician's hand and shuffled them. Picking three at random from different parts of the pack, he held them away. "Okay, smart guy. You tell me what I got here, eh?"

The magician had to fight to hold off a smile. "You doubt me? Then perhaps you'd like to place a little wager on my abilities? Say, twenty credits?"

"Sure!" the man snapped, fishing a banknote out of his pocket. "You ain't no psyker, and I'll prove it!" A couple of other folks in the crowd waved money as well, eager to test his skills.

"We shall see." The performer gave a broad wink to the rest of the audience, who chuckled. I've got these mugs eating out the palm of my hand, he told himself. The magician concentrated again and closed his eyes. A collective gasp arose from the watchers as he slowly began to rise off the pedway until his feet were just barely touching the perma-crete pavement.

He fixed the boyfriend with a hard look and spoke in a deep, sepulchral voice. "You have in your hand the queen of spades, ten of hearts and..." he gave a wry smile, "the joker."

To the man's irritation, the magician was completely right. The money was gone from his fingers in a flash and the performer nodded to himself. Where none of the marks could see it, a small optical imager was fixed to the inside of his hat, using a low-power laser to project a readout into his eye. Micro-thin circuits inside the cards transmitted their location to the hat and the imager relayed that to the magician; he didn't even have to look at him to know exactly what the guy was holding. "And now, I will stagger your imaginations with a new illusion that will confound your very reason itself!" Surreptitiously, he touched a control disguised as a cuff-link that powered up the short-range teleporter built into his kneepad; next, he'd do the pull-a-card-out-of-thin-air trick, maybe by 'porting it into the girl's blouse.

He looked back at the audience and saw that all of them, even the boyfriend, were silent and awe-struck before him. This is gonna be sweet, he told himself, I'm gonna milk these fools dry!

"Watch, as I exhibit powers that no mortal man could ever hope to achieve!"

And then from behind him, a voice all gravel and hard edges said, "I'll be the judge of that."

The magician's feet hit the ground and he whirled around. Too late, he realised that his audience hadn't been cowed by him. They were looking at a two-metre tall sentinel clad in midnight blue and adorned with gold armour pads. Colour drained from the performer's face and he felt his bladder loosen as he caught sight of the name on the Judge's badge: *Dredd.*

"Uh... uh," he managed.

Dredd extended his gloved hand. "Street performance licence?"

The magician looked dumbly at him.

"He conned me outta twenty creds, Judge!" said the boyfriend. "Bet me he could read my mind!"

Dredd gave the mark a brief look. "Betting is illegal, citizen. You're under arrest, one year in the cubes." He tossed a cuff-clip at the guy and waited. The boyfriend showed uncommonly good sense, meekly putting on the restraints and stared at the ground. "As for you," Dredd took a step toward the performer. "I'm guessing you don't have a licence."

The magician suddenly found his voice again and raised his hands in defiance. "You cannot hope to, uh, defeat me! I have uncanny powers of the mind!"

"I don't think so," Dredd retorted flatly. Unknown to this loser, a pair of real Psi-Division operatives were working a block away on a murder case and the presence of any real, unlicensed telepath would have registered with them like a flare on a dark night. "Fraud, unauthorised street perfor-

mance, gambling… Anything else to add before I take you
and that chump there downtown?"

In reply, the magician jumped into the air, rising up and
away, gaining height with every passing second. Dredd's
hand darted forward to grab the hem of his overcoat, but the
material ripped and fell away, revealing a small grav-pack on
the performer's back; the kind that kids used for aeroball
games.

"He wasn't levitating at all!" cried the woman.

Dredd watched the flyer wobble his way across the plaza.
The grav-pack wasn't designed to hold an adult's weight and
the motor was straining. It would be a simple shot for the
veteran Judge, a single standard execution round from his
Lawgiver pistol and the perp would come crashing to earth –
but instead he just watched and waited.

When the magician was about seven metres high, the grav-
pack belched smoke and spat out a nasty cloud of smoke.
The performer gave a strangled yelp and dropped like a
stone, tumbling head over heels to land in an ornamental
fountain. Dredd hauled the magician's dripping form out of
the water and slapped a pair of plastiform handcuffs around
his wrists. "Read my mind," he said.

"Uh, I'm… under arrest?"

"Six years. You can practice your card games in the cubes."

Lacking a convenient holding post, Dredd tethered the two
men to a bench in the plaza, where the local catch wagon
would scoop them up on its next pass through the area.

His helmet radio crackled into life. "Control to Dredd.
What's your location?"

"Waffle Plaza, east exit."

"Investigate reports of armed robbery with violence in
progress, Mobi-Cred Autobank, heading west on Dave
Fincher Overzoom."

"ARV, copy. I'm on my way." The Judge mounted his Lawmaster bike, sparing a glance up at the wide highway that
passed over the top of the plaza at the twelve-storey level.
There, on the city's high-velocity traffic lanes, massive computer-controlled transporters and mobile homes – mo-pads –

roared along at speeds of over three hundred kilometres per hour. A large proportion of Mega-City One's population lived on the roads, never settling in a single place, constantly circling the metropolis in a vast, unceasing migration. Where there were people, there were also schools, shops, leisure facilities and even banks, built into mobile platforms following the course of the massive twenty-lane megways that formed the transport arteries of the city. But, like the static buildings they flashed past every day, they were just as prone to crime.

The Mobi-Cred resembled a big, fat bug on eight clusters of wheels, low to the highway and broad enough to take up two lanes. A docking platform to the right allowed foot traffic to step off another moving vehicle and board, while a small slip-ramp enabled groundcar drivers to use a drive-thru terminal. Right now the mobile bank was cruising much too fast for anyone to disembark, thanks to a hasty reprogramming job at the hands of one of the Dexter gang. Up to now, that had been the only thing that was going right about the robbery.

In the bank proper, it was hard to see clearly. A low fog gathered around the knees of Big Dave Dexter and his men, making their legs cold and forcing the bank staff and customers to huddle together to keep warm where they sat on the floor. It was still raining inside, thanks to the small cluster of storm clouds that floated near the ceiling. Big Dave made a face and gave his cousin Larry a blunt look.

"How much longer?"

"Couple o' minutes, I reckon." Larry hefted the large, complex-looking rifle in his hand and patted it with a smile. "I set this to 'Sunshine' and burned off the vault locks."

"First thing that snecking piece of junk did right so far." Dave grumbled. "Why we couldn't just have used a plasma torch–"

"This is better!" Larry broke in. "What, you wanna be known as 'the plasma torch gang'? What kinda name is that? I told you, we got to have ourselves an identity. A gimmick, else we're just plain old bank robbers."

"Plain old, cold bank robbers," Royd, Dave's younger brother chimed in. "Plain old cold and *wet* bank robbers."

Larry was getting irritated. "You little spug! I didn't quit my job at Weather Control to listen to you whining! You're gonna be singing a different tune when we're all over the vid-news! Think about it, 'Judges Fail to Capture Weather Gun Gang'. It'll be great!"

"Uh-huh," said Royd, who then sneezed.

Dave's attention wandered to the drive-thru window and what he saw made his eyes widen. "Hey, you guys! We got company!"

Larry followed Dave's outstretched hand and saw the distinctive shape of a Lawmaster weaving between the trailing traffic, closing on the Autobank. "Crem! We ain't ready to go yet!"

"Royd, get Joe outta the vault," snapped Dave. "We'll take what we got and scram."

"No way!" said Larry, twisting the control setting on the weather gun to "Chill." "I'll deal with this. We take it all, right? I mean, we don't want to look like amateurs when they show us on *MC-1's Most Wanted*."

"Dredd to dispatch, am approaching with caution. Get traffic control to set up a roadblock at the Bleeker off-ramp. I'll deal with this."

"Control here, that's a roj."

Gunning the Lawmaster's engine, Dredd brought the bike in line with the drive-thru ramp and hesitated, calculating the angles of approach. Movement at the rear of the mobile bank caught his eye and a figure emerged from cover, the bulky shape of a weapon in his hand. Without conscious thought, Dredd's training took over and he veered the bike out of the firing line, just as Larry depressed the firing stud.

An actinic flash of blue light leapt from the muzzle of the weather gun and struck the road with a crackling discharge of energy. Where it hit, rimes of ice instantly blossomed into existence, spreading over the asphalt in a broad fan. Super-cooled air buffeted the Judge as sleet and snow formed around him. Dredd gripped the handlebars grimly and worked the bike with his knees and arms, turning into a fierce skid as the Lawmaster's Firerock tyres lost purchase on the road. Dredd was dimly aware of wheels screeching behind him as mo-pads and robo-trucks spun out on the ice field. Larry hosed the weather gun across the road, painting white swathes of frost along Dredd's path. Any second now, the Lawmaster would flip over and send its rider tumbling along the highway at hundreds of kilometres per hour; it was a chance the Judge refused to take.

Dredd revved the Notron 4000 engine and aimed the bike squarely at the Autobank's rear. Spitting wet slush and chips of ice, the Lawmaster rocketed forward, even as inertia dragged it down. Dredd coiled his muscles and pushed off the saddle, arms outstretched. For one agonising instant, he seemed to be suspended in mid-air, and the next, his gloves caught on to a maintenance ladder and held. The Judge hauled himself up to safety, turning in time to see his bike vanish beneath the wheels of a massive roadliner. Pausing to draw his pistol, Dredd considered the Lawmaster; how many of them had he lost in the line of duty since his first days on the street? Fifty, sixty? It would mean more paperwork to complete when he returned to the Sector House at the shift's end – but for now he had more important concerns.

Working his way over the vehicle's hull, Dredd dropped down on to the drive-thru ramp. A wrecked robot lay in a sizzling heap, torn out from one of the teller's stations and in a corner, the Judge found an injured man, his face and hands lobster-red from what appeared to be sunburn. "How many in there?" Dredd asked.

"Fuh-four, Judge. One of 'em got me with a huh-heat ray."

"Stay put. Help is on the way."

Dredd crouched and made his way towards the bank entrance. Parked on the exit ramp was a sleek Korvette Slabster on auto, doors open, the engine idling. Taking aim with the Lawgiver, Dredd selected an incendiary round from the magazine.

. . .

"I lost him!" Larry shouted. "He went around the back!"

"I saw the bike go. He's gotta be dead," Big Dave added, as Joe and Royd emerged from the vault. Joe had two large carryalls in each hand, the zippers straining to hold in the wads of currency and Dave forgot all about the Judge when he saw them.

Joe Dexter's face was split in a grin. "First thing I'm going to get me is one of those luxy-apts in Central. Then a face change, make me look like Conrad Conn…"

"You won't be getting nothing if that Judge is still around!" spat Royd. "Where's the getaway car?"

Big Dave opened his mouth to answer but the words he spoke were lost in the sudden report of an explosion from the vehicle ramp. Larry's jaw dropped as he caught sight of the car vanishing in a puff of orange flames. Joe clutched the moneybags like long-lost children and Royd swore. None of the Dexter gang were looking the right way when Judge Dredd came through the doors at a run, picking out his targets.

He gave a mandatory challenge. "Weapons down, creeps! I won't ask again!"

"Take him out!" Dave shouted, firing off a round from his shot-blaster.

Dredd ducked and rolled, coming up behind a display screen and fired on the move. "Leg shot!" The standard execution round cut a supersonic course across the bank and shattered Big Dave's left kneecap, exiting the other side in a puff of blood. The eldest Dexter crumpled, screaming.

Royd fired wildly, his autopistol chattering, bullet discharges chewing through plasteen wall panels and blasting apart desks. Some of the citizens and bank staff cried or whimpered, trying to lose themselves in the thin mist.

Dredd shot back at Royd, but the perp was quicker, dodging behind a pillar. The Judge watched as the gunman he'd encountered earlier ducked out of hiding to grab at the bags of cash.

"Spug off!" Joe hissed. "We go together or not at all, Larry!"

Larry Dexter made a pained face and reset the weather gun to "Gale". "Fine. We'll blow this helmet-head out the door!" He pulled the trigger and a concentrated blast of air boomed from the rifle, blowing a hole in the glasseen roof.

Dredd was ready when Larry's head popped up from cover and he fired; the bullet creased Dexter's cheek and embedded itself in the delicate electronics of his weapon. Larry tensed as the weather gun arced and vibrated. Without any intervention on his part, the gun's control switched over to "Hurricane" setting and hummed into life once more.

The weather gun coughed out a cone of force that tore across the inside of the bank, scattering papers and anything else that wasn't tied down into a vortex of racing wind. Larry held on to the weapon as the discharge slammed him back into Joe and sent the carryalls flying. The bags tore open and a storm of credit notes rippled into the air.

"Grud, no! The money!" Royd yelled, his gun falling away as he desperately tried to grab at armfuls of fluttering cash.

Larry struggled to deactivate the weather gun, but the weapon's gravity-energy coils were red-hot with overload and it continued to spit out a whirlwind inside the confines of the bank. Dredd wedged himself behind a stanchion and held on as the gale tore at him. Outside, a trail of debris spewed out into the Autobank's wake, thousands upon thousands of credits streaming into the air.

Royd hugged a million or so to his chest and grinned, but only for a moment. The edge of the continuous blast from weather gun caught his legs and threw him upward. Dredd watched the perp go tumbling past him in a mess of flailing limbs, up and out of the hole in the roof. The Judge's jaw hardened; the next victim could be an innocent.

Summoning all his strength, Dredd braced himself against the wall and aimed his pistol at Larry Dexter. It took just one shot.

"Armour piercing," Dredd shouted over the wind and the audio-selector in the Lawgiver obeyed, chambering the round. The bullet struck home, cutting through the weather gun's power core and into Dexter's chest. Like a switch being flipped, the miniature hurricane died away and drifts of paper and banknotes settled to the floor.

Joe Dexter swore and held up his hands in surrender. Beside him, Larry was coughing up blood but was still alive. "Joe! Joe!" he choked, his voice urgent.

"It's okay, cuz. You'll be fine," Joe said wearily, as Dredd cuffed him.

"Who cares about that?" Larry managed. "We got busted by Judge Dredd! That means we'll get on *MegCrimeWatch* for sure!"

The Mobi-Cred came to a halt at the Bleeker Street roadblock and Dredd found an H-Wagon waiting on the megway. The traffic control supervisor, Judge Evans, nodded at the blocky aircraft. "Got a call from Justice Central while you were busy in there. Chief Judge Hershey wants you in her office. Expedite immediate."

"I'm the arresting Judge. I need to stay on site until the situation's locked down."

"Negative, Dredd. I've been told to take over here. That H-Wagon will get you to the Grand Hall."

Dredd grimaced; he didn't like leaving a job half-finished, but orders from the Chief Judge were not to be ignored.

"Look on the bright side," Evans continued in a dour voice. "At least you won't have to do the paperwork. You won't have to be there when accounts division hear you let a few million credits blow over the whole of Sector 40. That honour's going to be mine."

Dredd shrugged and made his way over to the flyer. "It's an ill wind…"

Hershey steepled her fingers and gave Judge Chapman a level gaze. "This situation…" she said carefully, "has all the makings of a political nightmare."

Chapman nodded, stroking the thin stubble on his chin. "Agreed, Chief Judge, but I don't see that we have a choice. The request was made. We can't ignore it."

"No. But let's face it, Dredd's last trip to the Moon wasn't exactly a roaring success. A dead Psi-Judge from Casablanca. A viral outbreak."

"Oh yes, that zombie doppelganger business," Chapman grimaced. "But that was seven years ago. Things have changed a lot since then, what with the expansion of the Triumvirate council and the global partnership treaty–" His sentence was interrupted as Hershey's intercom beeped.

"Judge Dredd to see you, Chief Judge."

"Send him in."

Chapman stood as Dredd entered, as a mark of respect for the senior officer. Dredd gave him a cursory sideways glance and nodded to Hershey. "Reporting as ordered."

"Take a seat, Joe." Hershey indicated a chair. "Sorry to pull you off duty in the middle of a watch, but we've got something that requires your specific attention." The Chief Judge ran a hand through her hair, brushing the dark strands out of her eyes. She seemed fatigued, Dredd noticed. The pressures of the high office were no doubt taking their toll on her – the woman who had accompanied Dredd on the quest to find the Judge Child was long gone now and in her place was a seasoned veteran, older and wiser but still showing the same iron-hard resolve. "This is Chapman, Space Division. He's here to provide some additional background."

"What's the situation?"

Chapman touched a control on Hershey's desk and the lights dimmed as a holo-projector in the ceiling came to life. "Space-Div has been monitoring increases in incidents of large-scale armed violence across the Luna-1 colony over the last few months, but we haven't been in a position to get involved, not without stepping on the toes of a dozen other city-states around the world."

Dredd watched as a hologram of the Moon formed, with markers pinpointing confronts all over the lunar territories. "So, what has changed?"

"This morning, Justice Three intercepted comm traffic from an outlying complex, Kepler Dome," said Hershey. "The place was in flames. Then an emergency call was placed via encrypted channels to Earth from Luna-1's Judge-Marshal Tex."

"Tex…" It had been more than twenty years since Dredd had served his time as Luna-1's Judge-Marshal and on his recommendation it was Tex who had been installed as the colony's permanent Chief Judge. So many things had happened on Earth in the meantime – the Apocalypse War, Necropolis, Judgement Day – and through it all, the proud Texan lawman had retained his post as governor of the lunar city with a reputation for fairness and strength. "If he's calling us for help, the situation must be grim," Dredd said.

"Actually, he's calling *you* for help," Hershey noted. "Marshal Tex contacted the Triumvirate council and specifically requested the assembly of a Judicial task force under your direct command, to assist the Luna Justice Department with the current crisis."

"Because Luna-1 is an international zone, the team will be drawn from five of the signatories to the partnership treaty." Chapman worked the projector controls and the image of the Moon was replaced by a map of the world, with the cities that were party to the treaty picked out in green. "East-Meg Two have selected a Judge from their Kosmonaut Directorate and the Pan-Andes Conurb have sent a man as well. You'll be joined by representatives from Brit-Cit and Simba City when you reach the Moon."

Hershey held out a datapad. "I've made arrangements for your caseload to be transferred, Dredd. Your briefing is in here. Get your gear and report to Kennedy Starport. You've got a seat booked on the next NEO-Clipper to Union Station.".

"Why me?" Dredd asked. "Last time I set foot up there, the Luna Special Judicial Service tried to finger me for murder. I doubt they'll be happy to see my face again."

"You gave Tex his job, Dredd. He respects you and, more importantly, he trusts you."

"But there's more to it than that, isn't there?"

Chapman frowned. "Space-Div's intelligence unit has heard rumours that there are cracks forming in the global treaty. There's a chance that elements inside the international community are working to destabilise Luna-1. I don't have to tell you how valuable lunar territory is now, especially with the discovery of those new titanium deposits. If the Triumvirate... If *Tex* can't hold it together up there, things could get real ugly real quick."

"He wants you, Joe, because he knows you'll put the law above politics," added Hershey.

Dredd got to his feet. "When do I leave?"

3. UNION STATION

Dredd felt the familiar sensation of artificial gravity as he stepped down from the airlock and into the dock terminal. The floor curved away from him in a low slope in both directions, disappearing into the roof – or so it appeared – from his perspective. Like a lot of the larger Near-Earth-Orbit platforms, Union Station was a spin habitat, turning along its axis to provide gravitation for the transient population that passed through its halls. The Judge was familiar with the transfer procedure and made his way to baggage reclaim, snagging the heavy armourplas diplomatic case that contained the majority of his equipment, including his Lawgiver.

On a Freeport orbital like Union, Dredd had little jurisdiction to speak of, and in accordance with international space law the use of any projectile weapon he might carry was forbidden. The penalty for discharging a ballistic firearm on an orbital was quite severe, as he recalled – if convicted, the guilty party would be placed in an airlock and vented to space. Death by Lethal Ejection, they called it. Dredd approved: in an environment where one stray bullet could lead to the deaths of thousands from explosive decompression, the law had to be an effective deterrent.

The passport control droid scanned his ident card with a ruby laser beam, the thread of light flicking across his face and his badge. It paused as it examined the holo-pic on the card. "This doesn't show your face. Could you take your helmet off, please?"

"No." The force put into that single syllable made it clear Dredd would not tolerate an argument.

"Oh." The droid considered this, then decided not to press the point. "Business or pleasure?"

This time Dredd didn't even bother to reply.

"Business it is, then." The robot handed back the card. "Enjoy your stay."

Beyond the terminal, the station opened up into a vast, hollow cylinder, walls rising up to meet in an arched "ceiling". For the most part, Union Station was a waypoint; a place that people stopped at on their way to somewhere else and the interior reflected this. Much of the habitat was given over to eateries, capsule hotels and arcades full of stores. The scents of cooking, human sweat and other, less identifiable smells, mingled in the air.

The station had a slightly shabby look to it. Developments in single-stage-to-orbit rockets and trans-shuttles in recent years had meant that the higher-paying passengers going interstellar didn't need to use NEO transfer stations any more, but there were still droves of ordinary citizens who took suborbitals from EasyMek or SpaceTrain, heading out to the Moon or leisure stations like Bacchus at the LaGrange points. People from dozens of nationalities swarmed back and forth in broad rivers of bodies, breaking apart like frightened shoals of fish to filter into food bars or down the entryways into the departure lounges. A troupe of Sino-Cit eldos back from the spas on Ceres filed past a delegation of Uqquan traders from planet Qu, while a rowdy group of Oz skysurfers traded lewd stories with a party of dustboarders bound for the Martian sand-seas.

Dredd surveyed the crowd with a practiced lawman's eye. A place like this would be paradise for a tap gang or a pickpocket, but as he watched he saw little that set off his internal radar. Overhead, small oval watch-drones flitted about looking for troublemakers and, now and then, Dredd caught sight of a Duritz Securi-Bot ambling through the concourse. Dredd had little time for robot law enforcers – his encounters with the Justice Department's troublesome Mechanismo units had seen to that – but perhaps in an environment like this, machines were the best solution. He watched the droid as it clanked past him, a stun pulser at the ready in its grippers.

The chronometer overhead chimed the hour and Dredd took a moment to purchase a cup of synthi-caff in the waiting area; the dry, recycled air in the clipper had left his throat parched. Sipping the drink, he saw a flash of movement in the periphery of his vision.

A woman yelled something in Hindi that sounded midway between a curse and a sob, as two shapes vaulted away from her in opposite directions. A pair of juves, both with the wiry gait of orbit-born spacers, had grabbed her bags and bolted. They clearly knew the patrol schedule for the Securi-Bots – the area was clear of them – and they were sprinting for the drop tubes to the lower levels. Without putting down the caff, Dredd gave his case a swift kick and sent the container sliding across the plastic floor toward the closest thief. The juve ran straight into it and went flying, the lower gravity of the station granting him a graceful arc through the air just moments before he collided with a waste bin and crumpled into a heap.

Dredd finished his drink and strode over, recovering his case as he passed it. The thief was out cold. Dredd scanned the area to see if he could locate his partner, in time to see a figure in a helmet and a red rad-cape come from out of nowhere and drop-kick the second perp. The other thief took the hit hard, but didn't go down. Instead, he produced a wicked-looking knife from a wrist holster and made a savage swipe at his attacker. Spacers liked to fight with blades and melee weapons; there was no chance of a blow-out with a knife, a sword or a tonfa. The caped figure dodged the blade and stepped into the perp, planting a hard left cross to his cheek. The thief thrust the knife forward in a stab, but the other person drew the blade into the folds of the cape and twisted it, disarming him in one single action. Good technique, Dredd noted.

The caped figure gave the thief no pause and brought up a knee to strike him squarely in the crotch. Winded, the second perp dropped to the floor in a whimpering heap. Dredd took a handful of his thief's jacket and dragged him back to the victim, returning her bag. The caped figure did the same and only when they were closer did he recognise the outfit. The red and black cape was fastened securely at the throat with a bronze shield that bore a cluster of Cyrillic letters and the face beneath the bullet-shaped helmet reflected Dredd's own impassive gaze. It was probably the first time in Dredd's career he could ever recall sharing an arrest with a Sov-Judge.

The East-Meg officer gave him a nod – acknowledging a moment of shared purpose beyond national boundaries – and Dredd returned it, turning the criminals over to a brace of Securi-Bots that had belatedly arrived on the scene. He noted the small symbol of a stylised rocket on the Sov-Judge's uniform, the sigil of the Kosmonaut Directorate.

"Kontarsky?"

"Judge Nikita Kontarsky," she began, removing her helmet. "It is an honour to meet you, Judge Dredd." Her bright green eyes gave him a challenging look from a face framed with ice-blonde hair.

Dredd returned her appraising gaze. Justice Central's files had only had the vaguest details about the officer who would serve as his deputy on the task force, thanks to the typical East-Meg penchant for utter secrecy. Kontarsky was a high-flier in the Sov's space program and an expert in interplanetary law. But what the file had failed to mention was how young she was. The Sovs had sent a rookie. Looks like they're not serious about assisting Tex, he thought.

"I was approaching you when I noticed the crime unfolding," she continued smoothly. "I considered you would excuse a delay in our meeting in order for me to deal with it."

"Where's our third man, Rodriguez?"

Kontarsky pointed to the far side of the terminal plaza, where a dingy bar was situated. "There. He arrived just before you did." She paused. "May I speak freely, Judge Dredd?"

"There's little point in you being part of my team if you don't," Dredd answered as they walked.

"I believe that Judge Rodriguez may be unsuitable for this taskforce."

"Oh?" Dredd said. "What is the reasoning behind your assessment, Kontarsky?"

"His attitude is not... I feel he may not be a dedicated enough officer."

Dredd gave a cynical snort. "'Dedicated' is not a word you'll often hear applied to a SouthAm Judge."

Kontarsky chewed her lip as they entered the bar. Dredd spotted the Judge from the Pan-Andes Conurb at once, in close conversation with a female in a spacer's jumpsuit.

"Real big shot, chica, you understand?" he drawled, unaware of Dredd's approach. "It's a tough job, but when my brother cops on Luna called me, I had to come to their aid, you see? I, Judge Miguel Juan Olivera Montoya Rodriguez, am in charge of a special Judge squad and we're going to–"

"Do what?" Dredd grated.

Rodriguez turned a casual smile on the Mega-City Judge. "Hey, Dredd. Amigo. What a pleasant surprise." He held out a hand. "I heard a lot about you, man. It's a pleasure to be working with you."

Dredd ignored the offered handshake and eyed the glass on the bar. "Don't tell me you're drinking on duty, Rodriguez."

"What, we barely say hola and already you're busting my cojones? Don't forget, this is a Freeport, man. I don't have to follow your Mega-City rules."

Dredd nudged the half-full glass toward him. "Drink up, then. Go ahead, give me a reason to send you back down the well."

The SouthAm Judge's bluster faded as he realised Dredd meant every word and he gave a sheepish shrug. "Hey, well, it's just an eye-opener, you know? Those stratoflights, they really take it out of you. Look, Dredd, no need to kick me out before we even get Moonside, eh?" He gave the spacer girl a look, but she had clearly lost interest in him and stepped away. "Hey, chica, where you going?"

"You see my point now, Judge Dredd?" Kontarsky said.

Rodriguez sized up the female Judge with a leer. "Oh, hey. Maybe I can forget all about her and talk to you instead, eh? You look a little young for that uniform, though."

Kontarsky's eyes narrowed. "I am a fully qualified law officer of the glorious East-Meg State and a graduate of the Soviet Kosmonaut Academy," she growled, "and my age has no bearing on that fact!"

"Right," Rodriguez smiled. "So how many times you been into space, then?"

She bit out a reply. "This is my first assignment off-world."

Dredd frowned. Terrif. A wet behind-the ears Sov and a Banana City chancer. This team was shaping up to be a real set of aces. "I don't have time for this. Both of you, listen to me carefully, because it's the one and only time I'm going to say it. I'm in charge of this task force and I expect everyone in it to behave like a professional. If I see anything that looks like inexperience or disregard for protocol, you're on the next shuttle home. Am I clear?"

"Sí, amigo. It's no skin off my churro."

"Da."

"Then let's get to work. We have a transport to catch."

The spy kept watch on the bar until the trio of Judges had left, then he tracked them with care to the lunar departure terminal. He was very careful not to draw attention to himself, giving out the impression of a bored tourist wandering around as he waited for a connecting shuttle flight. Someone would have had to stand extremely close to him to have noticed the small holo-camera clipped to his air-cooled fan-hat; they would have to have looked very carefully to see the micro-miniature imaging lens as it recorded the movements and conversation of the two men and the young woman. Of course, if someone had been unlucky enough to have witnessed and understood what the spy was doing, soon afterward they would have suffered from some sort of terrible and unexpected misfortune. One that left absolutely no doubt they had died completely by accident.

He went as far as he could go, up to the gates to the terminal and watched Dredd, Kontarsky and Rodriguez disappear into the airlock. Then, still mindful to make his passage as insignificant and unnoticeable as possible, the spy stepped into a nearby vu-phone booth and dialled a number in Antarctic City. An automated relay in a vacant apartment there scrambled his call and bounced it off two hundred other randomly selected relays before finally broadcasting it to a target receiver a few hundred thousand kilometres away.

"Yes?" The voice at the other end of the line was indistinct, electronically masked into mechanical flatness.

"He's on his way. The girl and the South American too. Maiden Galactic, flight six-six."

"I will inform the rest of the cabal. Do you have the holo-scan?"

The spy connected a thin optic cable from the camera to the vu-phone's data port. "Transmitting now."

"Excellent. Dredd will never see his precious Mega-City One again. The Moon will be his grave."

Much to Dredd's irritation, Rodriguez seemed intent on talking all the way to Luna-1 and as their shuttle's countdown edged closer to zero, he continued to bait the young Sov-Judge.

"So you must be pretty special, chica, if you got shipped up here to help out with us big dogs, eh?"

"I was top of my class in space law and colonial legal statutes, Rodriguez. I am more than qualified to be part of this task force." She gave him a hard stare that all but rolled off the casual Judge's manner. "Tell me, why are you here?"

"Why are any of us here?" he replied airily. "The universe, she is a mysterious thing. I merely go where she tells me."

Dredd gave him a sideways look. "Kontarsky's got a point. Your file was real short on explanations about that."

After a moment of awkward silence, Rodriguez made a face. "Look, you wanna know why I got sent on this assignment? It's not some big secret, Dredd. I grew up in Luna-1's Puerto Luminia enclave, so the Moon, I know her pretty well." He paused. "That and also I was suspended for, uh, a liaison with another Judge."

Kontarsky gave a derisive snort. "As I understand it, those sorts of 'liaisons' are commonplace among the undisciplined law officers of the Pan-Andes. They are tolerated and ignored. Why would yours be any different?"

An insouciant smile crossed Rodriguez's face. "Mine just happened to be with the lover of the sector chief." He glanced at the Mega-City Judge. "So what about you, Dredd? This your first time up on la Luna?"

"Not quite."

"He was Judge-Marshal here for six months from 2099 to 2100," Kontarsky began, as if she were giving a lecture. "During his tenure, Judge Dredd cleaned up a lot of the criminal elements inside Luna-1 and the surrounding Badlands. Among these, he was responsible for the arrest and prosecution of CW Moonie, the exploitative capitalist crimelord who persecuted the hard-working lunar colonists."

"No kidding?" said Rodriguez. "I remember Moonie from when I was boy. My papa worked for him."

"Almost everyone worked for Moonie back then," Dredd noted. "He had his fingers in every part of the Luna-1 economy."

"Exactly," Kontarsky said. "He was a parasite feasting on the lifeblood of the workers."

"Something like that," added Dredd.

A two-tone signal sounded from the shuttle's public address system. "Your attention please. Trans-lunar injection will commence in two minutes. Please ensure your seat backs and tray tables are in an upright, locked position and please keep all hands, pseudopodia and tentacles out of the aisles until we have switched off the seatbelt sign. Thank you!"

"How come you know so much about Dredd?" Rodriguez pressed. "You a fan or something?"

"East-Meg Two's Judicial Directorate has very detailed files. It was deemed important to retain information on a man who was responsible for the total destruction of a Sov city."

"That was war," Dredd grated. "I took no pleasure in it. And let's not forget, it was East-Meg One that fired the first shots in that conflict. I did what was necessary to ensure the survival of my city."

"I do not disagree, Judge Dredd," Kontarsky said levelly. "Had the circumstances been reversed, I would have made the same choice. Just as you did once more during the madman Sabbat's assault."

"Madre de dios," said Rodriguez. "Now that was a dark day..."

"But the so-called Apocalypse War was not your first engagement with Sov forces, was it?" Kontarsky gave Dredd a piercing look. "You also fought them on the Moon, did you not?"

Dredd's jaw hardened. "Do you have a point, Kontarsky, or are you just going to keep listing my greatest hits? Yeah, I took part in a limited war. We used the old team-based system instead of all-out conflict. We won there, as well!"

A rumble began to build in the rear of the shuttle as the engines throttled up to full power and Dredd's voice rose along with it. "What else do you have to say? Come on, let's hear it."

"I was merely answering Judge Rodriguez's question," she snapped, her icy manner starting to slip. "I believe you returned to Luna-1 in 2118, where you were involved in a murder investigation. You were accused of a series of cannibalistic attacks, if my memory serves correctly."

"Did... did you say cannibal?" Rodriguez paled, edging away from Dredd as far as he could.

Dredd made an off-hand gesture. "I wasn't the perp. The killer was a zombie version of my future self from a parallel alternate timeline."

"Oh," said Rodriguez, in the same tone someone might use if they were speaking to an escaped lunatic. "Well, that explains everything."

"And now you're going back," Kontarsky noted, the roar of the rocket motors drowning out her voice. "I wonder, what history will you make this time?"

Dredd said nothing and let the G-force press him into his seat, as the shuttle powered away towards the grey disc of the Moon.

There were four men in the Silent Room. Two of them were subordinates, lackeys of the other pair, whose job it was to expedite the wishes of their masters. These servant men had servants and agents of their own and a degree of limited autonomy and command, but in all truth, theirs was a short leash. Neither man could move more than a little without the orders of his superior and although both of them were as different as two men could be, their polar opposite beliefs had come together for this one endeavour, in service for their masters.

The two men in charge faced one another across a table cut from black lunar basalt. The surface was so smooth, so finely polished, that it acted like a mirror, reflecting the sullen, watchful cast of their faces and the shimmering holographic display tank that filled the far corner of the room.

In actuality, the Silent Room wasn't silent at all, with the often heated discussions that had taken place between the two men in charge. It had the name only because it would appear silent from the outside. Millions of credits had been spent on just this one space, in order to render it utterly inert to any form of eavesdropping. Sensor baffles that could block radar, lidar, maser scans and tunnelling neutrino beams were embedded in the walls. Sound dampening panels in the structure meant that a nuclear bomb could be detonated inside it and the only thing a listener outside would hear would be the sound of their own breathing. The Silent Room had even been proofed against the more ethereal, less tangible forms of spying, blocking the probing psi-senses of telepaths with an array of cloned human brain tissue that broadcast the mental equivalent of white noise.

It was the ultimate sanctum from which to plot and scheme, an unbreachable preserve for these men, this cabal, to meet and to conspire against the Moon.

"I have the Justice Department report from the Kepler Dome uprising," said the thin man, the subordinate of the man who sat in the hoverchair. "Copies are on your panels, if you'd like to look at them."

The tall man, the opposite number to the man who sat in the hoverchair, smiled coldly. "I see your network of corruption still operates."

The man in the hoverchair gave a husky laugh. He was quite old and somewhat frail, but still potent enough to be dangerous. "There's always someone who wants a little more. Like you, my friend."

The tall man let the gibe pass unremarked, scanning the document. "This bodes well for us. The cause and effect still elude them and they are no closer to determining where the weapons came from. Perfect. We will soon be entering the endgame."

"You see?" the frail man said, sipping at a squeeze-bulb of water. "You had your concerns about mounting a full-scale test, but you understand now why I insisted on it. Kepler Dome was our last dry run. We're ready to begin."

The tall man's balding assistant smirked. "A 'dry run'? That's an interesting choice of words considering that the streets in Kepler ran with blood. I must admit I have my concerns that we may ignite a powder keg we won't be able to contain."

The tall man gave his servant a derisive look. "That is why you fail to move up in rank while I remain your superior. You lack the killer instinct."

"And killer instinct is what you need to survive in a place where nature herself is trying to murder you!" The frail man spat the words with vehemence.

The thin man interrupted with a polite cough. "At any rate, the process has proven itself to be a success. The only detail to be decided now is the date."

"If I may be so bold," the tall man said, "I have the very day in mind." When he told them, there was a chorus of grim laughter around the black stone table.

"Very theatrical," said the old man in the hoverchair. "That amuses me. Yes, yes, we'll proceed as you suggest. As the day dawns, we'll take the Moon for ourselves."

"There is another matter," said the bald man. "The secondary objective has been brought into play."

"Dredd." The old man spoke the name like a curse.

"Judge Dredd, yes. As we predicted, Judge-Marshal Tex requested his assignment and he will arrive within a day. Our operative on Union Station secured these images of Dredd and two of the task force sent to assist him." The bald man touched a control on his chair and the shimmering holo-projector began playing a loop of footage from the spy's camera.

"Who are these others?" said the thin man. "A woman and a Hispanic male?"

"They are known to us," replied the tall man. "They are of no concern. Plans have already been drawn to deal with them. Dredd is where our energies should be focussed."

The tall man shook his head. "I've said it before and I'll say it again. Why not simply use the contingency we set up for the Judge-Marshal and use it to deal with Dredd?"

"Oh, do shut up!" the old man growled. "I'll do everything in my power to ensure that Judge Joseph Dredd dies slowly and painfully. All of this," he waved a crooked hand at the holograms and the panels on the table, "none of it will be enough until I see Dredd on his knees, begging me for his life!"

"You'll have what you want, my friend," said the tall man. "We both will." He gave a nod to the bald man. "Let us extend a warm welcome to our guests from Earth. Send some of our associates to meet Dredd's party. I'm sure it will amuse us all to test their mettle."

4. THE EAGLE HAS LANDED

Kontarsky did her best not to show her excitement as she trailed Dredd and Rodriguez out of the shuttle gate and into the tunnel that led toward the starport. Outwardly, she was all business, her jaw thrust forward, helmet down over her face, the very model of a cool and composed East-Meg citizen; inside, she was bubbling with sensation, thrilling at her circumstances in a manner more befitting a child. Nikita tried to smother the butterflies in her stomach and failed – to be honest, some part of her actually liked the feeling. She was here, in space. At last.

They stepped on to the slidewalk to the port dome. As they passed underneath the world-famous Lunar Arch, a massive stone arc cut from porous moonrock, she couldn't help but read the words chiselled there and smile a little. *One Small Step for Man. One Giant Leap for Mankind.* It wasn't important that an American had said those words; the promise of a future in the stars they held was all that mattered. Kontarsky hadn't felt so alive since the day she had succeeded in making the grade for cosmonaut training, while still a Justice Academy trainee. They had praised her then, told her that she was a prodigy, a credit to the Motherland and she'd seen her own face on the cover of *Neo-Pravda* as yet another example of Sov superiority.

But it did not last. Young Judge-Kadet Kontarsky was just a momentary distraction for the East-Meg people, a propaganda subject one day, a forgotten footnote the next. It mattered little that she passed through space training with flying colours in the company of other kadets three or four years her senior. The State had chosen to give her a time in the spotlight and now it was over. She returned to her studies and excelled, but her teachers never made good on their promises of sending her to the stars. It would not be equitable to graduate you early, her mentors had told her. The State cannot give you special treatment. It seemed to Nikita that she had spent her entire life in training, in her orphanarium, at the Academy, at the Baikonur KosmoDome out in the Russian rad-lands, but now it had come to an end.

She would embrace this assignment and perform it flawlessly, she told herself. It mattered little that she would be forced to work alongside capitalists and opportunistic nyekulturni like Dredd and Rodriguez. These things were simply tests of her skill and her dedication. Sov-Judge Nikita Kontarsky would be a shining beacon to the people of East-Meg Two once again. Devoted. Strong. Indefatigable.

The SouthAm Judge made a weak joke and patted Dredd on the shoulder, his breezy demeanour rebounding ineffectually off the Mega-City lawman's hard gaze. Although Dredd was technically classified as an Enemy of the Sov Nation, Kontarsky had to admit that she harboured a sneaking admiration for him. It was something she would never dare to speak of in earshot of any other East-Meg citizen, but in poring over Dredd's files in preparation for the mission, she had learnt much more about him than the typical State-sanctioned portrayal of a heartless killer. Since childhood, Nikita had been in love with the thought of travelling into space, but that passion was twinned with another devotion: to justice. Despite the yawning gulfs of creed and nationality between them, Kontarsky saw that Dredd, too, held the law in the highest possible regard.

She halted this train of thought with a shake of her head. It would not do for her to consider Dredd as anything more than what he was – a grudging ally. Her briefing from Kommisar Ivanov, the East-Meg Diktatorat's lunar representative, had been quite forthright on that subject. Kontarsky was to fulfil her function as Dredd's deputy and monitor him for any signs of subterfuge or conspiracy against the Sov peoples. Any other motivations were not to be considered.

"Moon-U?" Rodriguez said suddenly, pointing to pieces of graffiti on the terminal wall. "What are they, some sort of new go-ganger crew or Free Luna activists?"

"There's a lot of these pro-independence kooks up here," rumbled Dredd. "They started making noise about 'liberation' a few years ago."

Despite herself, Kontarsky bristled. "Kooks, Dredd? You should not be so quick to dismiss those with a revolutionary fervour and desire for change. Was it not your own country that once sought independence from the nations that had colonised it?"

Rodriguez rolled his eyes. "Ay, Dredd, you've started her off again. Here we go, another political diatribe from the little red book, eh?"

Dredd did not reply, momentarily scanning a cleaning crew of four men who were working to erase more wall-scrawls further along the dome's inner perimeter.

"I was merely making an observation," Kontarsky retorted. "I make no apologies for my beliefs. The ordinary citizens of Luna-1 should be free to decide the path of their own future without the controls of a capitalistic–"

"Fine, fine, lovely chica, but listen. Keep it to yourself, eh? Dredd and me, we got more important things on our minds." He glanced at the other lawman, who seemed fixated on the work crew. "Say, Dredd, right?"

Kontarsky saw the subtle stiffening of the Mega-City Judge's shoulders and instantly caught the same sense of threat in the air. Something was wrong...

"The cleaners..." Dredd muttered. "No droids..."

Although Luna-1 had a far lower unemployment level than Mega-City One, it was still a common sight to see robotic street tenders at work on building maintenance instead of humans. Most people, even up here, preferred to find jobs that were less demeaning than scrubbing stonework. One of the men produced a remote control unit and stabbed at a key with his finger. A hundred metres away, something inside the slidewalk control box fizzed and melted.

As they passed the clean-up crew, the slidewalk suddenly slammed to a halt and the tourists and travellers it carried fell like dominoes. Completely oblivious, Rodriguez took a nasty spill, collapsing over a portly woman and swearing in furious Spanish. Only Dredd and Kontarsky remained standing, both snatching at the guide rail for support.

The four men turned in unison, each of them brandishing a backpack-mounted splurge gun. Designed to remove even the hardiest paints from a surface, the sud-throwers projected streams of concentrated, heated detergent – and they could strip bare flesh to bone with a foamy deluge.

"Hit 'em!" yelled the leader, training his sud-gun on the slidewalk. "Moon-U! Moon-U! Lunar liberty!"

The other men took up the chant and fired. Streams of bubbling liquid gushed across the terminal plaza in thick white streams, hosing the Judges.

"Kontarsky, cover!" Dredd took the brunt of the discharge as he shouldered the Sov-Judge aside, flattening her against a support pillar. Acidic liquid hissed and spat as it ate into his shoulder pad and badge. Kontarsky's nostrils stung as she smelt the harsh zest of chemicals and the sickly scent of seared flesh.

The splurge-gunners continued to project the foam into the crowd, striking anything that moved without concern for who they targeted. People died with gargling, wet shrieks.

"We're pinned down!" Rodriguez yelled. "They're gonna bathe us to death!"

Kontarsky resisted the urge to make a flippant comment about the SouthAm Judge's need for personal hygiene and gasped in a breath. She hesitated. This was different from the two perps up on Union Station; the only goal of these criminals were to murder them all.

Inwardly, Dredd cursed his lack of a weapon and pulled at his ruined badge, snapping off the gold shield where it connected to his chain of office. "We need to take them together," he told the other two Judges. "I'll get the leader.

Rodriguez, find a weapon! Kontarsky, you think you can handle this?"

The Sov-Judge's face reddened. "I am more than capable."

"Time to prove it, then, kid. On three! One…"

Rodriguez gave the obese lady a toothy smile and snatched up her plasti-cane. "Mind if I borrow this?"

"Two…"

"Moon-U! Moon-U!" chorused the shooters, spraying jets of hot foam over the pedway.

"Three!" Dredd sprang out from behind the pillar like a bullet from a gun, springing off the slidewalk guardrail at a shallow angle. He was ready for the lower lunar gravity and let it take him up and over the sud-gunman at the front. At the zenith of his jump, Dredd threw his badge like a shuriken and sent the plasteen shield streaking at the leader's bare throat. The badge struck his windpipe, embedding itself in the soft flesh and choking off his rabble-rousing chant in mid-flow.

At the same instant, Rodriguez popped up from behind the slidewalk and used the cane to swipe at the closest gunman. He struck the rifle-shaped weapon underneath the barrel and deflected it aside to aim at another one of the attackers, like a fencer parrying a sabre. Caught off-guard, the criminal inadvertently hosed his cohort with a point-blank blast of detergent, smothering him with boiling soap.

Rodriguez used the crown of his crested helmet to deliver a crippling head-butt to his target and sent him sprawling, blood spurting from his nose, to the ground.

Dredd came down hard on his shoulder and rolled, feeling the pain from the earlier chemical burn. Bad landing. I'm out of practice with this low-g stuff, he thought to himself.

The fourth man was waiting for him, splurge gun at the ready. "Moon-U!" he chanted, wild-eyed and snarling. "Moooooon-Uuuuu!" The sud-thrower barrel yawned before Dredd's face.

"Moon this!" Kontarsky's clipped voice snapped and Dredd caught the coughing report of a needler pistol. The fourth man slapped at a clump of thin metal spines that embedded themselves in his cheek and sank to his knees, eyes fluttering as a nerve toxin burned through his tissues.

Dredd got to his feet and stepped over the criminal's twitching body. The Sov-Judge stood nearby, gripping a small silver gun in her fist. "Give me the weapon, Kontarsky."

After a long moment, she handed him the firearm. Dredd studied it for a moment. "Volokov ZK-91 holdout pistol. How did you get this past the starport sensors?"

She patted her thigh. "Skin pocket."

"You know the law. No unsanctioned weapons inside the domes. I could have you put in the cubes for this." He weighed the tiny weapon in his hand.

"It only fires reduced velocity subsonic needle rounds. I'd never carry a weapon that could cause a blowout, Dredd. I'm not a fool."

"Hmmph." With a flick of the wrist, Dredd tossed the needler into the maw of a public garbage grinder. "Under the circumstances, I'll overlook this infraction. But don't test me again, understand? You can play with your Sov bag of tricks in your own time."

"Yes, Judge Dredd," she said, her cheeks burning with embarrassment.

"I think our friend here is also muerte," Rodriguez noted, nudging the foam-covered corpse with the tip of his boot. "I can see why they call it 'The Bubbly Death', eh?" He smiled. "So, tell me Dredd. Is this the kind of thing we can expect while we're working with you? Is this how it is down in Mega-City One?"

Dredd gave a shrug. "Different city. Same creeps."

A familiar face was waiting for him in the starport terminal and for a brief instant the sight of Judge-Marshal Tex standing there before him gave Dredd pause; twenty-five years earlier, he had stood in exactly that place and had welcomed him to the Moon.

Tex's face creased in a smile. "Well, howdy Joe." A glint of recognition told Dredd his old friend was thinking the very same thing. "Just like old times, ain't it?"

"Tex." Dredd took his hand and shook it. The Judge-Marshal still had the same firm grip, the same easy grin and trademark Stetson on his head, but the years had not been kind to the stout Texan. The hair that peeked out from under his hat was grey and his chubby face had turned craggy and drawn. He wore every day of his two and a half decades in office in the lines around his eyes. "Shame about the circumstances," Dredd added.

Tex nodded. "It is that." He studied the other two Judges. "I guess you'd be Rodriguez and Kontarsky, right?" Tex tapped his fingers to the brim of his hat. "Glad to have you both aboard."

"A pleasure to meet you, Judge-Marshal Tex," Nikita replied.

"So is this how you welcome everyone to the Moon?" Rodriguez jerked a thumb at the group of Luna Judges securing the remains of the sud-gunners. "Or maybe I'm thinking this is a special hello just for Dredd here?"

Tex's smile thinned to a tight line. "I reckon we'd better talk somewhere more private. Come on, I've got an L-Wagon waiting for us at the upper dock."

The low-grav flyer jetted away from the starport and turned in a long, lazy curve over the towers of Apollo Territory, heading towards the city core. Dredd glanced out of the window and watched the buildings flash by. A casual observer might mistake the view for a nighttime panorama of Mega-City One, with the same panoply of citiblocks and arcologies, but closer inspection picked out the spindly shapes of selenescrapers and skyhighways suspended on thin columns of lunacrete. Architecture throughout Luna-1 took advantage of the one-sixth gravity to create unique structures that would have collapsed under their own weight on Earth. The city's rapid pace of expansion from the early days of the Moon Rush had slowed, the nine original territory zones now filled, with new satellite domes growing like huge glassy mushroom caps around the vast half-sphere of the original settlement. Dredd picked out a few familiar landmarks as the craft threaded itself through aircar traffic: the bright lights of Main Street, the first road ever built on the Moon; the Spike, the glittering tower of the city computer hub; and in the near distance, the grey oval of Crater Stadium. Dredd noted that Rodriguez was maintaining a studied show of blasé disinterest, while Kontarsky was barely concealing her eagerness to drink it all in.

But things were different here. Not just the cosmetic changes in the growth of the city, but something deeper. Even from three hundred metres up, Dredd's seasoned street sense registered the telltale signs of decrepitude – zones where lighting was inactive, empty industrial compounds and run-down residential con-apts daubed with scrawls. Around the edges, the clean, model city he'd visited seven years ago was turning quietly back into the lawless colony he remembered from the turn of the century.

"Not like it used to be, is it?" Tex said quietly at his ear. The veteran Judge-Marshal read Dredd's thoughts in the set of his chin. "There was a time... Maybe we had our golden years, but now we're finding it hard."

Dredd didn't look away. "You're undermanned and underfunded."

Tex nodded ever so slightly. "You know I wouldn't have asked for help if I didn't need it, Dredd. But the fact is, we're on the ropes now. Some sectors are turning into no-go areas. We're having to send in Judges with Manta Prowl Tanks or not at all. The gang problem is getting worse, the usual punk juves are hooking up with organised crime..." He took a breath and rubbed at his eyes, clearly fatigued. "Hell, it's like the bad old days all over again."

The L-Wagon began to descend, passing by a vid-screen that flashed up a grinning Moon-U graphic. "What's that crud all about?"

"Pirate signal hackers bustin' into the comm channels. We've always had 'em up here, but these guys, they're real good. Luna Tek-Division are on the case but so far we're getting nowhere trying to jam it."

"Those yahoos at the starport, they were chanting it."

"Yup." Tex's face wrinkled, as if he'd smelt something bad. "They're stirring up all kinds of trouble in the barrios and the outpost domes. But this is bigger than some cockamamie cartoon. We're looking at an acceleratin' street war situation here."

"Then we'll have to stamp on it. Hard."

Tex said nothing for a moment, then reached into a belt pocket. "Oh, I almost plumb forgot. As you lost your badge back there, I reckoned I could spot you for a temporary replacement, like. Here." He held out a gold disc and Dredd took it. "You're gonna be a Luna Judge for the time bein'. It's my estimation you oughta look like one."

It was a Luna-City shield, a five-pointed star over an inverted quarter-moon, with four smaller stars on the crescent. "I accept," said Dredd.

Rodriguez craned his neck to see. "Hey, can I get one of those too?"

Nearby, Kontarsky frowned at him. "I think you will need to earn it first."

The L-Wagon drifted into a hover then descended into the imposing structure of the Luna Grand Hall of Justice; modelled on the shape of a castle keep, the massive tower was one of the tallest constructions in the entire city. The north face of the building was sculpted into the shape of an eagle, with a crescent moon held firmly in its claws – a multi-storey reminder of the law's grip on the Moon. The flyer docked at a concealed landing bay in the upper levels and Tex walked them to his office, set in the eagle's head. One whole wall was an elliptical glasseen panel in the eye of the sculpture.

Three men, each in a different uniform, stood as they entered. Dredd recognised Tex's second-in-command, Deputy Judge-Marshal Che. The former Mex-City Judge gave Dredd a grave, barely civil nod that confirmed what he had suspected: Tex's own officers objected to the request for the taskforce from Earth.

"Sit down, y'all," Tex drawled. "We're not going to stand on ceremony here. I got no time for it and, frankly, neither do you." He touched a control in the desktop and part of the window became a video screen, scrolling up pictures from street cameras and spy-in-the-sky drones.

"You all know myself and Deputy Che," Tex continued, "and that gentleman there is Joe Dredd, of Mega-City One. I'm sure you all know him, by reputation if nothin' else. As per my request to the Office of the Triumvirate, you five officers form the joint-nationality taskforce that is here to assist the Luna Justice Department with the current crisis. Che, you wanna take over from here?"

The Deputy nodded, "Sí, Chief Judge. The taskforce will be an autonomous unit inside the department reporting directly to myself and Judge-Marshal Tex. Dredd will act as force commander and his deputy will be Judge Kontarsky of East-Meg Two. Our Sov friends have chosen her for her expertise in space law." He nodded to the SouthAm officer. "To my right is Judge Rodriguez from the PanAndes Conurb and these two gentlemen here are Judge Foster from the diplomatic corps out of Brit-Cit and Tek-Judge J'aele from Simba City. J'aele will be handling technical liaison."

Dredd scrutinised the two Judges. Foster, dark-haired with a sharply chiselled face, had the watchful air of a career Street Judge about him; the African J'aele was a little shorter, bald and muscular with a bull-neck that accentuated the tiger-skin shoulder pads he wore. Neither seemed to be typical for their specialities as envoy and technician. Two more wildcards? Dredd found himself wondering why their governments had chosen them.

Che continued: "As you are aware, incidents of violent crime and rioting have increased in outlying domes by forty per cent over the past two months and there has been a corresponding surge in anti-Judge sentiment." He paused; the hard truth of what he would say next weighed heavily on him. "It is our belief that a concerted effort is being made by elements of organised crime and dissident factions to engineer an armed insurrection in Luna-1."

"There is no doubt?" J'aele asked. "You are certain of this?"

"It's just a matter o' time," said Tex quietly.

Dredd grimaced. "Then we have to tear these creeps out by the root before it goes that far." He saw Kontarsky framing another piece of pro-Communist rhetoric and beat her to the punch. "You say they want a revolution? Well, you know as well as I do that no matter what the brains behind this are promising, all it is going to lead to is blood on the streets."

There was a bleak chorus of agreement around the table, even a reluctant assent from the East-Meg Judge.

"The last flashpoint, whaddaya call it, in Kipple Dome–" Rodriguez began.

"Kepler," corrected Che.

"Kipple, Kepple, whatever. The point is, the last riot. What happened there?"

"If I may," J'aele said. "I have read the forensic report from Tek Central. There was an oxygen outage in the dome and panic drove the populace there to riot. It appears that Moon-U pirate broadcasts were used to transmit images of the event across the entire city."

"Sabotage?" asked Dredd.

"Inconclusive at this time."

"How do we know these Moon-U pendejos didn't start the whole thing?"

"They stirred it up, that's for sure," said Tex. "Got the whole damn Moon riled up about it. The media's puttin' the blame right at the door of the Oxygen Board for causing the panic and claiming it was the Judges who started shootin' first."

Kontarsky pointed at a data window on the vid-screen. "What about these weapons that were used in the riots? How were your citizens able to get them?"

"We have no leads," Che said bluntly, angry that he had to admit his failure. "If we did, we would not be seeking help from outside agencies!"

Foster cleared his throat. "Pardon my directness, Deputy Che, but if this bunch of blokes from 'outside agencies' can't help you out, then you're going to find yourself out of a job quite sharpish. Marshal Tex here has remained in charge of Luna-1 thanks to his twenty-odd years of keeping this slice of the Moon in check, but the rules of the International Treaty of 2061 are very clear."

"Clear to you, gringo," said Rodriguez. "Not to me. Explain, please."

"It's all in the small print, chum. If the Triumvirate council's current representative – which would be our esteemed Judge-Marshal Tex – demonstrates an inability to keep the lunar colony under control, then the treaty is automatically suspended. That means all the territories will be up for grabs for whomever wants to deal, cheat or invade their way into them."

Foster worked a control pad and the vid-screen shifted to show a display of near-lunar space. Several small platforms and starships in orbit were highlighted. He pointed upward. "At any one time there's about a dozen diplomatic courier vessels from all the major powers on Earth hovering overhead, ships from each of our cities as well as places like Hondo, the Stani-States, Midgard, Sino-Cit... They're all ready to stake a claim if the Moon goes to pieces." Foster leant forward and Dredd realised he was speaking directly to him. "This ain't just about knocking down some paint-spraying coffee-house rebels. It's about the future of the Luna-1 colony."

Dredd got to his feet. "Then we're wasting time every second we spend debating it in here. Kontarsky, you and J'aele secure me an L-Wagon with a full tech station rig. Foster and Rodriguez, you come with me. We'll get our equipment from the quartermaster and meet you at pad three in twenty."

To their credit, each of the five members of Dredd's team rose without hesitation to his commands. "Let's move like we got a purpose," he added.

"Dredd," Tex called as they were leaving. "Where you headin'?"

"Where else? Kepler Dome," he replied. "Scene of the crime."

When they were alone in the room, Che gave Tex an arch look. "I thought age might have mellowed him a little, but it hasn't. Dredd hasn't changed a bit."

"How do you figure?"

"He's still got the same iron rod up his backside he had when he was Luna-1 Chief Judge. If anything, I'll bet he's even more of a hardcase now."

Tex's mien softened. "No doubt he's one tough hombre, but he'll do what it takes to get the job done, Che."

"I hope so, sir. I'm just not sure there will be much of a city left after he's through with it."

5. STREET LEVEL

Foster looked Dredd up and down as they walked through the halls of Justice Central. The Mega-City Judge spoke without facing him. "Something on your mind?"

The Brit-Citter hesitated for a moment. "It's not important. I just... Well, I just thought you'd be taller."

Rodriguez bit his lip to stifle a chuckle.

Dredd ignored the comment. "You were posted here on secondment?"

Foster nodded. "Yeah and that Simba fella too. You know the drill, Luna-1's an international zone so forty per cent of the Judge force comes from treaty state members."

"So why'd you get sent up, huh?" Rodriguez asked. "Who did you sneck off to get a Moon posting?"

Dredd saw Foster colour slightly. The SouthAm Judge had hit a nerve. "There's a lot of opportunity for Diplo-Div work in space, what with all the alien traffic and so on. On top of that, there's coppers from a dozen countries up here and you need to know who's who and what's what."

Dredd mused on his first impression of the Brit-Judge and played a hunch. "International cooperation. It's a different ballgame to the street."

"No arguments there," Foster gave a nod. "Some days I wish I was back in the Birmingham Wastes on traffic patrol."

His suspicions were confirmed; he didn't have to read Foster's file to figure out what the Brit-Judge wasn't saying. A Street Judge, somewhere along the line Foster had been shuttled off Earth for some sort of infraction and left to cool his heels in orbit. Dredd was sure that he would find a similar situation with J'aele if he dug deep enough into the Simba City Tek-Judge's background. The other nations had promised Hershey that Dredd would get the best officers for the job, but now it was becoming increasingly clear that his taskforce was made up of whomever they wanted out of the way. He filed this information away for later consideration as they approached the quartermaster's stores.

Rodriguez's foot dragged and he stumbled, swearing. "Keep up," Dredd said.

The SouthAm Judge sneered and fiddled with a control on his ankle. "Okay, okay. It's these damn gravity boots we gotta wear. I haven't had to calibrate a pair of these since I got off this dull piece of rock." Like all of Luna-1's law force, the Judges had donned g-boots prior to their arrival on the Moon. The modified footgear enabled the wearers to walk as if they were in an Earth-normal gravity field, even in places where municipal grav-generators did not operate.

A spindly mechanoid with four arms rolled over to Dredd on clanking caterpillar tracks. The robot was an old Moderna Systems Model Eight, the same kind that Mega-City One had retired years ago after a spate of programming errors. It was another sign of the poor state of Luna-1's Justice Department.

"Gentlemen. Follow me to ordinance, please."

The machine rumbled over to a firing range, where belts and holsters were piled next to a rack of flat, compact handguns. "As you know," the robot continued, "projectile weapons rated at grade three and above are illegal on the Moon except with Justice Department special approval waivers. For the duration of your stay, you'll each be equipped with a Glock-Weptek S-54 STUP-gun firearm."

Rodriguez glanced at Foster. "You got one of these already?"

The Brit-Judge nodded and drew his sidearm. "You never used a beam pistol before? They're energy weapons. They shoot streams of highly-charged particles in microsecond pulses."

"STUP stands for Scalar-Tesla Uniform Pulse," droned the droid. "Palm print reader and self-destruct charge, trigger mechanism and safety catches all match those of a standard

Mark 11 Lawgiver. Battery magazines will auto-recharge while the guns are holstered."

Dredd and Rodriguez both took a gun and the weapons beeped softly to signify that they were now locked for their use only.

Foster took up a position on the range. "Let me show you how these things work." He flicked a thumb-dial. "They've got five levels of intensity, from a low-grade stun right up to a full power blast, manual or voice-active select. Hit someone with a level one shot and you'll make 'em puke or pass out. Go up to a five and–"

Foster squeezed the trigger plate and the gun bucked in his hand, the recoil washing back from the crackle of super-heated air as the pulse flashed into the target dummy. The plasti-flesh body shape blew apart like an overripe fruit. "Well, you get the picture."

Rodriguez gave the gun a cautious once-over. "Eh, give me my pistola rata any day. These space toys look like something from a sci-fi vid-slug."

Dredd said nothing and brought up his STUP-gun. The air snapped and hissed as he let off four precise shots from a modified Weaver stance.

"Four discharges registered. All range targets hit, ninety-four per cent critical strike percentage," intoned the robot.

"Hmm." Dredd considered the pistol for a second and then holstered it. "Seems okay to me."

"Show-off." Rodriguez rapped on the droid's carapace. "So, tin-head, where do we go to get our rides, huh? Come on, speedo. I feel naked without my wheels."

"The bike park is over here," Foster indicated the direction of the flyer bay with a nod. "Come with me."

With the robot trailing behind them, Dredd and Rodriguez followed Foster into an open atrium halfway up the building. Ranks of parked aircars painted in pursuit colour schemes and modified low-gravity H-Wagons sat next to hover-bikes in varying states of disassembly.

"Judge-Marshal Tex has assigned a Krait 3000 model zipper bike for your personal usage, Judge Dredd," said the quartermaster droid, as it worked a set of lift controls. From a garage level one floor below them, a launch cradle rose up with a sleek gunmetal and silver-blue speeder resting upon it.

"Ooh, hello baby," Rodriguez breathed, admiring the machine. "That is a fine piece of engineering. Too good for Dredd, I think. She needs a more caring rider, like me, maybe."

The Krait was an agile skybike, armed with its own array of STUP-cannons and a suite of full-spectrum sensors in addition to all the standard features of a Judge's motorcycle. While the Earth-style wheeled Lawmasters were sometimes employed in Luna-1, it was more typical to see the retrojet-powered zipper bikes cutting back and forth across the lunar skyline.

Dredd ran a gloved hand over the fuselage. He'd ridden one of these shark-like flyers before, on a previous mission to the Moon. "Just this one?"

"Affirmative." the robot clicked. "The rest of your taskforce has been assigned the standard Skymaster."

"The Krait bikes are few and far between these days," Foster broke in. "They used to be the front-line vehicle for Street Judges up here, but they've dwindled. Not enough replacement parts, you see? There's barely a tenth of the original number still airworthy."

"Ugh, so what do we get?" Rodriguez asked.

Foster gestured to another model of zipper bike nearby. The Skymasters were built around the ground-based Mark III Lawmaster's chassis, but replacing the tyres and power plant with a Teka-Tek anti-grav drive and thruster grid. A frown creased Rodriguez's face. "The ladies, they are not going to be impressed by a brute machine like this."

"You can always walk," Dredd snapped.

"We're lucky to get these," said Foster, mounting his bike. "The way things are going, by the end of the year the department will be back to using ground bikes."

"So where the drokk does all the funding from the Triumvirate go?" Irritation rose in Dredd's tone.

Foster gave a weary shrug. "Look around, Dredd. It ain't going here."

The trio of Judges circled up and out of the launch bay, climbing to the upper landing pads. Dredd saw a bulky L-Wagon lift off as they passed and the larger flyer moved up behind them to follow their three-bike "V" formation. In the lead, Dredd scanned the horizon as the city blurred by beneath him. The Krait responded smoothly, cutting through the air like a blade.

"Dredd, this is Kontarsky. Switch to secure channel, please." The Sov-Blocker's voice issued from Dredd's helmet radio speaker. He toggled the control on the zipper bike's dashboard.

"Dredd, responding. What's so important that you need to talk to me without the rest of the team hearing?"

"I am merely following command protocol. And I have also made an observation."

"Let's hear it."

"I was examining the incident reports and after-action arrest transcripts from the Kepler riots. Many of the survivors claimed that they felt compelled to fight, or that an irrational rage or intense fear seized them. I suspect there might have been some sort of psychoactive agent at work–"

"When does a rioter ever want to take responsibility for what they've done? Besides, the food, the air and the water were the first things that Tex's people checked," Dredd snapped. "Read the file, Kontarsky. Ever since East-Meg One tried that trick with the Block Mania virus, we've been ready for it! If any chemical or biological factor was there, we'd know it."

The Sov-Judge's voice went tight with annoyance. "I am well aware of that, Judge Dredd. But perhaps it could have been something else. A psionic effect–"

"Luna Psi Division haven't exactly been asleep over the past six months. A psyker strong enough to influence a few hundred thousand people wouldn't stay hidden from them for long." Dredd spotted the zipstrip tunnel to Kepler Dome and brought the skybike on to a new heading. "I want facts, Kontarsky, not speculations."

He switched back to the general radio channel, leaving the young Russian to seethe. "All units, form up, we're going down on the deck."

When they reached the skedway off-ramp to Kepler, the Judges were forced to halt in front of a massive set of airlock doors. The dome had been closed off completely from the rest of the Luna-1 network after the street fighting had threatened to spill over into the city proper and days later the place was still sealed, considered a giant crime scene. A Luna Judge at the gate control station waved Dredd over to him.

"You understand the dome has still to be re-certified after the riots?" he asked. "When things came apart in there, we had to evacuate and lock it down. There could still be booby-traps inside, maybe even a few stragglers still dug in."

"We could go in wearing environment suits," offered J'aele.

"If you come across a sniper or trip a frag mine in there, all an e-suit is going to do is slow you down." Dredd shook his head: "No, we'll take it slow and by the numbers. Open it up."

With a grinding hiss of hydraulics, the saw-toothed airlock doors yawned open, parting like the steel mandibles of some huge predatory insect. A puff of displaced air whistled out in a breeze and the scents carried on it sent alarm bells sounding in Dredd's mind. The acrid smell of smoke and cordite, melted plastic and the unmistakable odour of old, dried blood.

Just beyond the entranceway he saw the far end of the plaza outside the abandoned Kepler precinct house. The Justice Department building was a gutted ruin, black and skeletal. "Overwatch formation," Dredd called out. "Follow me."

The convoy of anti-grav vehicles kept low to the ground as it snaked across the lunacrete roadway, drifting up and over makeshift barricades and the shallow craters made by crude firebombs. "Be ready on your respirators, just in case," ordered Dredd. "Connect to your belt-pack oxy supply the instant you suspect any air leaks." If the dome did suffer a sudden breach, at least the Judges would be able to survive for a few minutes until rescue units could arrive. Dredd had felt the icy kiss of raw vacuum on his skin before and it wasn't an experience he wanted to repeat.

The Mega-City Judge studied the silent wreckage carefully, in his mind's eye reconstructing the confrontation that had taken place, figuring out what had happened when. Here was the burnt-out frame of a bot-cab, probably used as a ram to breach the precinct barricade. There were the circular impact marks typical of a close-range hit from a sonic disruptor rifle. Across the plaza, the stain of a broad heat scorch was visible, one that could have been from a hand flamer or a rocket-propelled grenade.

Foster cursed softly under his breath. "I saw the other incident sites before this one, but I had no idea this one was so bad... Dredd, you ever seen anything like it before?"

"Too many times." Something about the whole scene didn't sit right with Dredd and it bothered him. He brought the Krait to a halt and held up a hand. "Foster, Rodriguez, dismount. We'll check out this zone. Kontarsky, you and J'aele set up the Tek-station at the crossped to the west and get to work on figuring out where this all started."

The Sov-Judge hesitated. "I should accompany you–"

"The crossped," Dredd repeated. "Get going."

Kontarsky gave him a grudging nod and returned to the L-Wagon. As she walked out of earshot, she began speaking into a recorder rod in low, urgent Russian.

"If I didn't know better, I'd say the Sov there was more interested in you than she is in the job," Foster noted.

"I'm sure it's purely professional," noted Dredd. "Spread out. Look for anything out of the ordinary."

Rodriguez put his hands on his hips. "That's it? We just came out here for a look around? I can think of better uses of our time."

Dredd frowned. "It's called Judge work, Rodriguez. Perhaps you've heard of it?"

The Pan Andes Judge muttered something rude under his breath and set to work with a scanalyser. Foster took the central quadrant of the plaza and Dredd walked the length of the perimeter, taking it all in. Four decades of experience on the street had granted the lawman an almost uncanny sense for a crime scene, the ability to at once see the big picture and to also focus in on small, seemingly insignificant details. With grim determination, Dredd circled the ruins from the street fighting. He caught sight of Kontarsky observing him from the crossped, the red of her rad-cloak peering through the broken teeth of a fractured building foundation. An abrupt jab of memory passed through Dredd's mind. The last time he had faced a Sov-Judge wandering through ruined city streets, they had been shooting at one another.

Rodriguez stood up and beckoned him over. As Dredd approached, he noticed a change in the SouthAm Judge's body language. "I found something, I think." He was muted now, more watchful. "When Che was briefing us he had information up on the screen about weapons they had captured from the survivors?"

"Yes, nothing conclusive though. Everything they found was generic stuff, low-grade knock-offs without manufacturer's marks or serial numbers."

"Sí, just your typical gangbanger spit guns. But look here." He indicated a low wall discoloured with smoke. "See anything familiar?"

Dredd bent down for a closer examination. Embedded in the grey lunar brickwork was a cluster of bright silver needles, each as long as his finger. "Standard pattern dispersal," he noted, glancing over his shoulder. "Probably fired from close range. I'd say the shooter was one or two metres away." With care, Dredd pulled a handful of the needler rounds out and rolled them in his palm.

"Those are from a Volokov, right?" Rodriguez asked. "Like the baby needler gun that the chica was packing?"

Dredd nodded. He could just about read the telltale rifling pattern on the shards that was common to the Sov-made weapons. "East-Meggers don't sell a lot of these on the open market. Could be war surplus from the '04 conflict."

Rodriguez looked in Kontarsky's direction. "You think, maybe–" he began in a low voice.

"You can secure that line of questioning right now," Dredd interrupted. "We need facts, not speculation," he said, repeating what he'd told the woman on the flight in. The Judge's analytical mind was turning the small shred of evidence over and over in his mind, making connections, forming a hypothesis.

"Got something?" said Foster as he come closer to them. Dredd showed him the spent needler rounds. "That tracks with what I've been seeing," the Brit-Judge noted. "Most of the weapons that the rioters employed could have been made on the Moon back in the old days, but here and there I'm seeing anomalies." He nodded toward a torched vu-phone booth. "Heat diffusion traces on the glasseen over there matches the outputs from a Flesh-Blaster. These are both weapon signatures that look like off-world makes."

Rodriguez rubbed his chin. "Off-world? You mean from Earth, right?"

Foster nodded. "Guns like those Volokov needlers are very rare up here. You'd have to smuggle them in if you wanted one."

Dredd and Rodriguez exchanged a silent look.

"I just can't figure out where they got 'em," Foster continued. "We got no leads from the perps we pulled in. It's like these weapons were just lying around, ready for them to use."

Dredd secured the needle rounds in a belt pouch and strode back toward his bike. "If the guns were brought in from outside Luna-1, we've got a new factor to consider. Somebody spent the rocket fuel and the time to bring these weapons up the gravity well, which means there's gotta be more to this than just arming some cits for a pointless bloodbath." He paused. "Someone in Luna-City knows where these weapons came from."

"So we have to think about who we have to squeeze to get some results," Foster added. "Gun control's got pretty strict since the blowout in the Velikovsky botanical gardens dome, when you were here last. Most of the creeps who smuggle stuff up the well concentrate on low mass, high return products like drugs or Stookie glands. I doubt any of the usual suspects will cop to gun-running."

Dredd considered this for a moment. "Then maybe we need to concentrate on some of the old school Luna perps. And I think I know where to start looking."

"You got a lead you're not telling us about?" said Rodriguez.

"Just a feeling. You stay here and finish up. I'll meet you back at Justice Central at the end of the shift." Dredd gunned the Krait 3000's anti-grav motor and the skybike roared away, back toward the airlock.

"Huh," said Rodriguez. "He says he wants facts not speculation, then off he goes on a hunch. What do you make of that?"

Foster gave a wry smile. "He's Judge Dredd, pal. You know his record – if he says he's got an inkling on something, you can bet cold, hard credits it'll be on the ball."

Down by the crossped, Kontarsky looked up to see Dredd's zipper bike vanish into the zipstrip tunnel. She chewed her lip, then drew out her recorder and spoke into it once more.

Dredd held the throttle at cruising speed for a few minutes as he vectored down the tubeway back toward the central dome. He kept a close eye on his rearview scanner, watching for any sign of pursuit. He half-expected to glimpse Kontarsky trailing him on her Skymaster, but the Sov-Judge did not seem to be following him. That's the problem with fielding an international team, Dredd told himself, there's always the chance that people will put loyalty to their flag before justice.

It didn't take a genius to realise that Kontarsky was relaying every little decision that Dredd made back to the Sov-Block's diplomatic courier in orbit and the East-Meg Diktatorat on Earth. It stood to reason that there were probably dozens of covert agents in the pay of the Sov's Klandestine

Ops Directorate on Luna-1, even if Kontarsky wasn't one of them. Certainly, Mega-City One had its share of spies in the Moon colony and so did all the other major nation states.

Luna-1 was an international zone and that meant that every city on Earth had some kind of presence here, all of them watching one another, jockeying for position and playing political mind games. The lawman sneered at the thought of becoming caught up in this sort of intrigue. He wasn't a man for shady schemes or diplomatic double-talk. Dredd preferred a straight, stand-up fight to back-alley dealings and secret treaties. He was the blunt instrument of justice and he liked it just fine that way.

When Dredd was certain he wasn't being tailed, he opened up the Krait's throttles to maximum and pushed the flyer to the redline, weaving between heavy aerotrucks, darting through the traffic like a barracuda through a pod of whales. The East-Meg Judge had been constantly observing Dredd from the moment he'd arrived on Union Station, no doubt even from before they had met. He hadn't expected anything less – after all, he was the man who'd wiped out millions of her fellow Sov-Blockers with the push of a single button – but the discovery of the needle rounds threatened to shift the balance of his evaluation of Kontarsky. If the Sovs had some kind of connection to the Kepler Dome incident, then her position on the taskforce suddenly had a whole new dimension to it. Maybe all that wide-eyed rookie stuff was just a front. He even considered for a moment that Rodriguez might have planted the needler rounds to implicate the Sov-Judge, but then what would the Pan Andes Conurb have to gain by doing that? Besides, Foster had backed up the SouthAm Judge's discovery with one of his own and the idea of the Brits being in league with the Banana City boys was verging on the ridiculous, given current international tensions between them.

Dredd blew out a breath. All this second-guessing was distracting him from the real investigation at hand. The only course of action that presented itself was to keep himself at the forefront of things until he could be sure where the loyalties of the other Judges lay. Despite the professionalism – or lack of it, in the case of Rodriguez – shown by each of the foreign officers, the five of them were circling each other like wary tigers, watching one another for signs of weakness or malfeasance. It was up to Dredd to play the role of the pack alpha, to pull them into line, weed out any weak links and maintain discipline. Anything less and the group would fall apart before they could make any progress.

At the Santini flyover, Dredd took a sharp turn to starboard and throttled down the Krait, settling into a shallow cruise altitude over the quadrant formed by the edges of Verne Avenue and the Odyssey Loop. The locals called this place the Pink Crater and since the very first days of Luna-1's incorporation, it had served as the city's red light district where colonists could go to let off a little steam. The more relaxed laws set in place during the Moon's wild frontier heyday still granted this portion of the dome a little more freedom than other more upmarket parts of town, with licensed casinos on the edges of the zone feeding local pleasure-seekers and eager tourists alike into the null-grav nude bars, virtu-porn arcades and Lust-O-Mats. Mega-City One had similar districts, but the Justice Department kept them strictly regulated with regular crime sweeps on an almost daily basis.

The open immorality of the Pink Crater set the Judge's teeth on edge. It was in the interests of the businesses in the area to keep any serious crime off the streets, but he was willing to bet that untold numbers of lawbreakers and infractions were passing by beneath him right now, if only he could crack the place open to see them. He orbited around a gaggle of tethered floater boudoirs above the Satellite of Love massage parlour and located the building he was looking for, a fetish club at the rough end of the loop called the Harsh Mistress.

Dredd set the bike to hover mode and dropped down on to the roof, pausing to check the setting on his STUP-gun.

The holographic image of the club's signature female clad in black leather bondage gear leered over the rooftop, brandishing a cat o' nine tails and licking her lips. "Have you been bad?" the holo demanded of the revellers down on the street. "The harsh mistress knows you have! Come inside and get the punishment you deserve!"

Dredd gave a grim smile. "You have no idea how right you are," he told the sign.

6. VACUUM PACKED

Judge Dredd's boot made short work of the lock on the access hatch and he descended into the sweaty, ill-lit interior of the Harsh Mistress, the low-light image intensifier lenses in his helmet rendering the corridors of the club in green-tinted shades. Rastabilly skank music was currently enjoying a revival on the lunar cabaret scene and the grinding thuds of a particularly loud track's bassline resonated through the building. Dredd was thankful for the audio processing circuits in his headgear, which flattened the atonal pop music into a dull background hiss while still picking out the more important sounds of movement and activity. Correctly tuned, a Judge's helmet sensors could hear the sound of a spit gun being cocked amid the roar of a smashball stadium crowd.

A Bouncer-Mek met him halfway down the stairwell to the roof and grated out a stock warning in a metallic voice. "Your name's not down, you're not coming in. Hop it, you spugger!"

Dredd's reply was to fire a point-blank stun blast from his STUP-gun into the robot's braincase and it rocked back, spitting sparks.

"Awwk!" The pulse pistol worked just as well on mechanoids as it did on flesh-and-blood perps. The droid dropped to the floor in a clanking heap and lay there, twitching.

The Judge paused at the foot of the stairs to get his bearings. He was standing on a broad balcony that circled a packed dance floor below, where Luna-cits in various states of undress wrestled with things that could have been alien life forms or maybe just other people in bizarre fetish costumes. He shook his head and resisted the urge to arrest the lot of them. Off the balcony there were doors leading to private suites, soundproofed rooms where VIP club members could "entertain" or conduct clandestine trysts.

Dredd studied them carefully. The design of the club had been altered since he'd been here last and that had been a long time ago, with a force of two dozen Luna Judges and a fistful of warrants behind him. One of Tex's men at the time, Judge-Marshal Chico, had brought a tip-off to Dredd's attention and they had uncovered a smuggling ring bringing black market laser rifles up from Sino-City One. Two Judges had died in a firefight at the docks when they ambushed that cargo and Dredd had personally led the raid on the Harsh Mistress to arrest the man behind the deal, the night-club's owner-manager, Vik Umbra. He was a particularly odious perp, as Dredd recalled, with illicit tastes and desires that even the moderate laws of Luna-1's red light district paled at. If anyone could be sure to know something about the weapons from Kepler Dome, it would be him.

Dredd grabbed the arm of a woman who passed him. Her hair was a shock of bright electric blue and she wore a shiny black outfit of plasti-wrap, her neck covered by a choker adorned with rings.

"Hey, downshift, chummer!" she wailed, pushing at him. "What's your malfunction?"

"I'm looking for Vik Umbra. Where is he?"

"Vik?" she blinked. "He's in his g-room, wave me? You looking to spell with him? You a gravity-fun boy-boy guy?" She rubbed her hand over his uniform. "Oooh, deedee. This is real leather, wave? You gotta primo costume."

Dredd hissed in her ear. "It's not a costume, wave?"

"A real Judge?" her lip quivered. "I done nothin'!" The girl glanced at his badge and went pale. "Dredd? Dredd!"

Sometimes having his reputation precede him made getting what Dredd wanted a whole lot easier. "Show me where Vik is," he demanded and the blue-haired girl eagerly nodded her assent, ready to do anything to avoid time in the cubes herself.

She led him to an opulent room set back from the others and opened the door. Inside was an ornate, over-decorated antechamber where two human bodyguards were standing watch over a handful of frightened young juves, each chained to a spiked leash. The guards were quick and their hands were already diving for the triggers of their stump guns as he entered. Dredd wasted no time and fired two pulses into the meatheads, sending them sprawling. Sorting through their pockets, he handed the girl the keys to the leash and nodded at the teenagers. "You. Take 'em and get lost."

The girl did what he asked and Dredd looked around, finding and smashing an alarm keypad. It wouldn't do for Umbra to call for help before they had had their discussion. The Judge found a used injector that reeked of Stookie and a copious supply of Umpty Candy on a side table, more than enough to put the club owner behind bars for another long stretch.

He shouldered open the next door and found himself in a bi-gravity chamber.

Close to the doorway where Dredd stood, the g-plates in the floor simulated an Earth-normal one gee environment, but further in across a discreet line of yellow tiles, the room was completely weightless. The sole occupant was a pallid ball of skin at least six times the size of the Judge, a naked, corpulent pinkish mass floating just within reach of the padded walls. Sex toys, sense-dep masks and other less identifiable objects drifted around the huge fatty in a lazy shoal. "Has someone brought me a new playmate?" said a breathy voice. "My last one broke." The fleshy sphere of a man rotated slightly and presently a head appeared, peering owlishly at the Judge from out of a dozen rolls of neck-flab.

"Hello, Vik," Dredd sneered. "Long time no see. Have you lost weight?"

"Rot you, Dredd!" The fatty trembled. "I gained one hundred and thirty-six kilograms!"

"My mistake."

"I heard you'd come back to the Moon," Umbra said, spittle flying from his lips in little spheres. "Well, you can liposuck me, you drokker! I'm legit now! You got nothing on me!"

"Really? What about the youth drugs and addictive candy I found in here? I'm sure there will be more if I look for it."

"Not mine!" Umbra screeched, flailing at an inert alarm switch. "You can't prove it's mine!"

Dredd spotted a control panel on the wall and turned a dial on it. The effect of the gravity nullifier on Vik's side of the room began to decrease and by centimetres the bulbous man-shape slowly settled to the floor. "One-sixth gee has been good to you, Vik. I bet you couldn't even walk under your own weight on Earth." Umbra pooled on the tiles in a flushed pile of adipose meat.

He gave a weak cough as the dial passed the two gee marker. "Look, Dredd, stop it! My heart will pop like a balloon if you keep turning that up! What do you want with me?"

"I put you away for fifteen for dealing in illegal weapons back in '99, Vik. But even if you're not in the gun trade any more, I figure you still know who's bringing them into Luna-1."

"Sneck off, Dredd! All my gunrunning days are over. Like I told you, I'm out of it."

The dial turned to up three gravities. "I'm sorry, I didn't catch that."

"Please!" Vik spat out bloody drool. "My heart can't take it!"

"Then give me a name, or else they'll have to use a spatula to scrape you into a coffin." Dredd thought he could hear the sound of ribs cracking.

"You're crazy if you think I'll give you anything, helmet-head! I withered away in prison thanks to you, living on just nine meals a day! I'll die first!"

Dredd tap-tapped his finger on the gravity dial. "You sure about that?"

Vik's bluster wavered a little. "If I roll over for you, Dredd, I'll be a corpse before the next earthrise. These guys, they're connected."

"So you *do* know something," Dredd nodded to himself. His guess about Umbra still being in the smuggler's loop had proven right. "You've got a choice, Vik. You have to ask yourself who you're more afraid of. Me or them?"

After a few wheezing breaths, Umbra gave a wobbly nod. "All right, drokk you. Let me up and I'll talk."

Dredd dialled back the gravity to lunar normal, enough to keep the fatty down on the ground. "Spit it out, creep."

"You know about the rebel miners on Ganymede, right?"

A nod. "Sure. It was a Sov colony. They took the place over."

"There was a big cargo of weapons on the way out to them about three months back, so I heard. Nothing to do with me, part of some deal with the Diamante cartel in the Med Free States fronting for the Siberian Mafia." Dredd knew the name; the cartel were pirates and middlemen for a dozen larger criminal groups worldwide and the Siberian connection would have explained the Sov-issue guns like the Volokov needlers and Beria flesh blasters. "But they never made it there. Most folks figured that the load got caught by the East-Meg Judges, but one of my girls heard different from a, uh, client."

"Someone from the cartel?"

"Nah, this guy worked for M-Haul. They do interplanetary freight and salvage. He let slip that his crew intercepted the cartel ship. They cut up the freighter for scrap and kept the weapons."

"A name," Dredd growled. "Give me a name."

"Sure, sure. Yud Swindo, that was the guy. But don't bother looking for him, he's dead. A day after he spilled his guts, he was found out on the Sea of Vapours without an e-suit and the girl he blabbed to got done the same way too. Pretty soon after that, M-Haul lost all four of its ships in a tragic docking accident, if you get my drift."

Dredd shook his head and turned up the gravity again. "You're spinning me a line, Vik. Your story is so full of holes I could drive a roadliner through it!"

Umbra coughed and choked. "No, spug it! You didn't let me finish! When M-Haul went down, all their assets, including the storage dome where they kept their salvage, got bought out cheap by their major shareholder, see."

"Which was who?"

"Another old face from the past, Dredd. The MoonieCorp company got it all. The same business that used to be run by CW Moonie, the famous lunar explorer. Until you put him in prison for life, of course…"

"Moonie?" Dredd's brow furrowed. "But Moonie Enterprises was sold off when he was convicted. He lost control over all his holdings. It's an independent entity now."

"Yeah," Umbra gurgled sarcastically. "Sure it is." He wheezed in a breath. "So, I did what you asked, I talked. Now, how are you gonna keep me safe from these guys? I don't wanna end up freeze-dried out in the Oxygen Desert."

Dredd tapped the chin guard on his helmet and a wire-thin microphone pickup extended to his mouth. "Don't worry, Vik. Where you're going, there's plenty of bars on the windows to keep people out." He glanced around the room. "You're under arrest for multiple violations of Code Twenty, contraband statutes. Ten years in the iso-cubes."

Umbra began to thrash around on the floor in a desperate attempt to get up, his face flushing red, spitting and swearing at the Mega-City Judge.

"Dredd to control. Catch wagon required at the Harsh Mistress nightclub, Odyssey Loop." He paused, sizing up Umbra's obese form. "Better make sure you reinforce the hull first and bring a couple of anti-grav jacks."

It took another hour and a half for the Luna Judiciary to get Vik Umbra out of the building and into a vehicle big enough to carry him. In the end, Dredd had been forced to commandeer a couple of demolition meks from a construction yard off Buzz Aldrin Street to laser a hole in the nightclub's wall and remove the fatty with crane grabs. As he supervised the arrest, the Judge considered the chubby man's words. CW Moonie – it was a name he hadn't heard in years, but the Moonie bust had been the signature event of Dredd's tenure as Luna-1 Judge-Marshal.

Early in 2100, a couple of months after beginning his tour as the colony's Chief Judge, investigations into attempts on Dredd's life had led him to suspect the Moon's best known but most reclusive millionaire was intent on having him killed. Almost at the cost of his own life, the Judge had pursued and arrested the crime lord and incarcerated Moonie in the forbidding Farside Penitentiary, a prison dome on the lunar dark side. If Moonie had maintained some sort of connection to his old powerbase while he was in jail, he could be a valid suspect.

At last, Umbra's protesting form was inside the catch wagon and the vehicle's suspension squealed under the weight. Dredd waved them off and mounted his zipper bike, rising back into the air. It was just as likely that Umbra was trying to shift suspicion off himself as it was that an ageing criminal locked in a lunacrete vault was behind the Kepler Dome weapons, but Dredd couldn't afford to discount anything at this stage. He angled the bike at the distant shape of Justice Central and opened up the throttle. On the inner surface of the dome above him, Luna-1's solar reflectors folded closed, marking the start of the city's night-cycle.

The rest of the taskforce was waiting on one of the upper levels of the Luna Grand Hall of Justice, in a ready room where Judges going on or off shift could grab a quick cup of synthi-caff or a bite to eat. Windows around the edge of the room showed the glowing vista of the city as streetlights and holo-signs winked on. The sight momentarily captured Kontarsky and she lost a few seconds staring at it.

She caught Tek-Judge J'aele's eye and the African's face split in a smile. "It's really a sight, isn't it?" The Simba City Judge's voice was rich and deep. "I've been here for quite a while and I still find myself drifting off at the windows."

Kontarsky fought down a surge of discomfiture. "I was just observing."

J'aele's smile widened. "You don't have to impress me, Kontarsky. I'm not Dredd. I won't hold it against you if you behave like a human being now and then."

"I'm not trying to impress anybody," she said, a little too quickly than she'd have liked. "I'm just doing my duty."

The Tek-Judge let the sharp words roll off him. "Of course," he allowed.

Kontarsky's gaze dropped to the datapad in her hands. "Your report on the Kepler crime scene is very thorough. I don't think there's anything else I can add to it."

"If I may ask, are you not concerned by the evidence of Sov-made weapons at the incident site? Such a factor may reflect personally on your involvement in the taskforce."

He's testing me, she realised. "That information has no bearing on my role as deputy commander," she said in a practiced, clipped tone. "Besides, the larger percentage of the weapons were of NorthAm or Nu-Taiwanese manufacture."

J'aele was going to press the point, but a sharp expletive from across the room distracted them both. Rodriguez was close to the windows, hands clenching and unclenching at his hips, his body set and tense. "Madre de dios! Will you look at this snecking stomm!"

For a moment, Kontarsky couldn't understand what Rodriguez was talking about, until part of the city view outside the window moved – and she realised she was looking at a massive ad-blimp cruising over the Armstrong Hub Plaza. She and J'aele and a few other off-duty Judges, crossed over to get a better look.

The blimp was a big one, the size of a small sky-cruiser, shaped like an enormous cowrie shell with huge billboard screens sprouting from it on every side. Laser projectors cut slogans into the night air with neon-bright flickers and loud-speakers broadcast sales messages in a dozen languages; or at least, that was what the ad-blimp was supposed to be doing. The screens and holograms were flickering and blinking in and out of focus, as if something inside the craft were fooling around with the tuning.

"It's malfunctioning," said Foster.

"Yeah!" Rodriguez snapped angrily. "That's one word for it!" Even as he spoke, the blimp's display of garish off-world colony recruitment commercials reappeared for a few seconds, only to be suddenly replaced by a grinning cartoon figure.

"Kiss kiss, hi hi from Moon-U!" it squeaked, the synthesised voice carrying for dozens of blocks. "They try 2 stop me but they can't silence Moon-U!"

"Hackers," said J'aele with a grimace. "They're like a plague of rats. Every time we plug a hole in the network, they find another one." He plucked a hand computer from his pocket and worked at it. "These Moon-U people are the worst yet."

Scenes from the Kepler Dome riot – including images that Kontarsky knew were supposedly secure footage from Justice Department spy cameras – were running over the screens now. Far below, traffic was coming to a halt and pedestrians were craning their necks up to see what the giggling cartoon had to tell them. Moon-U gave them all a comical wink and beamed. "Here's what the Judges don't want U 2 know! It's not enough that they wanna shut us all down down down!" The caricature put a finger to its lips in an exaggerated gesture of conspiracy. "Now they gotta secret death squad on the streets – and they're coming for U!"

"Death squad?" said Foster, "What is this drivel?"

"Where's the anti-aircraft cannons?" Rodriguez said, becoming increasingly agitated. "Shoot the drokker down!"

"Over the most heavily populated area of the city?" J'aele retorted.

Moon-U produced a picture-in-picture and held it up. It was all Kontarsky could do to stop her jaw dropping open in shock as she recognised the faces in the image: it was her and Rodriguez, but slightly distorted and behind them were J'aele and Foster. The warped screen-Judges were feral and hateful-looking, weapons drawn with a blood-hungry cast to them. As she watched, the screen showed the four of them dashing down a corridor in the starport, gunning down citizens left and right with vicious abandon. The fake Foster ignored the dying pleas of an old woman and shot her squarely between the eyes; the screen J'aele produced a Masai war spear from out of nowhere and ran three men through with it, skewering them like a shish kebab.

Under other circumstances, the affable Simba City Judge might have found the ridiculous image amusing, but here and now it was enough to make his stomach turn. Up on the billboard, an obviously drunk Rodriguez flailed around, randomly shooting explosive bullets into the crowds and the virtual Kontarsky looked straight into camera before firing her weapon into the lens. Static flickered, then Moon-U reappeared, shaking his head sadly and wearing a black armband. "That was taken earlier today, my friends! 2 many people were killed, just for speaking their minds! And U could B next, so we have 2 make them stop! Tell them, we want free elections! If Judge-Marshal Tex don't step down, then we'll fight 'em!"

The dart-like shapes of two L-Wagons flickered through the air toward the ad-blimp and Foster saw the glints of sucker guns as the crews fired boarding cables at the floater. He shook his head. "What is this rubbish? Nobody's going to be dumb enough to fall for some doctored video footage!"

"Don't be so sure," said Kontarsky, pointing to the street below. Already, there were citizens yelling and waving their fists at the Hall of Justice. "Propaganda can be a very powerful tool. It is most insidious."

"It's not just the ad-blimp," J'aele noted. "They're also broadcasting on a dozen public vid-channels and street-screens."

Rodriguez's face was crimson with anger. "It's gotta be silenced! They make me look like some slack-jawed idiota drunkard!"

"Oh! Oh!" cried Moon-U, big tears forming in his saucer eyes. "They're coming 2 shut me up up up!" The cartoon character loomed large and brushed at the edges of the screens, as if he were trying to flick away the Judges crawling over the blimp like bothersome insects. "U have to know B 4 it's 2 late! Dumb old Marshal Tex has called in the most vicious killer of all to lead the death squad! He's a menace 2 society!" And with those words, a massively over-muscled but uncannily accurate imitation of Judge Dredd appeared over Moon-U's shoulder, a Lawgiver the size of an artillery piece in his spiked-gloved hand. Hellish red light glowed under the eye-slits of the false Dredd's helmet. Barbed wire was wrapped around his forearms and the Eagle of Justice on his shoulder pad was sickle-clawed and vicious. "It's Judge Dredd! The man who killed a million billion people... just because he could!" Moon-U screamed like a girl and cowered as the monstrous lawman turned the gun on him. The words *No Justice, Just Us* were clearly written on the barrel.

"Better Dredd than dead!" roared the screen Judge and with an ear-splitting roar, the gun spat white light that over-whelmed the screen.

From behind Kontarsky and the other Judges, a voice remarked, "That's not a bad likeness."

The real Dredd studied the blimp, now silent and dark, as it began to drift slowly toward the ground. Rodriguez took a step toward him, a balled fist smacking into his palm with an audible thwack.

"Dredd! How can you let that happen, man? These hacker pendejos make us a drokking laughing-stock!"

"Get a grip, Rodriguez," said Dredd. "There are worse things to have than a bruised ego."

"Says you!" the Pan Andes Judge retorted hotly. "This whole taskforce is turning into one big La Luna Loca!"

"You have a better idea of how to run things?" Every one of the other Judges caught the warning tone in Dredd's voice, but Rodriguez seemed oblivious to it.

"Sure! We tool up, not with these toy guns, but some proper pistolas and make a few examples of these punka-mentes!"

"So your advice is to do exactly what those hackers are accusing us of?" Dredd's lips twisted in a sarcastic sneer. "I'll take it under advisement. In the meantime, get yourself down to the barracks and take an eight-hour stand down. I'll be generous and assume the poor judgement you just dis-played is a side-effect of your space-lag."

Rodriguez pulled off his helmet and gave Dredd a hard look; then the ire seemed to drain right out of him and he gave a tight nod. "Sí, sí. You're right, Dredd. It just rattled me, seeing my face up there like that."

"That goes for all of you," Dredd addressed the other Judges. "All taskforce personnel are to have the mandatory eight. We'll pick up on the morning shift. J'aele, accompany me to the docks. The rest of you will check out the offices of M-Haul, over in Von Braun Territory. Dismissed."

All the team members nodded their assent and drifted away. Dredd caught a snatch of quiet conversation between Foster and J'aele as they passed him. "What was with Rodriguez back there? For a second there, I thought he might do something stupid."

The Tek-Judge answered with a shrug. "It must be that fiery Latino temperament I've heard of…"

Kontarsky lingered a moment, before passing Dredd her datapad. "Here's the summary of the Kepler Dome investigation. I hope you'll find it in order."

"I'm sure I will."

"If I may ask, what is the connection you have found to this M-Haul group?"

Dredd paged through the files. "I'm not sure yet. You've got a good eye for detail. You'll know it when you see it."

The Sov-Judge accepted this without comment, then asked: "Anything else?"

He nodded. "Rodriguez. Watch him, Kontarsky. If he steps out of line once more, I want him locked in the cargo bay of the next transport Earthside, understand?"

"I concur."

"Good. Now, go take your down time. I want you at the top of your game tomorrow."

She turned to go, then hesitated. "What about you? Or is it true what my kadet instructors told me, that you don't need to rest and dream like other people?"

"I'll take my ten minutes in the sleep machine," Dredd told her gruffly, turning to direct all his attention to the pad. "I gave up dreaming a long time ago."

7. OFFICER DOWN

The perp ducked as he wove between the oil drums, a heavy calibre spit gun in his hand. As three more go-gangers in identical colours rushed up to join him, Dredd snapped a command out of the side of his mouth: "Level three."

The STUP-gun gave an answering beep and the Judge fired: a sun-bright flash of yellow crossed the distance to the perp and hit him in the chest. He fell back, the spit gun vanishing as it left his fingers. The ganger's pals weren't fazed and kept on coming. The insect buzz of low-velocity bullets sang past Dredd's helmet as they fired. Dredd mentally picked out a shooting order for the men and squeezed the trigger three times. The last man took a pulse blast in the face before the first ganger had even hit the ground. Their inert bodies lay there on the floor for a few seconds before they popped out of existence in a blink of glowing pixels.

"Four discharges registered," said the range monitor droid. "All targets hit, ninety-seven per cent critical strike percentage."

"Better," Dredd said aloud. The lightweight beam gun took a little getting used to, but after an hour or so on the firing range picking off holographic criminals, the Judge was almost up to the same level of proficiency he exhibited with the heavier ballistic Lawgiver. "Reset," he told the robot. "Let's try for ninety-nine per cent."

Even as he spoke, Dredd became aware of someone else in the room. "Always the perfectionist, huh Joe?" Judge-Marshal Tex walked out of the shadows and joined Dredd at the firing stalls. The Texan was carrying a heavy silver revolver and a box of bullets.

"Tex," Dredd greeted the other man with a nod. "It's late. What are you doing down here?"

Tex loaded his pistol. "I could ask you the same thing. Ah, you know what it's like, Joe. The older you get, the less you sleep. Sometimes I come down here in the middle of the night, take in a little practice."

Dredd nodded. "Good discipline."

"Keeps me sharp," added Tex. "These days, it's the only chance I get to field a weapon, what with me flyin' a desk." He cocked the gun with a well-oiled click. "Targets up!"

This time, eight perps emerged from the corners of the simulator chamber and the two Judges made short work of them, both Dredd and Tex placing careful shots into shoulders to disarm or heads and chests to kill. In as many seconds, the eight holo-targets were dispatched. "All targets hit. Judge Dredd registers ninety-eight per cent critical strike percentage, Judge-Marshal Tex registers ninety per cent critical strike percentage."

Tex swore softly. "Gettin' slow in my old age."

Dredd studied the gun. "That's not a standard firearm."

"Nope, this here's an heirloom." He handed the pistol to Dredd. "Been in my family for more than two hundred years. It's gotta micro-thin diamond layer sealed over the metal, so she'll stay in perfect order for two hundred more. A genuine Colt Model 1873." Tex nodded down-range. "Go ahead, try her out."

Dredd ordered up two targets and fanned the Colt's hammer, blasting the last two bullets out of the barrel. "Both targets hit. One hundred per cent critical strike percentage," reported the monitor.

Tex removed his hat and ran a hand through his greying hair. "Shoot, Dredd. You can even handle an antique like a pro! Y'all never cease to amaze me."

Dredd handed back the pistol. "It's a good weapon. It doesn't matter how old it is. It can still do the job."

The comment hung in the air between them for a long moment, before Dredd finally broke the silence. "What's on your mind, Tex?"

"You know, it's funny. Seein' you step off that shuttle, seein' you wear a Luna-1 star. It's like no time has passed since you were Judge-Marshal yourself... Then I realise it's been a quarter century and I'm feelin' every damn day of it."

Dredd did not speak, letting his old friend give voice to his thoughts.

"Why'd you do it, Joe? Why did you make me the sheriff of this godforsaken rock? Back before you were marshal, we had a new Chief Judge every six months, but then you came in and the last thing you did before you went back to the Big Meg was make me the honcho, permanently."

"You know why, Tex. Luna-1 needed someone like you back then, someone who knew the city and could keep it in line. You were the right man for the post and you did it better than anyone before you. You've served longer than anyone since the days of Fargo."

For a moment, a glow of pride glinted in Tex's eyes. "Yeah. Damn me, but I love this airless piece o' dirt." He gave Dredd a troubled look. "But I'm caught, Joe. I'm getting too old for this and my judgement's startin' to slip. I'm like this here piece," he hefted the Colt for emphasis. "Just a damn relic."

"You're a fine lawman. Your service to the city has been exemplary. You could step down and no one would deny you a peaceful retirement."

Tex snorted with dry laughter. "C'mon, Dredd. You and me, we're too much alike to believe that quittin' ever works. We got the law in our blood. And you can't exactly go take the Long Walk on the Moon. Beside, there's no one I could trust to do the job after me... Che's a good Judge, but he's too soft on the international zoners. Heck, Joe, you're about the only other man I'd trust with this city and I'd never ask you to give up Mega-City One."

Dredd accepted this with a nod. Although in manner and personality, the laconic Tex was poles apart from Dredd's rigid disposition, the Judge-Marshal was one of the few men he knew that shared the same unswerving dedication to justice as he did. "We'll get to the root of this," Dredd told him. "Count on it."

Tex replied with a weary nod. "It's not me I'm worried about, Joe, you understand? It's my city. If I turn my back, if I give those lawless punks out there even an inch more, then Luna-1's gonna go to hell in a goddamn handbasket."

"Not while I'm here."

The Judge-Marshal forced a smile and turned to go. "Ah, listen to me! You must be thinkin' ol' Tex here is going soft in the brain! I reckon I'll get me some shut-eye."

"Good night, Chief Judge." Dredd watched his former partner amble away into the gloom, weighing his old friend's words with careful, taciturn consideration.

In the Silent Room, things were anything but quiet.

"Again I find myself forced to question the validity of this alliance!" snapped the bald man, addressing his tall superior officer but speaking as much to the old, frail man in the hoverchair and his thin, gangly assistant. "We entered into this partnership after receiving certain promises, one of which was the assurance that Luna-1's criminal fraternity would not be an issue–"

"I know what I said!" the old man said, his voice like nails down a blackboard. "I made good on that!"

"Did you?" retorted the balding man. "Did you really? A few of the, what do you call them, the 'little fish' are dealt with, but you let the big ones roam free to flap their mouths to the Judges? To Dredd?"

The thin man blew out a breath. "That was an unfortunate development. We were not aware that the information had proceeded beyond the targets we had already eliminated."

"Unfortunate," repeated the tall man. Until now, he had been content to let his subordinate speak, but now he weighed in with an exact, cold tone. "That is an extremely weak description of something that may jeopardise our entire project, especially when we are at such a critical juncture." He steepled his fingers. "Tell me, my dear friends, what masterful and completely foolproof plan do you have to deal with this blunder?"

The thin man exchanged nervous glances with his aged boss. "Well, uh, we thought we would just, you know, have him killed."

"And how do you propose to do that?"

The old man in the hoverchair recovered a little of his poise. "Like I've told you time and time again, I have loyal men in every part of this colony. The Luna Grand Hall of Justice is no exception."

The tall man raised an eyebrow. "So, what then? Some crooked Judge will simply walk into Umbra's cell and scramble his brains with a pulse blast?"

"Nothing so theatrical," the frail figure shook its head very slightly. "Our friend Vik is a big eater, but I'm afraid he'll find something in the prison food that will disagree with him. Permanently."

The bald man drummed his fingers impatiently on the obsidian table. "But this is too little too late! It is closing the barn door after the cow has bolted!"

"Horse," growled the tall man in exasperation. "After the horse has bolted. If you're going to copy their idioms, at least get it right..."

"I apologise, sir. Cow, horse; perhaps pig would be a better euphemism for that bloated sack of fat Umbra. My point stands, however. For better or worse, we must assume that because of this oversight, Dredd has moved closer to uncovering our operation."

"Indeed," his superior added. "So how shall we ensure that he is thrown off the trail? We cannot afford to have Dredd or that decrepit cowboy Tex disrupting the scheme until the grand finale is ready."

The frail old man gave a thin, predatory smile, his teeth emerging from behind his pallid lips like a knife being drawn from a sheath. "Oh, I have something in mind. With the technology you provided as your part of the alliance, I think we can set an incident in motion that will tie up Dredd and his little posse until we're ready to deal with them." He touched a control on the arm of his chair and the face of one of Dredd's taskforce formed in the holo-tank. "I believe you have already begun to turn the screws on this one?"

The bald man's expression was one of disdain. "I find your terminology crude. The protocol is subtle and carefully controlled, far more so than any clumsy physical torture methods."

"You Teks, you're always preening yourself over your damn hardware." The old man gave an airy wave. "The fact remains, we'll give this Judge a good, hard push and see what breaks. Dredd will be so busy scrambling over the fallout that he'll be looking the other way when we come for him."

The bald man was about to complain once again, but the tall man cut him off. "Yes, I concur. This approach makes good use of our resources. I had hoped to play this card a little later, but circumstances demand otherwise. We will proceed as you suggest."

"I'm so glad you approve," the frail man replied, with thinly veiled sarcasm.

"One more point," the bald man pressed on, ignoring the narrow-eyed look from his superior officer. "The installation of the secondary device, the reserve contingency against Judge-Marshal Tex... Was it successful?"

"Completely," said the thin man. "The unit sent a burst transmission of telemetry after activation earlier today. It should remain undetected until we need to use it, if at all."

The tall man rubbed his chin thoughtfully. "Perhaps we could deploy it sooner rather than later. We may be able to combine it with our colleague's plan to disrupt Dredd's investigation."

The old man's smile grew wider. "That," he grinned, "is the best idea you've had all day! Dredd must be made to pay for his misdeeds and for the life of me, I'm damned if I can't think of a better way to do it than this!" He laughed, a dry and dusty sound like the crackling of old, dead leaves and presently, his fellow conspirators joined him in harsh, ruthless amusement at their plans.

· · ·

Even the polished sheen of Kontarsky's helmet couldn't disguise the tight sneer of disdain that creased her face as she strode purposefully across the main atrium of the Green Cheese Shoplex, Judge Foster at her side and a muted, wary Rodriguez a couple of steps behind. From all sides, hard sell holo-commercials and the braying voices of advert drones were bombarding her.

"Get Ugly! Get Sump! Because you're worth it!"

"Plasti-Flakes – taste the difference! Now with flavour!"

"Mom's Robot Oil! An Oil... for Robots!"

"Wear Clothes By Qwecko... Or else you're a loser!"

The sheer, unadulterated consumerism of it all sickened her to the very core of her Soviet soul. The Shoplex was a broad, thick disc, forty storeys tall, from the outside resembling a gigantic wheel of Swiss cheese; inside, it was a loud, offensive temple to the capitalist ideal of money. Luna-citizens swarmed around her, pushing and shoving, forcing themselves into stores and vendor cubicles to snap up products they didn't need. The pure greed of the place seemed to leak into the very air itself and it made Kontarsky's guts knot. "Look at this place," she growled. "These people are like pigs at a trough."

Foster shrugged. "It's just shopping. Some people gotta have a hobby and it's better this than murdering their neighbours."

Kontarsky shook her head. She should have known better than to expect a sympathetic viewpoint from the Brit-Cit Judge. His corrupt nation was just as bad as all the others. She flicked a quick glance over her shoulder at Rodriguez, who was continually scanning the crowd, watchful and tense. Kontarsky doubted that he would feel any different, either.

As they approached the main bank of turbolifts, the Sov-Judge passed through a flickering scan-beam and triggered another advert. This one was a "cred-seeker," a targeted commercial that spoke directly to potential consumers. "Hello there!" it said, as a holo-image formed in front of her. "Wouldn't you look dynamite in the new Luna collection from Kalvin Klone?" The hologram morphed into a version of Kontarsky, but dressed in a sumptuous formal gown; the only incongruous note was that the holo-version of her was still wearing her Judge's helmet. For a split-second, Nikita found herself admiring how the clothes hung on her, wondering if she could afford the dress on her pay. In the next moment she waved the image away, annoyed at herself for briefly falling for the sales pitch.

The waiting shoppers parted before her stern gaze and the three Judges took the first lift to arrive. "M-Haul Incorporated," Kontarsky told the vox-control.

"Level thirty-six," said the lift and the capsule jetted upward.

"So," Rodriguez said suddenly. "What's the plan? We go in, rough a few of these spugs up, lean on them?" His fingers were drumming on the side of his helmet in a rapid tempo.

"We secure the company records," said Kontarsky, "and keep a look out for anyone who might have more information than they're letting on."

Foster nodded. "We got the better assignment, I reckon. Dredd and J'aele have got two whole warehouse domes to check out by the shipping docks."

Kontarsky nodded but said nothing. Before they had set out this morning, Dredd had given them a briefing on his interrogation of the criminal pervert Vik Umbra and the M-Haul connection to the weapons. She had her doubts that the MoonieCorp clue was anything more than a false lead – Kontarsky suspected that Umbra had used the name to play on Dredd's suspicions – but rousting the staff at the M-Haul offices might still have some value to the investigation.

The lift chimed and the doors opened to their destination floor. The moment they stepped out, the cacophony of commercial jingles and invasive advertising hit them squarely in the face. A robot bearing a tray of mock-meat patties began to follow them. "Hey there, citizens! How about a free sample of the new Flame-Grilled Fungi-Snack from Burger Me?"

"Go away," Kontarsky snapped.

"It's fungus-tastic!" continued the machine. "Fortified with extra synth for that char-broiled taste! Mmm-mmm!"

Without warning, Rodriguez rounded on the machine and knocked the tray out of its grippers. "You got mushrooms in your audio pickup, you tin-head clicker? She said get lost!" To underline his point, the SouthAm Judge gave the robot a bad-tempered shove that sent it squealing away on its castors.

Kontarsky let that slide for a moment and pushed open the doors to M-Haul's small office. "Justice Department," she said, her voice clear and hard. "Crime sweep."

The receptionist was a human – a rarity, Kontarsky noted – and she visibly paled as the Judges approached her. "C-can I help you?"

"The manager. Right now," said Foster. Kontarsky was impressed at the Brit-Judge's control and tone. The right amount of force and authority in a Judge's commands often spelled the difference between a pliant citizen and an obstructive one. The receptionist was already on her way into the office proper, a cluster of desk cubicles further back into the building and the trio of Judges advanced.

"Foster, watch the doors," Kontarsky said, sotto voce. "In case we get any runners."

The manager returned with the receptionist. He was a portly man, florid and sweaty with surprise. Kontarsky automatically tagged him as someone hiding something. She held out a hand computer to him. "I want all your office files downloaded to this unit."

"What's this all about?" he asked. "We've done nothing wrong. We've only just taken over this business." He dabbed at his forehead with handkerchief. "Perhaps your concerns were with the previous owners–"

"I won't ask again," said Kontarsky. "Unless you'd like me to believe you are obstructing a Justice Department investigation?"

That was enough. The manager took the computer and she watched him link it to the M-Haul mainframe. In a matter of seconds, the dense memory core in the portable unit had flash-copied the office's entire file store, simultaneously broad-casting it back to a team of data analysts in Tek-Division.

"Now perhaps you can tell us something about the salvage stored in M-Haul's warehouses. What happened to the last consignments?"

The manager blinked. "What consignments?"

Rodriguez made a spitting noise and closed the distance to the overweight man in two long strides. "Do we look like we have time to waste with you, idiota?" he barked, his fists balling. "Spill it, you worm!"

"I-I don't—"

"What?" His colour rising, Rodriguez shouted in the man-ager's face. "Are you going to lie to me again?"

Foster and Kontarsky exchanged glances and the Sov-Judge made a small halting gesture with her hand. If the Pan Andes lawman wanted to play up the role of bad cop, then let him. It would make things move quicker.

"There was no salvage in the company inventory when we took it over!" the sweaty man spluttered. "The storage domes were empty!"

Kontarsky studied her portable lie detector, the East-Meg version of the device the Mega-City Judges called a "Birdie". The needle was buried in the "Nyet" end of the scale.

"You're lying to me!" Rodriguez bellowed.

"He's telling the truth," began the Sov-Judge, but Rodriguez didn't seem to hear her.

"You stinkin' bastardo!" The SouthAm Judge gave the manager a vicious backhanded slap that sent him staggering. "You're in it with those other pendejos, right? Making me look like a fool!"

"Rodriguez!" she snapped. "Back off!"

"No, no, no," he growled and with one swift movement pulled the manager into a headlock and pressed the barrel of his pulse gun to the back of his skull. Judge Rodriguez flicked the power dial to level four and the pistol hummed with power. "He talks or he loses his head!"

"Rodriguez, you're out of line!" said Foster. "Let him go!"

"Shut up, Brit-boy! And you too, chica. You let me do this my way!"

"Rodriguez, put away that weapon."

"I don't think so!" he said, his face crimson red with barely restrained anger. "Talk, you fat slug! Talk!"

The manager whimpered, his synthi-wool slacks darkening as his bladder loosened. "Please! I don't know any–"

The pulse blast cut through the air like a thunderclap. At point-blank range, the manager's entire head vaporised into a mess of hot goo that blew out across the room in a spray. Kontarsky flinched as bits of brain matter pattered over her helmet. Then she was diving for cover as Rodriguez fired wildly, sending particle bursts into computer terminals, walls, the receptionist and other screaming workers.

Judge Foster stood his ground and tried to bracket the outlaw Judge with a brace of stun-level discharges but Rodriguez was too fast, fuelled by adrenaline and anger and sent a high-energy bolt into the Brit-Judge's chest. Kontarsky saw him go spinning away behind a charred desk.

She took a breath of heat-seared air and spoke into her helmet mike. "All units, we have a rogue officer at the Green Cheese Shoplex, level thirty-six! Foster is down. Judge Miguel Rodriguez has gone rogue!"

Broadcast over the general frequency to all Judges within a sector-wide radius, Kontarsky's urgent message crackled over Dredd's helmet speakers. His jaw hardened when he heard the name of the Pan Andes Judge.

I should have sent him home when I had the chance.

A few metres away, at the storage dome entrance, he saw Tek-Judge J'aele freeze, hearing the same call for help. Neither man said a word; they both turned and sprinted for their zipper bikes.

Dredd reached the Shoplex as the first H-wagons arrived, a few moments ahead of J'aele thanks to the superior speed and handling of the Krait 3000 he rode. Without stopping, he piloted the nimble grav-cycle through the main doors of the shopping mall, sounding the whooping sirens to scatter the droves of frightened civilians coming the other way. Inside, fire alarms were blaring and a soothing female voice asked politely for everyone to exit in a calm, orderly fashion.

No one was listening and people were falling over one another to get out. Dredd caught the sound of pulse-fire from the upper levels and the smashing of glasseen. As he swooped around, the Judge saw a juve using the confusion to steal a Tri-D projector from an electronics store. Dredd knocked him to his knees with a kick as he passed the opportunist thief. "Control, gotta kid in a blue radorak down outside the Gizmonics store, level one. Have someone pick him up. Looting, two years mandatory." Twisting the Krait's throttle, Dredd guided the bike up in a spiral climb. "Am in pursuit of Rodriguez."

"Copy, Dredd," came the voice of the dispatcher. "J'aele's on the way from the roof. He'll meet you there."

On the thirty-sixth floor, Dredd set the zipper to hover mode and dismounted, weaving through burnt planters and the heat-scorched corpses of citizens. He found the M-Haul offices a smoking ruin. Kontarsky was at the doorway, fumbling at a medpack. Foster lay nearby, groaning weakly.

"He'll live," the Sov-Judge said. "The shot just grazed him." She nodded in the direction of a large kneepad boutique. "Rodriguez went in there. He's got hostages."

"What the drokk happened?"

Kontarsky gave a weak shrug. "He was fine one second and the next..."

J'aele approached from the stairwell with a trio of Special Judicial Service Judges. The Justice Department's internal affairs division, the SJS were notorious for their ruthless nature and the zeal with which they pursued errant Judges. The silver skull designs on their uniforms earned them the nickname "Reapers" from street officers. "We'll take it from here," said one of them. "SJS Chief Kessler's orders."

Dredd shook his head. "Negative. Rodriguez is one of my team. I'll deal with him. Kessler can take it up with me if he doesn't like it."

The SJS officers hesitated. Each of them knew Dredd by reputation and each of them knew he and Kessler had crossed swords before. Before any of them could object, J'aele handed Dredd a laser rifle. "Take this. It's more accurate than the STUP-gun. You'll be able to knock him out with one shot."

Dredd accepted the weapon with a grim nod.

8. CORPUS DELICTI

Dredd passed through the archway and into the garishly lit interior of Forbidden Knee – The Kneepad Store For Those Who Dare! – crouching low to minimise his silhouette. The Mauley laser rifle was pressed close to his chest, charged and ready to spit searing coherent light with a single trigger-squeeze. The Judge paused, weighing his options and considering the terrain. Forbidden Knee was one of the larger retail units in the Shoplex, with favoured positioning on the thirty-sixth floor. As such, it was crammed with hundreds of display cabinets and racks of high fashion kneepads that dangled down from the ceiling on thick cords. Even on distant Luna-1, the twenty-second century's most popular item of clothing was still a hot seller.

A high-pitched scream cut through the air and Dredd tensed. Stores like this tended to attract juves and he was sure that if Rodriguez had hostages, they'd be young ones. A small flicker of movement caught his eye and Dredd raised the rifle, bringing the vu-sight to bear. J'aele had already configured the weapon to urban fighting mode and Dredd toggled the compact scope from normal vision setting to X-ray. Someone was moving behind one of the larger displays and the gunsight rendered the solid object in a misty, see-through form. The Judge could clearly see the figure now, a woman on her knees, shoulders gently shaking as she sobbed.

Dredd made a mental note of her position and moved deeper into the store. Once in a while, Dredd heard a random series of pulse blasts and saw energy bolts lancing into the ceiling. One lucky shot caught a suspended display rack and sent a dozen Tommy Mutiefinger kneepads tumbling to the floor, to burn there in an expensive little bonfire. Rodriguez was shouting and ranting, but it was difficult for Dredd to get a sense of what he was saying – some of the words were in English, but the majority of his tirade was being conducted in a guttural SouthAm street-speak dialect.

A quiet voice whispered from his helmet speakers. "Dredd, Kontarsky here. I've handed Foster over to the Med-Judges. I am making my way up the service corridor behind the kneepad store."

"Understood." Dredd subvocalised, letting the sensors in his helmet mike enhance and relay his words. "Keep him from using the back way to make an escape. I'll take him out of play."

"Copy." Dredd sensed the weariness in Kontarsky's voice, the self-doubt. She had been in charge here and now Rodriguez's sudden burst of insanity would reflect badly on her judgement.

Dredd shifted the rifle again, part of him considering the number of other Judges that he had seen go off the edge in his career. Officers who used to be good law enforcers like Sleever or Gibson, men that Dredd had personally had to deal with. It was perhaps one of the worst tasks that a Judge could ever be faced with, something that no civilian outside the kinship of the law could ever truly understand. The constant pressure of upholding the legal system, of passing judgement on hundreds of thousands of people throughout the course of a single career, sometimes these things proved too much to handle. Rodriguez, with the lax morals in-bred from years of living in the licentious Pan Andes and his volatile temper, had clearly crossed that line. Dredd shut down the train of thought with a grimace. In these circumstances, doubt could be a killer. Dredd resolved to mention this to Kontarsky later in his field report.

"Stop crying!" Rodriguez bellowed at someone out of Dredd's line of sight, the SouthAm Judge suddenly appearing in a gap between two cash terminals. "I'll kill you if you don't stop your stinkin' noise!"

With the X-ray scope, Dredd could see the shape of a cowering teenager behind the tills and he pulled the rifle's stock firmly into his shoulder as Rodriguez raised his STUP-gun to press it against the weeping juve's head. "You're all in it against me, eh?" the rogue Judge spat. "Every one of you filthy putas trying to get into my head with your chattering!" He pressed his free hand to the side of his helmet, as if he were trying to block out a noise that only he could hear. "Shut up!"

In the instant Rodriguez's index finger tightened on the trigger of the pulse pistol, a handful of outcomes raced through Dredd's mind: he could call out, distract Rodriguez, try to reason with him. With a careful shot, Dredd might be able to hit the SouthAm Judge's hand and sear off his fingers with a laser bolt, disarming him, or he could take the safety shot, the clearest and simplest approach that wouldn't risk the lives of any more citizens.

The rifle sent a pencil-thin streak of hot light down an ionised tunnel of air, making a sound like bones cracking. Dredd's shot melted a penny-cred sized hole in the faceplate of Rodriguez's helmet, cutting instantly through the cartilage in his nose and into the soft interior of his addled brain. The laser bolt made the Judge's skull pop as the superheated steam inside it expanded. All this occurred in less then a thousandth of a second, before Judge Miguel Juan Olivera Montoya Rodriguez collapsed to the floor of Forbidden Knee like a discarded rag doll.

"All units, be advised," Dredd said aloud. "Threat has been neutralised. Repeat, neutralised."

Although Chief Judge Ortiz was hundreds of thousands of kilometres away, broadcasting from the Pan Andes Conurb's Justicia Centrale, the distance did nothing to mute the volume with which he roared at his opposite number on Luna-1. "What kind of rinky-dink operation are you running up there, Tex?" he asked, his face filling the monitor screen in the Judge-Marshal's office. "You come crying to us for assistance and when we send you one of our best men, you kill him!"

Standing at attention next to Dredd, Sov-Judge Kontarsky fought to hold down a sneer. Best men? Rodriguez had been anything but that, a loutish oaf that Ortiz had wanted out of his hair, but given the direction the conversation was taking, she realised it would be impolitic to point out that detail at the moment.

Tex was fighting his corner as hard as the SouthAm Judge. "You're blamin' Luna-1 for this? Perhaps you didn't read that report that we sent you, Ortiz, but I reckon you'll find that it was your man who assaulted fellow Judges and murdered a half-dozen citizens!"

Ortiz seemed not to hear. "What did you do to him, huh? How did you make it happen?"

Judge-Marshal Che spoke up from where he stood. "You're not saying you think that we caused Rodriguez to go insane?"

Ortiz gave Che a filthy look. "Oh, so now you've got something to say?" The rivalry between the Judges of South America's Pan Andes and Mex-City was always a source of friction between SouthAm and Luna-1. "Hundreds of our people live in the lunar barrios of Puerto Luminia and if we can't be sure that Luna-1's Judge force is looking out for Pan Andes interests, things are going to get mui furioso!"

"Speak plainly!" Tex growled. "What in Sam Hill are you gettin' at?"

"This isn't the first time you NorthAm and Eurasian types have put the Pan Andes cities at the bottom of the pile. This is, how do you say, the thin end of the wedge! I'm recommending that the Pan Andes Conurb and Ciudad Barranquilla councils consider full withdrawal from the Triumvirate and diplomatic relations with Luna-1!"

"You've been looking for a way out of the lunar treaty for ages, haven't you, Ortiz?" rumbled Dredd, speaking for the first time. "And now you're going to blow up this incident in order to justify your needs."

"The killer himself speaks at last," snapped Ortiz, masking the moment of hesitation that Dredd's words forced from him. The Mega-City Judge had touched a raw nerve. "You should be happy that I'm not demanding your extradition for trial and execution, Dredd! If Tex has any sense, he should have you suspended!"

"Judge Dredd was following standard–" began Kontarsky, but Ortiz spoke over her.

"If I want to hear the whining of little girls, I'll go find myself a streetwalker." He fixed Tex with a gimlet eye as the Sov-Judge fumed. "I want Judge Rodriguez's body on its way home within the hour and I'm ordering our courier ship to prepare for departure. Our business, Señor Tex, is at an end."

"Rodriguez's autopsy isn't complete," said Che. "We must give his corpse a full–"

"Within the hour," Ortiz repeated with force. "Or else I'll send an armed cruiser to recover it. Judge Rodriguez deserves a hero's funeral." Before anyone else could speak, the comm-link cut and the screen flickered into a grey rain of static.

Tex sat heavily in his chair and shook his head. "Y'know, Joe, when I called you up here I expected to have a few deaders lyin' around because of it, but I never reckoned you'd be shootin' your own men."

"You saw the security tapes from the Shoplex. Rodriguez lost it. I had no choice."

Tex glanced at a monitor on his desk, where a loop of the SouthAm Judge's trail of destruction was playing. "Damn it, Dredd. Couldn't you have winged him?"

"Not without losing another innocent life. I made the call, Chief Judge. I take full responsibility for it."

Tex chewed his lip. "It ain't that simple, Joe. I'm responsible for what happens up here, not you." He stabbed a finger at the screen. "This is the last thing I want right now. It's already being broadcast city-wide by those Moon-U hackers."

"I was against this taskforce from the start," said Che. "Perhaps we should consider dissolving it."

Dredd gave him a hard look. "Thanks for the vote of confidence," he said bluntly. "Chief Judge, my team is making progress with this investigation. I need to follow this through to the end."

The Texan's eyes narrowed. "You're on thin ice, Joe. Luna-1 ain't like Mega-City One. We gotta half-dozen nations

cheek-by-jowl here and that means keeping everyone happy
– or else what little support we get from Earth is gonna dry
up."

"I don't think what happened to Rodriguez was a fluke,"
Dredd said. Beside him, Kontarsky's brows knitted in surprise. "His breakdown was engineered. Someone did it to
throw a spanner in the works."

"How could you possibly be sure of that?" said Che. "The
Med-Division's initial examination of Rodriguez showed
nothing untoward."

"Call it a hunch," Dredd replied. "And you yourself said
that his autopsy was incomplete. We need to examine the
corpse in more detail."

"Can't do it," said Tex. "I'm sorry, but I'm not going to risk
an international incident with Ortiz and his boys just on the
basis of your hunch." He nodded towards the door. "Get
back on the trail of those guns. I'll try to smooth things over
with the Banana City gang."

As Dredd and Kontarsky reached the exit, Tex called out
again. "Joe? I know it ain't your style, but can you try to keep
the bodies to a minimum from now on?"

Kontarsky studied Dredd for a moment before speaking, as
the two of them walked through the corridors of the Luna
Grand Hall of Justice. She barely covered her surprise when
Dredd had announced he suspected something unusual about
Rodriguez's aberrant conduct. Kontarsky had considered the
same thing herself, but dismissed the possibility as a wild
supposition; her kadet instructors had always drilled into her
that facts and facts alone were what made law enforcement
work. East-Meg Judges did not believe in "hunches". Yet, the
fact that Dredd had also come to a similar conclusion gave her
a swell of pride that was very un-Soviet.

"So ask me," Dredd said, without looking at her.

"Why do you think Rodriguez was... influenced?"

"You were there. You tell me."

She chewed her lip. "It... It was more of a feeling than anything else," Kontarsky managed. "Something about him just

seemed to be off." She shrugged. "Well, more off than his usual behaviour."

Dredd nodded. "Last night when we saw the hacker attack on the blimp. And again in the M-Haul offices."

Kontarsky gave a small smile. "Didn't you tell me earlier that you wanted facts, not speculation?"

"When you've been on the street as long as I have, you'll learn how to tell the difference."

She accepted this with a nod. "So, has your conclusion caused you to alter your opinion on my theory about an outside influence on the Kepler Dome rioters?"

Dredd gave a small shrug. "I'm keeping an open mind."

"The point is moot, anyway. Without a chance to study Rodriguez's body in close detail, any conclusions we have remain unfounded."

The senior Judge rubbed his chin, thinking. "Can't figure out why Ortiz is so eager to get the body back."

"I'm sure it is to prevent a deeper autopsy. It's not that I believe the Pan Andes Conurb are involved with our investigation, but it is common knowledge in East-Meg Two that SouthAm Judges have illegal bio-modifications banned by the global cyberware treaty..."

"Oh?" Dredd said carefully.

"Strength enhancements, cybernetic brain implants, penile extensions... All of which I'm sure would be discovered on a deep scan by a Med-Tech. Use of stimulant drugs is also prevalent among their law enforcement community."

Dredd nodded. "Ortiz would be hard-pressed to make claims about treaty violations if it was found out his men were doing the same thing," he sneered. "I'm getting sick of all this political garbage."

"It is sometimes necessary–" Kontarsky began, but Dredd cut her off with a growl.

"What's necessary is to solve this case. Anything else is of secondary consideration." The Mega-City Judge fixed her with a hard stare and Kontarsky felt his eyes boring into her. "Understand?"

"Yes, sir."

They reached an intersection, one corridor leading up to the flight bay, the other down into the lower levels where the Tek Labs and medical centre were located. Kontarsky took two steps toward the upper levels before she realised Dredd wasn't walking with her. "Sir?" she repeated. "What are you doing?"

"What is necessary. Come on, let's go talk to J'aele. I've got a job for him."

The Simba City Tek-Judge placed his hands flat on the desk-top and shook his head. "Out of the question. Frankly, Judge Dredd, I am shocked that you would even ask me to do such a thing."

"Too difficult for you?" Dredd asked lightly. "I'll under-stand if it's something beyond your skills."

J'aele's eyes narrowed. "I can do it. I just don't want to."

"Remember when Che said we were an autonomous inves-tigation team? That means we have free rein to pursue this matter wherever it leads."

"Even if that risks an international incident?"

Dredd gave him a level look. "You know as well as any of us that all secured records of Judge Rodriguez will be purged from the system the moment his corpse leaves the city. I'm not asking you to break the law."

"No, but you are asking me to bend it and bend it a lot."

"I could make it a direct order."

"I would refuse."

"Really?" Kontarsky broke in, watching him over the top of the monitor screen in the Tek Lab cubicle. "And then what? You would be relieved and shipped home on the next flight... and I think that the reception you would get there would not be a warm one, da?"

J'aele's expression darkened. "No," he said at length. "It would not. I... was not favoured by the commanders of the Simba Justice Division."

Dredd mentally ticked off another conjecture. As he sus-pected, J'aele was another problem case, an officer sent to Luna-1 as some kind of punishment for a misdeed back home. But for now that didn't matter. He leaned forward. "You know as well as any one of us that we're on the clock, J'aele. I need to see the autopsy report on Rodriguez."

"Why don't you just ask Judge-Marshal Tex?"

"He has other concerns right now... And I'm not sure we can trust Tex's people," Dredd said quietly. "I'm not going to take the chance."

J'aele crossed his arms. "And what makes you think you can trust me?"

"I'm a good judge of character," retorted Dredd, "and besides, if you're willing to admit it to me or not, you want to bust this case as much as the rest of us, if for no other reason than to show the folks back home how wrong they were about you."

A broad grin crept across the African Judge's ebony features. "You have an eye for people's flaws, I'll give you that. All right, I'll do it." J'aele began to work the keyboard before him, swiftly tapping into the medical centre's data core, descending though layers of stored information. "What do we tell them if the South Americans catch us with our noses in their business? If they detect me, it could be very bad."

"Then don't let them catch you," said Kontarsky.

Dredd watched the holo-screen in front of the Tek-Judge writhe and flex like a live thing, panels popping open and closed as he navigated through dense storehouses of material, circumventing pass codes and security protocols. "You're good at this," he remarked. "You've done it before."

J'aele nodded. "I'm part of the central computer division's tiger team. One of my duties up here is to monitor data defence strength from outside hack-attacks. We regularly simulate data penetration by staging mock raids on our own systems, looking for loopholes." He frowned. "No matter how hard we try, though, those Moon-U perps are still getting in. It's infuriating."

Kontarsky said what Dredd was thinking. "Do you suspect the involvement of an insider?"

J'aele shrugged, still typing at a furious rate. "There are Judges from all over the world stationed here. Odds are that some of them will have viewpoints opposed to the people in power..." His words trailed off as a scroll of text began to march up the screen. "Here. We're in."

"That was fast," noted Dredd.

The Tek-Judge made a casual gesture. "I told you I could do it."

Kontarsky scrutinised the data. "It may have been for nothing. I don't see anything unusual here. It is as Che said, just the basic report."

"Freeze it there," Dredd interrupted. He pointed a gloved finger at a blank section of the virtual document. "There should be a comparative DNA scan listed. It's a standard stage-one post-mortem procedure."

"You're sure?" asked Kontarsky.

The senior Judge nodded. "I've signed off enough death certificates in my time to know the difference. Any Med-Tek examining Rodriguez would have done that, even on a quick check."

J'aele studied the display, working the console. "Dredd is correct. This is suspicious. I'm finding broken data tags in this part of the file."

"Which means?"

"The comparative DNA scan was entered here, but then it was erased. Rather sloppily, too." The Tek-Judge ran a few more commands and a cluster of red indicators blinked into life on the screen. "And that's not all. This file has been tampered with. Someone altered Rodriguez's autopsy report after the fact."

Dredd's brow furrowed. "Who has access to these records? Who could do that?"

"Senior medical department staff..." J'aele tapped out another string of commands. "The senior technician on duty today was Sanjeev Maktoh."

Kontarsky was already speaking into her helmet mike. "Control, query and locate Sanjeev Maktoh."

"Checking..." came the reply. "Confirming, Maktoh, Sanjeev. Justice Central medical department civilian auxiliary, Indo-Cit resident on lunar placement. He checked out from work a couple of hours ago, logging absent due to sickness."

"It's him!" she snapped. "Dredd, he must be the one."

"I need an address," Dredd told J'aele.

The African Judge nodded and flickered through to a personnel file. "Here it is. Ventner Boulevard, con-apt 44/LK/31."

Dredd threw J'aele a nod. "Good work."

J'aele sighed heavily. "Just don't tell anyone I gave in so easily."

Ventner Boulevard was in the midst of one of the central dome's mid-level residential districts, well appointed with a handful of block parks and shopperias between the stubby half-ovoids of the con-apt buildings. Maktoh's small two-pod habitat module was on the thirty-first floor, facing outward. Dredd and Kontarsky made a landing on a nearby Multistack, giving them a clear line of sight into the medical technician's apartment.

Kontarsky studied the windows through a compact pair of Sov-issue binox. "I see movement inside. A single person, I believe. He appears quite agitated."

Dredd accepted the field glasses and took a look for himself. "He's packing a bag. What do you reckon, he's already bought a ticket back Earthside?"

She nodded her agreement. "If he's running scared, that might explain why he made such a bad job of doctoring the autopsy report. His disquiet could be helpful in interrogation."

"Agreed. We'll take him now. You go through the front door."

"You're not coming with me?"

Dredd gunned the Krait 3000's gravity drive. "I'll be around."

Sanjeev caught his foot on the trailing cuff of a shirt dangling out of the pile of clothes in his hands and tripped over. He landed on the suitcase that lay open on his folda-bed and it flipped, spilling out the contents he'd frantically packed into a mess of unkempt clothing. He fell to his knees and had to struggle to keep from crying. Sanjeev's stomach turned over and he felt the same about-to-throw-up sensation that had been dogging him since the phone call.

That voice at the other end of the line. Menacing him, intimidating, making veiled threats about what would happen to his mother and father, his wife and the pod where they lived in Indo City. He had done as the voice had asked, time and time again. He had hidden things in rooms in the Grand Hall of Justice. He had given things to shady people in dark alleys. He had slipped the tasteless, odourless capsules into the food of the fat prisoner in iso-cube 576. All of this he had done, gradually getting more and more afraid, more terrified by increments until today, the dam of his fears had broken. The voice had made him change things in the dead Judge's file and even as he did, Sanjeev was suddenly struck by the absolute certainty that this time he would be caught. When it was done, he closed up his desk and left, every muscle screaming in him to run, run, run!

And running was what he was doing… Just as soon as he could pack his bags. When the knock at the door came it was as loud as a gunshot and Sanjeev almost soiled himself in fright. It wasn't the casual, how-are-you knock of a neighbour or the hopeful entreaty of some robotic salesman. It was a cop knock, hard and forceful and without pity. "Sanjeev Maktoh?" asked a woman's voice. "Justice Department. Open the door."

If Sanjeev thought he was panicking before, then the absolute terror that descended on him after he heard those words showed that everything up until now had just been a taster of the real thing. He twisted on the spot, hands flapping at the air like distressed birds, mouth agape. Mad, insane plans raced through his mind – could he hide in the fridge? Barricade himself inside the toilet? Feign unconsciousness until she went away? But with a physical effort he shuttered his fear away and made himself focus. He ignored the banging on the door and the shouting woman outside. Sanjeev grabbed the billfold that held all the credits he had withdrawn from Luna Bank 6 and stuffed the one-way ticket to Delhi-Cit in his pocket, then he sprinted for the hab's window.

He heard the door crash open under the steel toe-caps of Judge Kontarsky's boot, heard the high-pitched whine of her STUP-gun going active. But he was at the window, it was open and he was through it, hundreds of metres up over Ventner Boulevard.

Sanjeev's fingers snatched at the box on the wall where the emergency floater was stored, the one-shot parachute-balloon combination that high-rise residents could use in lieu of a fire escape. It was empty.

A new sound reached his ears: the high-pitched motors of a zipper bike.

Dredd let the flyer drop down from where he had been hovering. He held out a bright orange bundle of plasti-fabric. "Looking for this?"

With crushing certainty, Sanjeev realised he had nowhere else to go and he closed his eyes, letting himself teeter forward and surrender to the lunar gravity. Before he could fall, however, something hard and rigid snapped into place around his wrist and suddenly he was yanked back into the apartment, landing once more in a pile of his own clothes.

Judge Kontarsky held the other ring of the cuffs she'd just snapped shut around Maktoh's hand. "Do not move," she told him, "or I may be forced to injure you... permanently."

Sanjeev gave a nod of acceptance and then threw up.

9. BREAKING STRAIN

As a Judge-kadet, Kontarsky had studied the techniques of interrogations very carefully. She'd learned how to give them and how to resist them, how to tell if someone who was answering was actually replying or just saying what they thought you wanted to hear. She watched Dredd take two long steps across Maktoh's hab and decided to treat this as another lesson, a chance to observe an American Judge in the midst of a cross-examination. As she expected, Dredd went for the direct approach.

"Spill it!" he barked, his face a few centimetres away from the medical technician's. "We know you tampered with the Rodriguez autopsy!"

Sanjeev said nothing, eyes flicking to Kontarsky as she wiped off her boots with one of his shirts. He gulped down air.

"Silent type, huh?" Dredd pressed. "Fine. We'll take you back to Justice Central and Psi-Division can pluck it out of your head the hard way."

"Nooo!" Maktoh suddenly found his voice. "Please, no! It's not safe there! They can get me anywhere!"

Dredd's eyes narrowed. "They? Who are *they*?"

The thin man's vu-phone chirped and with a weak, apologetic smile in the direction of his boss, he stepped away from the conference table and answered it with a husky snarl. "What? I told you never to call me here–"

The caller's voice was muted by distance. "Uh, sorry, Sellers–"

"No names!" the thin man snapped. "Are you even using an encrypted channel, you dolt?"

"Sorry, uh, sir, but it's the mark. He's got company."

The thin man winced and gave the other men in the Silent Room a wan look. "Judges?"

"Yeah. Two of 'em."

"Ah, sneck." He hesitated, he was glad he had put some men on Maktoh just to cover himself, but now he was afraid that things would get out of hand. The last thing he needed was for one of their assets to start blabbing so soon after Dredd had squeezed information out of that corpulent slug Umbra. The thin man decided not to take any chances. "You got the hardware with you?"

"Sure, boss. Right here." He could hear the rush of traffic in the background.

"Good. Waste him and then get the drokk out of there."

The trembling perp blinked fear-sweat out of his eyes. "I... I want protection," he said in a querulous voice.

"From what?" Kontarsky followed Dredd's lead, keeping her voice level and ice-cold. "Who are you working with?"

Words tumbled out of his mouth. "I needed the money, you see... I had gambling debts, I couldn't afford to let my family be shamed..."

"So you sold out," Dredd grated. "You'd better come clean. The more you hold back, the harder it's gonna be."

"I stole equipment for them, for the money. But then they wouldn't let me stop, they threatened my family..." The medic was on the verge of tears now. "Made me... do things. Change things."

"Like the autopsy," Kontarsky added.

"Yes... The analysis droid found anomalies in his brain tissue. I was told to blank the robot's memory, but it had already uploaded the data to the central file. I... I had to erase it..."

Dredd glanced down at the Birdie lie detector in his hand. Maktoh's stress levels were high, but his readings were still in the green. He hadn't said anything untruthful yet. "Tell me what you changed."

"I replaced the neurological scans. There were unusual readings in the aural centres of his brain. Very high levels of dopamine, serotonin and epinephrine…"

"Neurochemicals," said Kontarsky. "They stimulate adrenaline production and aggression."

The Mega-City Judge gave a slow nod. "Someone was pushing Rodriguez, making him crazy. How?"

"I… I can't be sure…"

"Take a guess!" Dredd growled.

Maktoh stared at the floor. "I think… Subsonic pulses, perhaps. Just beyond the range of human hearing, but powerful enough to affect the victim."

Kontarsky considered this for a moment. "This is quite possible. Sonic weapons technology is certainly capable of such a function."

Dredd grabbed the technician and dragged him to his feet. "Who was paying you, creep? I want a name!"

"No names!" Maktoh screamed, flailing in the Judge's iron grip. "Just a voice! A voice on the phone! The money came through Luna Bank! It's untraceable!"

"Dredd," Kontarsky said carefully, "Luna Bank is one of several subsidiaries owned by MoonieCorp."

"Well, well," said the Mega-City Judge. "What a surprise." He let Maktoh drop to the floor. "You're under arrest, pal. Conspiracy. Gambling. Computer hacking. Theft. I'm sure there's more. You won't be seeing your family for a long time."

The medic threw up his hands and yelled at the top of his lungs. "But I told you what you wanted to know! You promised me protection!" He stumbled backward, away from the Judges and swore at them in gutter Hindi.

"I never promised you anything," Dredd retorted.

"You're coming with us," Kontarsky added.

"No! No! NO!" Maktoh stamped on the floor like a child throwing a tantrum.

Something flickered on the edge of Dredd's vision and his head snapped around toward it. A thin tail of white smoke arcing around in a half-loop, something grey and bullet-quick spiralling towards the window.

"Down!" He shouted, reaching out to shove Maktoh to the floor.

Dredd was a half-second too slow. The compact mini-missile struck the glasseen window of the con-apt and the detonator triggered. Inside the warhead, a dense weave of monomolecular wires were projected outward in an expanding sphere and tore through Maktoh's apartment in a razor-edged hurricane. Dredd's right-hand glove was cut cleanly down the middle by a spinning fragment and behind him, Kontarsky lost a triangle-shaped section of her rad-cloak from another screeching piece of shrapnel.

Sanjeev was standing directly in the path of the detonation and took the full force of the weapon on his unarmored body. Dredd saw the medical technician jerk and spasm under a hundred hits before his body fell apart, irregular chunks of meat tumbling apart in a pink mist of fluids.

Kontarsky choked down a churn of hot bile in her throat and looked away. "I am uninjured..." she said, thanking her luck that the sofa she'd dropped behind had absorbed most of the damage.

"There!" spat Dredd, his now-bare hand stabbing out at something in the distance. Through the torn rent in the con-apt wall where the window had been, the Sov-Judge saw a black Skylord aero-sedan race away from a standing hover. "Blitzer team!" snapped the Judge. "In pursuit!"

Before she could react, Dredd was already vaulting out of the gap, dropping smartly into the saddle of his skybike where it floated below the balcony level.

The Krait 3000 handled well, turning sharply into the banks and angles as Dredd twisted the throttle, narrowing the gap between his flyer and the sleek shape of the dark aircar. He could see little of the interior through the sedan's tinted windows, but the bike's sensors swept an infrared frequency scan over the vehicle, showing three figures inside. Behind the driver, he could clearly see two human heat-shapes fumbling over a long, tubular object. The missile launcher. They're reloading, he thought.

The driver of the Skylord was good and Dredd could see that he knew the layout of Luna-1's streets. Against anyone else, that might have been an advantage, but with a Judge on his tail and the Krait's direct link to the city's central traffic net, Dredd was more than a match for the perp. Other vehicles were getting out of their way, yellow air-cabs and hover buses pulling aside to let them flash past. Dredd had the zipper bike's sirens and lights on the full power setting, the keening wails and flickering colours bouncing off the concrete canyons they sped down. The aircar turned sharply, pivoting around the offices of Interplanetary News and down into the stream of oncoming vehicles from a one-way sky-highway.

Slow and ponderous oxy-tankers passed by with horns blaring and a trio of egg-shaped floater pods collided with one another as Dredd's Krait cut through their formation like a diving falcon. For a moment, the Judge thought the aero-sedan was going to go full tilt toward the lower city levels, but then it angled upward and twisted into a side alley. Dredd executed a brutal wing-over and turned the zipper to follow them. His thumb flicked the bike's STUP-cannons from the "safe" to "armed" setting and he waited, counting down the seconds until the sedan's rear appeared in his target scope.

A flare of orange flame blinked out of the aircar's near side passenger window and Dredd jerked the handlebars by reflex, standing the Krait up on its stubby winglets. Heat from a jet of burning solid fuel seared the Judge's cheek as the rocket lanced past him, crackling through the air at near-supersonic speeds. His head whipped around to watch the missile spin past the zipper bike's underside and clip the upper floors of a Selenescraper. A fat bulb of yellow fire erupted out of the building where the warhead struck home, instantly immolating two whole floors of the tower.

"Grud!" Dredd said aloud. "Creeps have switched to hi-ex!" The Judge squeezed the pulse-cannon triggers and sent streaks of coherent particles stabbing out at the aero-sedan, bracketing the flyer. A well-aimed salvo punched through the trunk of the aircar and tore off the rear quarter fender and a stabiliser vane. The Skylord's driver pulled hard on the flight yoke, but the aircar lurched to starboard and began an uncontrolled turn.

Dredd gunned the Krait's thrusters and pulled parallel with the sedan, drawing his STUP-gun from its holster. "Level two!" he ordered. With these perps clearly eager to discharge military grade explosives as well as anti-personnel weapons inside the Luna-1 dome, Dredd's options had quickly changed from "arrest and detain" to "stop at all costs". Grud knew how many more shells they had to hand in there.

"Put it down, now!" he bellowed, his voice amplified by the helmet pickup and broadcast through the Krait's loud-speakers. "This is your only warning!"

The answer Dredd got was a snarl of spit gun fire as the Skylord sped over the roof of a tall, broad office block. Unable to turn as quickly with its stabilisers damaged, the aircar smashed through a video ad-screen, shattering it like glass. Dredd avoided the same obstacle and fired his pistol.

Pulse blasts punched out the windows on the driver's side of the flyer and tore ugly holes in the bodywork. Shots from a spit carbine sang out in reply, missing wide of the mark. Dredd returned fire and heard the clatter of a weapon dis-charge from inside the car. The thermographic scan of the sedan interior showed the gunman with the spit carbine twitch as he was hit, spastically emptying his weapon into the back of the seat in front of him.

Riddled with bullets, the driver slumped forward and his dead weight pressed on the steering column. The aircar obeyed and stood on its tail, the trunk flapping open like a gaping mouth as it soared vertically. Climbing on a powerful column of anti-grav thrust, the Skylord became a missile itself, heading straight towards the glasseen dome hundreds of metres above.

Dredd saw the danger coming. "Drokk! Control, Code black! Code black!" The two-word signal was an alert spe-cific to space habitats and orbitals that simply meant explosive decompression imminent. Heedless of the speed of his own flyer, Dredd steered the zipper bike with his knees and used both hands to steady and aim the STUP-gun, firing full-power shots into the aero-sedan, desperately trying to knock out the gravity drive, but the Skylord was a favourite choice of Luna-1's criminals for a good reason. The thick fuselage could easily soak up energy weapon fire that would tear apart a weaker aircar.

The other occupant of the vehicle, the gunman who had interrupted his boss in the Silent Room, was desperately trying to load another high-yield explosive rocket into the launcher tube when the aero-sedan collided with the inner surface of the Luna-1 dome. The shock made him jerk the trigger and the missile added its destructive force to the explosion of the Skylord's fuel cells.

Dredd saw the aircar vanish in a ball of fire before it was snatched away by the hard vacuum of space as a hole blew through the dome and out into the lunar void. The sudden tornado of screaming air ripped him from the saddle of the Krait 3000 and the bike followed the car out into the darkness. Time seemed to slow to an agonising trickle as he tumbled up toward the gap, the hole shrinking even as emergency jets of cellu-foam from nozzles on the dome frame raced to seal it closed.

Forcing all the air from his lungs, Dredd screwed his eyes shut and braced himself to be projected into space, but the sucking vacuum quit as quickly as it had started. The emergency seals had shut, leaving Dredd airborne and alone, hundreds of metres over the streets of Luna-1.

And so he fell.

"Bolze moi!" Kontarsky swore out loud, a rare expletive escaping her lips as she threw her Skymaster bike after Dredd. Her heart hammered in her chest when she saw the aero-sedan explode and for a moment she thought that the Mega-City Judge would perish along with the blitzers in the car; but then she saw the dark streak of a body falling back toward the ground and knew he had cheated death once again. She angled her zipper bike toward him and unbidden, a memory of something her mother used to say popped into her mind. *That one has a charmed life.*

Certainly, luck was on Dredd's side today. The lower lunar gravity meant that his fall was slower than it would have been on Earth, which gave Kontarsky time to cross the distance and loop her Skymaster beneath him. She felt the rigid grip of his fingers snapping into her leg and, with a single swift motion, the senior Judge hauled himself up and into the saddle behind her. He made it seem easy, as if nearly getting blown out into space and falling hundreds of metres was something he did on a regular basis – but then, Nikita considered, given Dredd's record of repeatedly defying the odds, it probably was.

"Good timing," Dredd said, after he got his breath back. Kontarsky smiled to herself; that was the closest she would get to a thank-you.

L-Wagons and emergency tenders were already closing on the impact point on the dome, ready to patch the temporary cellu-foam plug with a new piece of glasseen. Dredd watched them go, contacting Luna Justice Central and ordering a moon rover unit to search for any remains on the void-side. He frowned. A detonation like that and an explosive decompression probably wouldn't leave a lot of evidence to sift through, but there was a chance that the vacuum might freeze-dry something that could give them another lead. A crew of lunar Judges in e-suits would find whatever was left of the Skylord sedan somewhere out in the moondust – and, Dredd hoped, the guns the blitzers had been using.

The Sov-Judge's mind was clearly on the same track. "That missile launcher was military grade weaponry. This is a serious escalation from the small-arms we saw evidence of in Kepler."

"Agreed. It's time to step this investigation up a notch. We're wasting time chasing the little people while the creep who is pulling the strings is staying hidden."

"What do you propose, Judge Dredd?"

"Maktoh was being paid by a MoonieCorp shell company. MoonieCorp bought out M-Haul after they took possession of that weapons load. Those guns turn up in the hands of rioters. Do I have to draw you a picture?"

"It will be difficult to pin anything on them. MoonieCorp have worked very hard to disavow themselves of any connection to their founder following his incarceration. I took the liberty of checking the corporation's files – there are no records of any kind of infraction since they became an independent entity. They have... what is it you Americans say? They have kept their noses clean."

Dredd snorted. "Just because no one has found anything yet doesn't make MoonieCorp innocent. One connection might be coincidence. Two is enough for me to start kicking down doors and busting heads." He tapped her on the shoulder. "Get us back to the Grand Hall of Justice."

The blowout in the main dome had echoed across half a dozen sectors and broken windows on the upper levels of six citi-blocks in the prosperous parts of Luna-City North. Normally, news of something like a penetration of the dome would be kept rigidly suppressed by the Justice Department in the interests of public safety until the matter had been dealt with, perhaps adding a small report to one of the Judge-sponsored channels once everything had been cleared up, but other forces were watching and waiting for something like this to happen. Seconds after the emergency Code Black call went out, intelligent software subroutines and image processing engines went into play, creating footage and matching live feeds from co-opted street cameras to synthetic fakes.

Like a malignant imp, the crater-faced, computer-generated Moon-U mascot reappeared on screens all over the city, bringing with him a warning of terrifying disaster.

"Oh no!" cried the cartoon character, stopping traffic with his wails and turning thousands of people from their daily routines to watch him. "U won't believe this! Look at what the Judges did!"

Shaking his head and blubbering big wet tears, Moon-U played a scene of Dredd, laughing like a madman, as he fired a massive shoulder-mounted laser cannon at a bus full of screaming children. Teeth bared and spittle flying, the monstrous Dredd sent the energy bolt clean through the grav-transport and punched a huge hole in the city dome. The hover bus cracked open like a piñata, spilling kids of all ages and types into the whirling slipstream of the vacuum. People on the street watched in rapt horror as Moon-U's video showed the children sucked out into the blackness of space, their little bodies popping into too-red splats of gore.

"Dredd is crazy!" Moon-U shouted, imploring the audience to listen. "He's gonna kill U all unless U stop him!"

There were those among the crowds of viewers who saw through the display for what it was and some of them even had the wherewithal to say so out loud, a few even laughing at the ridiculous notion. But every single one of them was drowned out by the shouts of anger and hatred, as cries for justice echoed back and forth under the Luna-1 dome.

Tex snapped off the vid-screen with an angry flick of the wrist and stood up, fixing Dredd with a hard glare. "Grud damn it, Dredd! Were you even listening to me? I said I wanted minimum casualties, not massive property destruction! What the hell were you doin' out there?"

"You wanted results, Tex. I'm getting them for you."

"Results?" the Judge-Marshal exploded. He snatched up a data pad from his desk and read out what was displayed there. "A Justice Department medical technician dead, a wrecked con-apt and a half-dozen minor injuries in neighbouring apartments. Six separate airborne traffic accidents resulting from your pursuit of a criminal. Eight more deaders on the top floor of the Rent-A-Robot Agency tower, plus two more killed by falling masonry!" He slammed the pad down on the desk. "And then to top it all off, you punch a hole in the dome! You call that getting results?"

Dredd's eyes narrowed. "Let's be clear about this, Chief Judge. You requested my assistance up here because you wanted someone who could get the job done. I regret any innocent loss of life as much as the next Judge, but I had no choice but to go after that aircar. They murdered Maktoh right in front of me."

"All right, partner…" Tex took off his hat and rubbed his brow. "Let's say we forget the chase for a second and talk about this med-tech. What the drokk led you to him, huh?"

"Maktoh handled the autopsy files for Rodriguez. Something was rotten there and I followed it up."

Tex shook his head. "Don't give me that famous 'Joe Dredd hunch' bull! I know you leaned on that Simba City fella to hack the records, even after I told you to keep your damn nose out! You're lucky Ortiz and his cronies never found out about that lil' detail!" He threw up his hands. "Jovus! Che was right about you! You ain't mellowed in your old age, you've turned into a bigger hard-ass than you ever were!" The Texan waved a stern finger in Dredd's face. "You know, back home in the Big Meg you might be the big dog, but up here you're on my leash! We gotta different way o' doin' things on the Moon and you ain't towin' the line!"

Dredd ignored the accusing tone in his former partner's voice. "I don't have time to debate my methods with you, Tex. MoonieCorp are in this and they're in it deep. I put J'aele on a full sweep though their data records and Foster's going to join him when he's out of speed-heal–"

"You did what now? You're investigain' one of the biggest corporations on the Moon without my authorisation? You're barkin' up the wrong tree there, Joe! MoonieCorp ain't like it used to be in the past when ol' CW was honcho – they gotta good rep now, supporting charities, public works…"

"I'll bear that in mind," Dredd said dryly. "In the meantime, I'm taking a hopper out to Farside Pen to talk to Moonie himself."

"Oh no you ain't," Tex growled. "You disobey orders and disregard procedure like it ain't no thing and now you're on some kinda revenge kick, raking up perps from twenty-five years back? Moonie's a sick old man wastin' away in a cell on the dark side and you're layin' all this at his door? I reckon the low gravity is foggin' your brain, Dredd! If that's the best you can do, then you're not the Judge I remember…"

Irritation flared in Dredd and his jaw hardened. "I'm not here to play nice for you, Tex. If you wanted a softly-softly approach, you should have called in someone else!" He made a derisive grunt, looked at Tex and saw nothing but his age and his weakness. "Maybe you were right when you said your judgement is getting rusty. You and Che sit up here in your office and you have forgotten what life is like down on the streets. You got soft and now Luna-1 is going to pay the price!"

"You arrogant son of a bitch!" Tex shouted. "I've held this chair for half my grud-damned career! I kept this city from self-destructin' while you played the yahoo on Earth, tossin' around nukes like they were spit-balls! Remember this, Dredd, you ain't been Judge-Marshal up here for a long, long time! I'm the sheriff of Luna-1 and I say how it goes down, not you!"

Dredd slammed his hands down on the desk and stared Tex in the face. "Then do your damn job, old man! Or else step aside for someone who has the guts to enforce the law!"

"You callin' me out?" Tex retorted fiercely. "You stone-faced drokker, you think you can take me-" The Judge-Marshal's hand darted towards the antique six-gun in his belt holster.

Years of training automatically made Dredd go for his own weapon, muscle memory working his fingers before he was even conscious of it.

"Dredd!"

"Tex!"

Both men turned toward the source of the voices behind them. Che and Kontarsky entered the Chief Judge's office and beyond them through the open door, Dredd could see a dozen more men all watching with concern. Belatedly, he realised that every heated word he and Tex had exchanged must have been heard in the anteroom and corridor beyond. The hot anger that had raced through him just seconds earlier ebbed and Dredd carefully stepped back from Tex's desk, aware of the tension tightening every muscle in his body. The Judge-Marshal's expression held in a grimace of anger and disappointment.

"What is going on here?" Che demanded. "They can hear you out on Hestia!"

"Just a... difference of opinion." replied Dredd.

Tex sat heavily in his chair and drew a hand over his face. "I've got the Triumvirate breathin' down my neck, the citizens callin' for your blood... It's time to cut my losses." He gave Dredd a long, measuring look. "By order of the Judge-Marshal, you are to stand down from your position as taskforce leader. I want you on the first shuttle back to Mega-City One."

Kontarsky gasped. "Chief Judge, that is a mistake!"

Tex ignored her. "Luna-1 is gonna have to sort out its problems without your heavy-handed help, Dredd."

10. INTO DARKNESS

The old man in the hoverchair nodded slowly, the faint red lights of the Silent Room casting a demonic illumination over his craggy, pock-marked face.

"Perfect," he purred, drinking in the word. "I couldn't have asked for a better outcome. And with witnesses too." He gave a mocking salute to the bald man sitting across the room from him. "You're an artist, do you know that?"

The bald man seemed uncomfortable with the compliment and looked away. "I am merely an instrument of destiny. My skills serve only our cause."

His superior, the tall man, suppressed a cold smile. "Ah, you truly are a model Judge, are you not? Obedient and strong. Sometimes I wonder if you ever harbour dreams of taking power for yourself..."

"Sir, I would never–" the junior man began.

The tall man waved him into silence. "No, no, I know you would never dream of it. You do not have the instinct to lead, do you?"

His subordinate looked away, barely covering the anger he felt at being mocked in front of the other cabal members. The bald man said nothing and simply accepted the insult. In time, he would show his superior just who it was who could lead and who could not...

"I have to admit, for a second there I almost thought Dredd and Tex were going to shoot one another!" said the thin man, sharing his words like a ribald joke with his chairbound master. "A few moments more and Dredd might have done the job for us!"

"There's still time," smirked the tall man, joining in the gallows humour.

"I swear," began the old man. "I've seen it work a dozen times now and still it fascinates me. Watching a normal man slip over the edge into rage, at just the push of a button... Planting one of the devices in Tex's office, though, that was a master stroke."

"We have spent many years perfecting the hypno-pulser technology." Pride swelled in the bald man's voice. "On low-level settings, like those we used on Dredd and Tex, the subjects don't even realise that they are being manipulated. That's the beauty of it, you see. The pulser just amplifies emotions that are already present."

"Well, however it works, it's genius. That gizmo is gonna make the Moon mine again."

"You're too kind." said the tall man, "But let's not forget it was your pet turncoat who did the deed. I trust that particular loose end will not come back to bother us any more?" he asked, addressing the old man's assistant.

"Not unless he can sew himself back together," the thin man said flatly. "And the men who were sent to kill him are corpses as well. There will be no repeat of the Umbra situation."

"I am gratified to hear that. Perhaps now we can resume our plans without any further unforeseen obstacles?"

"What about Dredd?" the bald man asked. "He'll be on the next ship to Earth. Are we going to just let him go?"

"Nothing is leaving until the solar flares have died down," the man in the wheelchair shook his head. "And besides, you don't know Joe Dredd like I do, son. That stubborn law-dog is too dumb to just down tools and go. He's gonna put himself right where we want him, you can count on it."

"We're monitoring Dredd's movements," added the thin man.

"Good," said the tall man, smiling once more. "In the meantime, order the assassin to prepare. We will begin phase two immediately."

. . .

"Is it true what I heard? About Dredd?" Foster said as he approached the table in the mess hall where J'aele and Kontarsky sat. The Tek-Judge gave him a sullen look and nodded. Foster sat heavily, wincing as he unwittingly put pressure on his recently healed arm.

Kontarsky gestured at the limb. "You are fit for duty?"

"More or less," Foster replied. "The skin is still a little tender but it's nothing I can't handle. I just have to avoid any flying bullets for the time being." He hesitated. "I reckon I owe you some thanks, Kontarsky. The Robo-Doc told me I might have lost my arm if you hadn't been there to slap a med-pack on me."

The Sov-Judge gave a tight nod of acceptance. "I would have done the same for anyone. Just because our cities may not be allies, there is no reason why we cannot work together on amicable terms."

Foster raised an eyebrow in mild surprise. "Blimey. What happened to you quoting East-Meg doctrine at the drop of a helmet? I thought all Sovs considered us Westerners to be decadent and contemptible."

Kontarsky sniffed. "Perhaps my exposure to different law enforcement cultures on Luna-1 has broadened my viewpoint." She gave Foster a sideways glance. "Besides, I never said I did not think you were decadent."

"What we are is high and dry," said J'aele, absently smoothing a hand over his bald head. "With Dredd's removal from the taskforce, we're cut adrift. With all due respect to you, Judge Kontarsky, I doubt very much that Judge-Marshal Tex will allow you to take charge of the crisis investigation."

Foster nodded. "I heard talk from one of the Med-Judges that Deputy Che will be taking over where Dredd left off."

J'aele gave a cynical grunt. "Then we can be assured that nothing will get done. Che was once a fine officer, but he is nothing but a desk man now. This investigation needs a senior Street Judge to lead it."

Kontarsky shook her head. "If I had not seen it myself, I would not have believed it. Dredd and Tex, the two of them were near to blows when we entered the office. In all honesty, I had expected better from him."

"Dredd's served for longer than some of us have been alive," said Foster, pointedly giving the Russian a brief look. "Tex too. Maybe they're both candidates for the old Long Walk, eh?"

"I refuse to accept that!" Kontarsky snapped hotly. "First Rodriguez and now this... There is a conspiracy at work here, I am convinced of it!"

"Perhaps," J'aele agreed, "but without firm leads we have nowhere to go. Dredd might have had the latitude to follow his instincts, but we do not. I have no doubt Che would not hesitate to ship us home too if we ignore protocol."

"What about Umbra?" Kontarsky said. "Perhaps we could interrogate him further–"

"Umbra is dead," said Foster flatly. "You didn't hear? He was stuffing his face and his ticker gave out. Pop! Just like that and the fat bloke was a goner. They had to take off the cell door just to get him out."

"A heart attack?" the Sov-Judge's lips thinned. "How convenient."

J'aele sighed. "It matters little. Dredd will be on his way back to Mega-City One within the hour and in a few days we will be knee-deep in the Apocalypse Day anniversary celebrations. Perhaps all of this unrest will have blown over by then."

"You think these riots are just the run-up to A-Day then?" asked Foster. "Just the usual war vets and troublemakers we get every year?"

"Wait a moment," Kontarsky broke in, holding her hand up in front of the Simba City Judge. "What did you say before? About Dredd?"

J'aele blinked. "I said Dredd is on his way back to Earth."

She shook her head. "No, you said within the hour. You said that Dredd would be on his way back to Mega-City One within the hour."

"Yes. I passed him in the flight bay just before I came down here. I tried to talk to him about what happened, but he told me he was on the next Earth-Direct out of here. He took a Skymaster and headed off toward the spaceport."

The confusion on Kontarsky's pale face was suddenly replaced by a dawning realisation. She bolted up from the table and made for the door. "I have to go!"

Foster watched her depart in surprise. "What was all that about?"

J'aele shrugged and sipped his synthi-caff. "I think that for Dredd, the girl has a 'thing'."

"A 'thing'?" Foster repeated. "For Old Stony Face? Jovus, it must be that chin, or something…"

Kontarsky vaulted up the stairwell, taking the stairs two at a time, dodging past a pair of chattering servo-droids as she reached the vehicle park. Without waiting to get confirmation from Justice Central flight control, the Sov-Judge straddled the saddle of her zipper bike and kick-started the anti-gravity motor. Her Skymaster shot into the air, making a beeline for the spaceport terminal in Armstrong Territory.

On its lowest setting, the STUP-gun still packed enough charge to neutralise the prissy desk-bot in the landing bay office and Dredd carefully stepped over the twittering machine to work the controls that released the security lockout. The Justice Department command code that Tex had issued him had yet to be revoked, despite the fact that the Judge-Marshal had ordered Dredd home – a piece of luck that was working in his favour.

Dredd threw a glance out of the window to the spaceport bay below. There were three moon hoppers parked on launch cradles, each one an identical wedge-shaped craft resting close to the ground on a cluster of thruster modules. At full burn, cruising low over the lunar surface, one of them would be able to get him across the terminator to the far side in a couple of hours. The Mega-City Judge recovered a control key card and took the elevator down to the bay.

There were no humans down here, just a handful of maintenance droids and a bulky overseer unit working to strip down the drives of another hopper. Dredd had ensured that his timing was spot-on, in the ten-minute gap between shift change over between the human supervisors. As long as he didn't run into any problems, he would be well on his way before anyone realised that the moon shuttle was missing.

Dredd stepped up the ladder to the hopper's airlock and used the key card to open it. The security lamp flashed green and the outer door obediently opened. He was already clad in a Justice Department-issue environment suit, the helmet held under the crook of one arm and he had to shift his weight to move his suited form inside. Outside the influence of the gravity-field generator plates in the city proper, Dredd was careful not to let himself stumble under the lunar G-force. He was reaching out to tap the "close" control when he heard her words echoing through the launch bay.

"You told J'aele that you would be on the next Earth-Direct flight home," Kontarsky's voice issued out from above him, "but the port authority reported a magnitude nine solar flare today. Every Earthbound transport is grounded until the all-clear."

Dredd looked up and spotted her, the red rad-cloak catching the strip lights as she descended in the maintenance lift. She kept speaking. "Piloting a moon hopper alone under severe flare conditions is not recommended. A navigational malfunction could leave you stranded."

The lift deposited the Sov-Judge on the lower level and she approached him. Dredd's hand drifted toward the butt of his pulse gun. Knocking out a robot was one thing, but firing on another Judge? He wasn't sure he wanted to cross that line unless he was forced to. "Thanks for the tip. I'll bear that in mind."

"You're going out to interrogate Moonie? What do you hope to find?"

"Answers," Dredd replied.

"What if there are no answers, Dredd? What if Tex was right when he said that Moonie isn't involved? At the very least, you'll be deported from Luna-1, at worst you'll be up on disciplinary charges."

"I came up here to do a job," he grated. "And I'm going to see it through. You know as well as I do, Kontarsky, CW Moonie has some connection to the Kepler riot, to Rodriguez and Maktoh. If I can't find out what it is, this city will tear itself to pieces."

She nodded. "You are right, Dredd."

"Good. Now move back. The thrusters on these hoppers burn hot and you'll get fried if you're too close when I take off."

Kontarsky shook her head. "No, I don't think so." She took a step closer. "You're not going anywhere alone in this thing. You need a co-pilot."

"I can manage just fine on my own, rookie. I don't need your help."

"Really?" she said sharply. "Which one of us has the better training for this kind of vessel? You, someone who hasn't been inside a lunar craft for over two decades, or me, the winner of the Baikonour KosmoDome space pilot excellence medal for three years running?"

"And if I don't agree?"

She shrugged. "Then you are going to have to shoot me, because otherwise I'll alert Justice Central and you'll barely make it over the Sea of Rains before you are discovered."

"You're bluffing."

Kontarsky shook her head, the ghost of a smile on her lips. "No, I'm volunteering."

Dredd gave her a long look, measuring her sincerity. "I doubt that will look good on your spotless record with the Kosmonaut Directorate."

The Sov-Judge stepped up into the airlock, gathering an e-suit in her hands. "Like you said, Dredd, there's a job to be done. I can worry about my records later."

"Take your station, then," he said, with a curt nod.

They kept off the main aerial corridors between Luna-1 and the outlying domeplexes, flying nap-of-the-moon over craters and between mountain ranges. Kontarsky proved her worth immediately by programming in a new, faster course that skirted the Heraclides Promontory and took them up and through the Jura Mountains. The solar flare was at its height now and with their suits and the hopper's rad-shields they would be able to survive the brief exposure to the sun's hard radiation; nevertheless, the trip was a risk. If the hopper got into trouble and ditched on the surface, both the Judges would be cooked before any rescue craft could reach them.

Other vehicles were few and far between and Dredd made sure to keep any mining rovers or transports at the extreme edge of sensor range. The flare meant that any communications except hyperchannel and landlines would be severely curtailed for the duration, preventing word of their abscondment spreading too quickly. The added bonus of the solar radiation was its disruptive effect on lunar orbital spy-sats, enough to make a visual or sensor sweep of the Moon's surface difficult. They dropped into the Bay of Dews and Dredd pushed the hopper's engines to full burn, skating the shuttlecraft over the compacted grey dust at high speed, the gravity-repulsors along the ventral hull pushing a thin bow-wave of powder out behind them.

At last, they crossed over the terminator and as the Earth disappeared behind the curvature of the Moon, a wave of shadow embraced the hopper. Kontarsky felt her breath catch in her throat as she peered out of the shuttle's windows; looking up at a star-filled sky that was brighter and denser than anything she'd ever glimpsed from home.

"Incredible…" she whispered, losing herself for a moment in the sight.

"Look sharp," said Dredd abruptly, interrupting her reverie. "Registering approach pattern to Farside Penitentiary."

Kontarsky shook off her moment of distraction and nodded. Now was not the time for sightseeing, she had to concentrate.

Judge-Warden Lee had to concentrate just to be sure that he'd heard the hailing message correctly. He asked the communications monitor to repeat the signal and the droid obediently did so. When he heard it the second time, his mouth went dry. *Dredd*? A surprise inspection by Judge Dredd? Lee had noted the Justice-Net dispatches that the former Judge-Marshal was in Luna-1, but like most things that took place on the near side of the Moon, Dredd's arrival was far off and none of Lee's concern. Never in a million years had he expected that Dredd would stick his nose in here.

Farside Pen was an outpost in the outer face of the Moon, virtually alone except for a couple of nearby mining concerns and the massive radio telescope array to the south. Judge Lee liked it that way. It was quiet here out in the dark, there was little or no trouble and it gave him time to put his feet up and read while the sentry-bots patrolled the prison proper. It was calm and controlled at Farside Penitentiary, but the warden instantly felt a sick feeling in his gut: Dredd's arrival was about to change all that.

Lee met Dredd and Kontarsky at the main airlock. The senior Judge wasted no time and ordered the warden to take him into the secure iso-cube blocks. "Had I known you were coming, Judge Dredd—" Lee began.

"If you knew I was coming, it would hardly be a surprise inspection, would it?" Dredd surveyed the corridors branching off as he strode along the main thoroughfare. "How many officers have you stationed here and what's the inmate count?"

"Ten Judges, including me. We have four hundred convicts spread over five sub-blocks."

"Ten men to handle forty times that number?" said Kontarsky.

"My staff are the best," Lee added defensively. "And we have an extensive force of servo-droids and armed sentry drones. Farside is secure."

Dredd halted at an intersection and pointed to a sign. "Block E. Special Conditions Unit. That's where you're keeping Moonie, right?"

"Moonie? Oh, of course, you were the arresting officer," nodded Lee. "That was before my time, but yes, he's being detained there. In fact," the warden smiled, warming to the subject, "a number of the felons that you were responsible for apprehending are incarcerated here. Lucius 'Geek' Gordon, the Weatherspoons Gang, Luufy McMarko, William Carmody, aka 'Wild Butch' Carmody–"

"But why is Moonie in there and not in the general population?" the Sov-Judge demanded.

Lee beckoned them to follow him. "Come with me." The warden led them through a double set of airlocks and into a hermetically sealed access tunnel. "Prisoners in the Special Conditions Unit are kept isolated from the rest of the convicts for medical or biological reasons. Some of our inmates have genetic traits or peculiarities that prevent them from associating with other people. Prisoner Moonie is just such a case." He gave Dredd a look. "Did you explain Moonie's, uh, condition to Judge Kontarsky?"

Dredd shook his head. "Feel free to clue her in."

They reached an observation gallery, located high over a deep pit. Ten iso-cubes radiated out from a central dais like points on a star. The warden picked up a data pad from a monitor station and studied it. "Clinton Wendell Moonie, aka Mister Moonie. Former owner of Moonie Enterprises, he was an independent astronaut explorer who came to the Moon in 2014 during the Lunar Rush. Moonie was responsible for many ore discoveries and ice finds, but he was mostly known for winning a ten million credit prize from the International Astronautics and Space Administration. He discovered alien life here, a form of primitive bacteria in Cleomedes Crater."

"Da, that is a matter of historical record. He became a crime lord by exploiting his fellow workers and attempted to take clandestine control of the Moon through his ruthless capitalist-imperialist business empire."

"Uh, yes," said Lee, "but what's not on record is why he became a recluse after winning the prize." The warden touched a control and a monitor screen lit up. Kontarsky's eyes widened as she saw the frail human figure displayed there. For a moment, she thought the screen was distorted in some way, but then she realised that the prisoner it showed had a hugely disfigured head, well over two or three times the size of a normal person's. The bony balloon-skull was pinkish-grey with veins pulsing visibly beneath the papery skin and the surface was pockmarked with lesions that looked like tiny lunar craters.

"Chyort Vozmi! What happened to him?" she asked, unable to look away.

"We call it Selenite Hydrocephalus Syndrome, more commonly known as Moonie's Disease. The bacteria he discovered did that… It softens the bone matter of the skull and causes it to swell until it pops. Most victims died, but Moonie, well, he was rich enough to keep himself alive. Immunisation wiped out the virus, or so we thought."

"You thought?" snapped Dredd. "Explain."

"The alien bacteria was only dormant. It mutated and became active again a few years ago and we couldn't cure the new version, so we were forced to put Moonie in an isolation module. He's been there ever since, cut off from human contact and tended by robots." Lee tapped a finger on his temple. "There's not a lot of him left up here, if you get my drift."

Dredd studied the monitor grimly. "Get me a hazmat suit. I want to go in and have a little chat with our friend."

The multiple airlocks slammed shut behind Dredd and he took a step into the isolation cell. Two droids slowly orbited the aged man lying on the recliner-bed, one a spidery Robo-Doc, the other a simple servo-droid that hand-fed the prisoner thin vitamin gruel. "Hello, Moonie. Remember me?" Dredd's voice was hollow and muffled inside the thick polypropylop of the one-piece hazard suit.

Moonie slowly raised his bulbous head and blinked. "Who?"

"Judge Dredd. I've got some questions for you, Moonie."

The frail little man made a sad face. "Oh, I can't help you, Judge Dredd. I'm old, old, old, now. Forgotten so much. So much. Ha ha."

"I told you," Lee's voice said in Dredd's earphone. "He's senile. It's a side-effect of the virus."

"I don't buy it!" Dredd growled.

"Buy?" said Moonie, suddenly animated. "But I'm not selling! Oh no, I only bought the Moon! And bought it all, all of it was mine, mine, mine! Ha ha."

"You never let it go, did you?" Dredd approached him, stern and serious. "Publicly you were cut off from MoonieCorp, but behind the scenes you're still pulling the strings, right? How did you do it? Who is your contact?"

The prisoner made the same sad face again. "I'm old, old, old, now. Forgotten so much. So much. Sorry, Judge Dredd. Sorry. Ha ha."

"Don't test me, creep!" Dredd spat. "You're not fooling anyone. I know you're behind the riots and the guns, I know you're trying to turn Luna-1 into a bloodbath!"

"Bath?" Moonie repeated. "Blood? Bath? Sorry, Judge Dredd. Sorry. Ha ha."

Dredd grabbed a handful of the convict's shirt and hauled him up off the bed. The skinny little man was surprisingly heavy. "You wanna do this the hard way, Moonie? I'll be happy to oblige."

"Dredd!" Kontarsky yelled. "Restrain yourself! He's just a feeble old man!"

But even as the Sov-Judge spoke, something like hate and anger flickered across Moonie's distorted face. "Unhand me!" He shouted and with a snake-fast movement, the prisoner snatched at Dredd's hazmat suit and viciously shoved him backwards. The attack caught the Judge unawares and Dredd stumbled, his plastic-booted feet losing purchase on the smooth cell floor. He fell and landed hard, the breath singing out of him in a gasp.

"Grud! Creep's got a punch like a pile-driver!" The Judge could feel the familiar sensation of a bruise forming on his sternum.

"Dredd! Your suit!" Kontarsky's voice contained an emotion he'd never heard from the Sov-Judge before – panic. His gaze dropped to his chest, where Moonie had grabbed him. There was a ragged tear where a fist-sized piece of the hazard suit had been torn away. "Y-You... You've been exposed!"

"That's impossible!" he heard Lee shout. "Those things are rip-proof!"

Dredd looked up to see Moonie, back to his earlier manner, sitting down on his bed. "Oh, I can't help you, Judge Dredd. I'm old, old, old, now. Forgotten so much. So much. Ha ha." Moonie repeated the exact same words he had spoken before, the patch of orange material falling unnoticed from his hand.

"Lee. What are the symptoms of Moonie's Disease?"

"Uh, the first signs are bleeding from the nostrils, muscle cramps, acute headache…"

"How long?"

"No more than two minutes from contact until the virus takes hold."

Dredd eyed Moonie and then shrugged off the rest of the hazmat gear. He looked up to where Lee and Kontarsky were watching, horrified, in the observation gallery. "That isn't him," he said simply.

"How can that be?" Kontarsky demanded.

"We'll know for sure in…" Dredd flicked a glance at his chronometer, "just under ninety seconds."

11. HIGH NOON

"Is he insane?" Judge-Warden Lee watched Dredd kick his discarded hazmat suit into one of the cell's dim corners. "He's just willingly exposed himself to an incurable alien viral strain!"

Kontarsky found herself hesitating before she answered. Ever since she and Che had walked in on Dredd's argument with Marshal Tex, a doubting voice in the back of her mind had started to question the Mega-City Judge's stability. He was taking a serious risk down there in the cell, just to prove a point. She shook the thought away with a turn of her head. "How long has he been in there for?"

Lee checked the clock on the monitor console. "Too long. If he's infected, he'll be feeling it right any second."

The Sov-Judge tapped her helmet microphone. "Dredd. What is your condition?"

There was a long second when Dredd did not speak and Kontarsky saw him rub a gloved hand over his upper lip, looking for any telltale traces of blood. If he collapsed in there now, it would all come down on her shoulders.

"Four-square," Dredd's voice grated over the comm. "No infection, just like I thought."

Lee shook his head. "But... but that can't be. Moonie is the carrier, he's patient zero! How can you be all right? Unless the virus has gone back into a dormant state again..."

For his part, the prisoner seemed to be oblivious of Dredd and the conversation going on around him. The Judge indicated the Robo-Doc. "If that were true, your droid would have reported it, right?"

"Well, yes..." The warden's brow furrowed. "But these inmates are checked by an independent, off-base medical technician every six months. The last visit was very recent and Moonie here was still classified as dangerously infectious."

"A medical technician?" repeated Kontarsky. "From where?"

"The Luna Grand Hall of Justice. It's a standard operating procedure–"

"What was his name?" snapped Dredd, although he knew the answer already.

"An Indo-Citter, I think... Mac-something..."

"Maktoh." Kontarsky said the word with a frown. "Sanjeev Maktoh."

"Yeah, that's the guy."

Down in the isolation chamber, Dredd's teeth bared in an angry snarl. "We're being played for chumps!" He advanced on the prisoner, drawing his daystick from where the baton rested on his belt-loop. "Get up!" he ordered.

Moonie blinked at him. "Oh, oh, oh. Sorry Judge Dredd. Sorry. Ha ha."

"That act is getting real old and my patience is just about through. Stand up, creep and let's see what you're really made of!" Dredd's hand darted forward and hauled Moonie off the bunk, knocking aside the servo-droid in a clatter of utensils.

"Don't touch me!" the old man shouted, a vicious light flaring in his eyes. Moonie raised claw-like hands to defend himself, but Dredd deflected them with the daystick.

"Not this time, pal!"

The prisoner lunged, his big spherical head bobbing on his skinny neck like a bouncing beach ball. Dredd's daystick connected with Moonie's temple and there was a cracking sound, like ice breaking.

Watching on the monitor, Kontarsky's stomach turned over. For a moment, she was sure that Dredd had caved in the criminal's skull. Moonie then shook himself like a wet dog and a palm-sized piece of bony matter clattered to the floor.

"You've done it now!" the prisoner shrieked in a shrill, high voice. "You've damaged me!"

Moonie turned to face Dredd and there, through the rent torn in his scalp, the Judge could see delicate electronics and mechanical workings. "An android. I knew it!" He snatched at the duplicate's throat. "Where's the real Moonie?"

"Gone gone gone!" the robot chimed in a singsong voice. "Free, free, free! Mister Moonie is going to be back on top, you'll see! He'll have his revenge! He'll have the Moon, Moon, Moon!"

Dredd shoved the droid to the floor and left it there, chattering and babbling away to itself. Behind him, the hatchway irised open to admit Kontarsky and Lee, who nervously scanned the air with a bio-sensor.

"Not a trace of disease contaminants anywhere!" he said. "The Robo-Doc must have been reprogrammed to give false readings."

Acrid smoke issued from the android and it let out a thin screech. With a flash of seared plastic it deflated, melting into a pool of unidentifiable wreckage. "If this machine has been standing in for the criminal Moonie, then how long has it been here?" asked Kontarsky.

Lee's face was pale. "I... I don't know. Like I said, most of the prison's systems are automated. Whoever swapped this robot for the real man must have been able to bypass our security hardware."

The Sov-Judge shook her head, taking in the enormity of it. "Dredd, do you realise what that means? Moonie could have been free for months, or even years!"

Dredd nudged the molten remains of the robot's head with his boot, the frozen rictus of the android's sick grin staring back up at him from the floor. "We can worry about how and where he escaped later. All I want to know is where Moonie is *now*."

The frail man in the hoverchair sipped from a glass of water and looked up as his assistant approached him. "What is it now, Sellers? Cheer up, boy, you look like a moon-cow with chronic gas."

"Sir, there's been a development you should know about," said the thin man. "The decoy? The android at Farside prison?"

The old man made a dismissive gestured. "Yes, yes, what of it?"

"It's been discovered, sir. Dredd was there."

"Show me."

Sellers handed over a data pad and thumbed a button. A few moments of footage shot through tiny cameras inside the eyes of the duplicate played. The blurry form of a Judge's helmet filled the picture. Dredd's voice emerged from the pad's speaker. "An android. I knew it! Where's the real Moonie?"

The frail little man laughed softly to himself. "Where?" he said to the air, his face splitting in a feral grin. "Why, I'm right here, Dredd. And soon I'll be exactly where I'm supposed to be... with the Moon in my hands!"

"Mister Moonie, uh, sir," said his assistant. "How do you wish to proceed?"

"Our operative is in place, yes?"

"He returned from Union Station this morning."

"Then proceed as planned."

"Sir, respectfully I feel I must go on the record and protest this decision in the strongest terms."

Tex turned sharply and threw down the Judge-Marshal's Rad-Cape of Office, crossing the distance to Che in a few quick steps. "Oh, you do, huh? Grud damn it, man, protestin' about what I do seems like all you're good for these days!"

Che kept his face neutral and stood his ground. "You asked my for my opinion, sir. I'm giving it to you."

Tex made a negative noise and picked up the cape again, straightening it over his broad shoulders. Che used the opportunity to take a look at the monitor screen set up in the corner of the anteroom. The display showed a view of the area outside, the broad fan of steps leading into the Grand

Hall of Justice, where public announcements and important press conferences were held – just as one was to be given today.

"There is no need for this sort of display, Marshal. The public media office could have simply set something up to broadcast on the city-wide communications net."

Tex picked up his favourite hat and absently flicked a piece of lint from the brim. "Oh yeah? With them Moon-U hackers cuttin' into every signal whenever they want? What kinda message would it send if all o' Luna-1 thinks I'm broadcastin' from a safe little bunker somewhere, cowerin' behind a desk?" He spoke the last words with venom. "No, Che, we gotta step up to this, do it out in the open and show no fear." He donned the hat and straightened his badge. "That's the frontier way. Things are going straight to hell out there and we gotta show that the Judges mean business."

"I know that but we are less than forty-eight hours away from the annual Apocalypse War holiday. Could it not at least wait until after that? Or at least, you could consider using a force field or a las-screen."

"Damn it, man, why are you doggin' me on this?"

Che's lips thinned to a hard line. He knew that Tex would not be swayed. "Because I am your deputy, Judge-Marshal and it is my duty to point out alternatives to you."

Tex gave him a tight nod. "And that you have and respectfully, you can shove 'em."

"Yes, sir."

The Chief Judge of Luna-1 straightened and walked purposefully out of the anteroom and into the glare of the camera drones and spotlights. "Any word on Dredd?" he asked out of the corner of his mouth.

"Nothing. We have been unable to locate him or the Sov-Judge Kontarsky within the city limits. However, a hopper shuttle was launched a few hours ago from one of the outer docks at the spaceport. Dredd's ident code was used."

Tex smothered a growl. "Don't that beat all? That's Joe all over – he's like a damn pit-bull. Tell him to let go and he'll still hang on there and bite all the way down to the bone."

"What are your orders for when he returns?"

Tex stepped up to the podium. "I'll deal with him when the time comes."

The Judge-Marshal looked over the wide plaza that stretched out between the front of the Justice Central to the south and the Luna Academy of Law to the north. A milling throng of people were gathered there, easily a thousand citizens. Most of them were quiet, but there were a fair number brandishing placards and banners. There was a seventy-thirty mix of slogans visible, leaning in favour of mottoes about *Moon-U, Luna Liberty* and *Judges Out!* vying with a sprinkling of pro-government demonstrators. Voices were raised and there were some angry words being thrown around, but mercifully violence had not broken out. That might have had something to do with the rank of Judges wielding daysticks and STUP-guns spread out in a thin black line along the bottom of the stairs.

Tex gave the careful nod and smile to the audience that had become his trademark. "My fellow citizens of Luna-1, I thank you for your time and attention tonight. I have called this public address to answer some of the concerns that have been risin' to the fore here in our good city over the past few months…"

Foster stood at J'aele's side in the Grand Hall's overt media control centre, a dozen floors above the steps where Tex was speaking. A live feed from each of the hovercams recording him was displayed on a large wallscreen, each shot fixing Tex carefully under the powerful, clean light of the floods. All of Luna-1's media were present in some form, from Tri-D channels like LCTV and IPN to newsfax services like the Luna Module and SeleNet.

"You know, when I watch him talk I realise why he's done this job for so long," said Foster.

"And why is that?" J'aele asked, glancing at a console.

"The man has integrity. Honesty just comes off him in waves. He's nobody's fool and he's tough with it, but you get the sense he'll give you a fair shake. Every city should be so lucky to have a man like Tex in charge." Foster looked away. "It's funny. I heard he never even wanted the job of Judge-Marshal in the first place."

"That is correct," J'aele said, his attention elsewhere, "but those who seek power are usually the ones who are least suited to have it."

"True enough," Foster nodded at the console readout. "You got a problem there?"

"No, not at all and that worries me," the Tek-Judge replied, indicating the screen. "Because of the importance of this public address, Tek-Division has brought in all its counter-intrusion specialists to make sure the broadcasts are not interrupted–"

"You don't want those Moon-U punks breaking into the transmission?"

"Exactly. But we're monitoring all available wavebands across the comm-net and there's nothing going on out there. Not a single pirate signal or attack program in sight."

Foster shrugged. "Maybe you scared them off…"

J'aele shook his head. "I think not, Judge Foster. The jackals do not stay in their den when a meal is within their reach. Moon-U are simply choosing not to disrupt this broadcast."

"Isn't that a good thing?"

"No. Mark my words, Foster, they're planning something. I have a very bad feeling about this."

Tex knew that the crowd were hooked now and while he was sure that there were plenty of folks out there who hated what he stood for, he knew that they were at least listening to him. "Luna-1 is a proud city. We're a nation-state of folks from all over the Earth and just as much as we're part of our home planet, we're also independent. We're Selenites, Lunarians, whatever name you choose, many of us Moon-born and Moon-bred. Some folks out there are sayin' we ain't free, that the Judges are keeping you prisoner. Well, that there is a lie and I'm here tonight to tell you that Luna-1 is the freest damn city off Earth!"

A soft murmur of agreement moved through the crowd and Tex smiled a little to hear it. Any disquiet that Che's earlier comments might have brought up in him faded as he watched the strength of his words influencing the citizens. "There's folks out there who are screamin' for free elections, but we already got those. My name's been on that ballot time after time and you good people have always voted me back in to office, 'cos you know I'll do right by you. Now these same folks think I'm a tired old cowboy, long in the tooth and slow in the brain, but let me tell you this – I'm sharp enough to know that Luna-1 ain't gonna rip itself apart on the say-so of some cartoon goofball!"

Tex flashed a grin as a ripple of laughter crossed the plaza, before his expression hardened. "I'm gonna keep this city safe. It's my life's work. And no amount of rumours and half-truths are gonna get in the way of that." He tapped his badge. "This here means Marshal and that means I'm the law–"

At that moment, something high on the upper floors of the Luna Academy building glittered brightly and caught Tex's attention. The Chief Judge had a fraction of a second to register the vibrant crimson flash before a high-energy collimated laser beam lanced through his chest, the crack of superheated oxygen breaking the night air a moment later. The powerful bolt of coherent light melted through the middle of his badge and tore through skin and bone to flash burn his heart into cinders. Judge-Marshal Tex tumbled away from the podium, trailing a thin pink stream of vaporised blood. He was dead before he hit the lunacrete steps.

Shock and terror broke through the crowd like a wave and the panicked citizens surged in all directions, the line of Judges distending under their weight. Che was the first to the body and the sight of the ruined corpse of his old friend and commander made his guts knot with anger and sorrow. "Seal off the plaza!" he bellowed. "Now!"

In the media centre there was a stunned silence until J'aele snapped out an order to one of the camera operators. "The

Academy – the shot came from the Academy! Get a hovercam
up there!"

Several of the views that had been trained on Tex now
swooped giddily around and flickered over the crowd, catching blink-fast images of fighting, screaming, hysterical
people. Then the Justice Department's training facility filled
the sub-screens as the flying camera drones closed in on it.

Foster spotted the gunman first. "There! Unit six, upper
quadrant! Send men over there right now!"

The hovercam could see little; it was unlit on the office
level where the sniper had fired from and the drone's low-
light lenses were insufficient to show anything but gross
shapes and shadows. The figure, clad in a dark outfit with
bulky shoulder padding, was sprinting for a null-grav drop
tube and it turned as the hovercam closed in. Foster got the
impression of a pistol in the killer's hand and then with a
flash, the drone's live feed became a rain of static.

"Replay!" J'aele barked. "Freeze that last frame!"

One of the other Tek-Judges did as he was asked, halting
the video feed at the exact instant before the assassin
destroyed the drone. The picture was blurry and dim, but the
clothing the gunman wore was distinct, even in the gloom.

It was the uniform of a Mega-City One Judge.

In the hours after Tex's murder, the panic at Justice Plaza
turned into a crisis that soon expanded far beyond the death
of one man. Che's orders and a poorly considered command
given later by a watch commander led to the use of neutral-
ising stumm gas and riot foam on the people who had
gathered to hear the Judge-Marshal speak. Under the glare of
all Luna-1's media, a few Judges were injured and dozens of
citizens were killed in the deadly crush of bodies; every
bloody incident and moment captured and broadcast across
the city.

As the solar shutters across the dome interiors began to fan
open to announce the lunar dawn, the last of the bodies
trapped in the hardened foam were being cut free. Parked
medi-flyers and emergency porta-domes were serving as field

hospitals for those people too badly crushed to be moved and Judges of every stripe were everywhere, combing the plaza with serious and careful intent.

Tex's body had been one of the first things to be removed, but the brown smear of his blood, heat-dried by the laser bolt, was still there, a dark streak across the centre of the Grand Hall's stairs. Che stood to one side of the podium, which had miraculously survived the events of the night untouched. The Mex-City Judge was fixated on the upper floors of the Law Academy, watching the L-Wagon floating outside the room where the gunman had hid.

Foster and J'aele approached, gingerly giving the blood-stain the widest possible berth. "Reporting as ordered," the Brit-Cit officer announced.

Che nodded. "Quick thinking with the camera drone." His voice was flat and toneless. "Good work. What's the word from the other sector houses?"

The two men hesitated.

"Spit it out!" Che snapped. "I gave you an order!"

"It is bad, sir," J'aele began. "Multiple demonstrations across the city were taking place during the speech and the majority of them lit off into full scale riots the moment Tex was killed. Pro-justice and anti-government activists clashed. There have been a lot of deaths."

Che closed his eyes, as if the words were causing him physical pain. "Containment?"

"Ongoing," added Foster. "Riot units are in deployment in all nine territories and a curfew is in effect in most sectors. Manta prowl tanks and pat-wagons have been mobilised." The Judge paused. "The... the Moon-U broadcasts have begun again, city-wide."

Che gave J'aele a withering look. "Your division's performance has been pathetic, J'aele! Can you do nothing to block these chattering fools?"

The Simba City Judge looked uncomfortable. "They are not common hackers, sir. The Moon-U signals are using military-grade encryption technology... It is far beyond the capacity of the equipment possessed by the Luna Justice Department."

The Deputy Judge-Marshal made a spitting sound. "Our systems are so out of date it's a wonder we can still keep air in here!" He thumped one fist against the podium. "Damn them!"

"The pirate transmissions are inciting disorder in a dozen places. They're claiming that Tex's killer was Judge Dredd, sir and they're denouncing you as the instigator."

Neither Foster nor J'aele had any grasp of Che's native language and so they were spared the full impact of the string of invective he let out in response. His swarthy complexion flushed crimson with barely restrained fury. "This will not stand!" he growled. "I want you both to join the crime scene investigation team in the Academy building and evaluate the situation there! Get back to me with a preliminary report in fifteen minutes."

J'aele and Foster said nothing and acknowledged the command with nods.

The twenty-eighth floor of the Luna-1 Law Academy was primarily devoted to offices handling conscription and evaluation. By day it was busy with servo-droids, Judge-Tutors and a small staff of civilian specialists, but during the evening it was silent and inactive. Visitors to floor twenty-eight were typically parents looking to induct their children into the fifteen-year program that would turn them into Judges, but tonight someone else had entered by stealth with a plan for murder.

The darkened corridor Foster and J'aele had seen from the hovercam's live feed was now starkly lit by floating glow-globes and pin-spots, stark magnesium-bright light banishing all shadows and any places where even the tiniest speck of evidence might hide. Spider-like investigator robots prowled slowly over the floors, walls and ceiling, scanning the surfaces with fans of green laser light. J'aele gave a nod of greeting to another Tek-Judge, who sat crouched by a black-ened disc of metal.

"Here's your camera droid," said the officer. "Close range pulse blast hit, I'd say a level four setting."

"I concur," agreed J'aele. "What else do you have?"

The Tek-Judge stood up and Foster caught the name Tyler on the glint of his badge. "Not much. We checked the security camera footage and whoever this guy was, he knew exactly where all the sensors were located."

"He? You're sure the suspect is male, then?" Foster replied.

"Yup. Body kinetics and motion track ties in with a male, approximately two metres tall, aged between thirty to fifty years-old."

"That fits the description of hundreds of Judges," J'aele was dismissive, "and that's even if the assassin was actually a Judge and not just a jimp."

Tyler indicated the window from where the shot had come. "Well, Judge impersonator or not, the shooter was a professionally trained marksman. Takes a good eye to make a heart-shot from this distance. Which brings me neatly to the weapon of choice."

"You found the gun?" said Foster. "Where?"

"Garbage grinder in the maintenance room. There wasn't a lot of it left by the time we got here, but we lucked out. The grinders clogged up when they chewed through the battery packs and they left a few pieces relatively intact." Tyler picked up a plastic-sealed packet and handed it to Foster. Inside, the Judge could clearly see the shape of a pistol grip and a trigger assembly.

"Any markings?"

Tyler nodded. "Oh yeah." He tapped the packet with a stylus. "That's part of a Mauley M500 Hunter-Stalker. We're running the serial numbers down right now, but it's my guess that the weapon is Justice Department stock."

"I know these rifles," said J'aele. "I've used them myself–"

"Yes," said a new voice. "Yes, Judge J'aele, you have." As one, the three men turned to see four more Judges exit the drop shaft that the killer had used to make his escape. Only the Simba City lawman was able to keep a neutral expression; Foster's and Tyler's faces both soured as they recognised the uniforms of the Luna-1 Special Judicial Service. The man who had spoken advanced on them. The harsh floodlights glinted off the clear disc of a cyberlink monocle over his right eye and under their luminescence the lengthy pink scar that crossed the left side of his face glowed red.

Foster's eyes drifted to the skull-shaped sigils on the SJS officer's shoulder pads and badge. He could never figure out why the Justice Department's internal affairs division had such a thing for death imagery. "Judge Kessler. So glad you could join us."

Kessler scrutinised Foster through the monocle for a moment and the Judge knew that the SJS Chief was using the device to call up his records. "The pleasure is all mine, Foster," he said, a humourless, icy smile playing over his lips. Kessler's reputation was well-known throughout the city: a ruthless, vicious man, the SJS-Judge was more than willing to go to extreme lengths to get the results he wanted and unlike the internal investigations divisions of other Mega-Cities, Luna-1's SJS had full discretionary powers. Quite rightly, other Judges spoke Kessler's name with dread and antipathy. "I'm here to inform you that as of now, in accordance with Justice Department regulations 46-A through 48-F, the SJS are taking direct control of this murder investigation. From this point on, you may consider yourselves under my command."

12. POLITIKA

Instead of hugging the lunar surface as they had on the journey over the terminator, Dredd ordered Kontarsky to get them back to the domed city as quickly as she could. The Sov-Judge programmed in a speedy sub-orbital trajectory that took them up and over the Pole, approaching the city's starport dock.

As they descended, Kontarsky tapped the side of her helmet as a message broke in over the guard channel. "Dredd, I am getting a signal from Traffic Control. There is a curfew in effect across all of Luna-1."

Dredd came forward into the cockpit from the rear cabin, a half-finished cup of synthi-caff in his gloved hand. "Any details?"

She shook her head. "No, just a warning. I will tap into the civilian video network for more information."

"Give me a feed on the monitor."

Kontarsky did as she was commanded and presently a grainy image broadcast on LCTV's news feed came into focus. "Reception is poor," she noted. "It's not the solar flares. It must be localised interference."

"Probably Moon-U trying to jam them." Dredd fell silent as a newsreader, grim-faced and severe, appeared on screen.

"For those of you just joining us, we apologise for the pre-emption of SportsTime and bring you this ongoing report of the current breaking story across Luna-1..." The display cut to footage of rioting near the water reclamation plants. "Tonight, a city is in uproar as millions of lunarians take to the streets in anger and fear after the brutal assassination of Chief Judge-Marshal Jefferson J Tex…"

Kontarsky's heart suddenly leapt into her throat as she watched the murder of Tex play out, the flash of the laser piercing the lawman like a lightning bolt.

"Tex…" Dredd's voice was a low growl.

"Recent incidents of civil disobedience by members of the Luna Liberty group Moon-U have spilled over into full-scale street warfare in all nine territories, as the Justice Department struggles to maintain an enforced curfew to stem the tide of lawlessness…"

"They killed him." Kontarsky breathed, hardly able to take in the enormity of what she had just seen. "They must have planned this all along."

Dredd crushed the metallic cup in his hand with a snap. "Moonie," he snarled. "He's behind this!"

The screen changed to show Che placing his hand on a giant star-and-moon sigil in the Grand Hall's central chamber. "Former Deputy Chief Che was sworn in as Judge-Marshal of Luna-1 a few hours ago and he promised that the current disorder would be dealt with as swiftly as possible, in addition to apprehending Tex's killer. Meanwhile, rumours continue to circulate that Mega-City One's Judge Joseph Dredd is the prime suspect in this heinous crime. Judge Udo Kessler, head of Luna's Special Judicial Service, had this to say…" The SJS chief stared into the camera. "We will capture Tex's murderer, you may be assured of that. He will not be able to hide, even behind the shield of a Judge's badge…"

Kontarsky muted the channel, the soundless footage of more rioting and street fighting taking on an unreal quality. "I… I am shocked…"

Behind her, Dredd was staring out of one of the hopper's windows, his jaw set with implacable resolution. "I'll find him, Tex," Dredd said softly, giving his old friend a private farewell. "Count on it."

The Sov-Judge spoke. "I have linked into a local Justice Department data-nexus. The SJS have us both at the top of a priority watch-list."

"Figures. Kessler's got no love for me. If he's on the case, he'll do whatever he can to lay the blame on me."

"You think the SJS could be involved in Moonie's conspiracy?"

"Maybe. Or he could just be using Kessler's natural antipathy toward me. Either way, it puts a king-sized block in our way."

She tapped her fingers on the flight yoke, thinking. "Judge-Warden Lee will be able to vouch for your presence at the prison and I can testify that I was with you during the assassination–"

"It would never get that far," Dredd rumbled. "If Moonie can get a Chief Judge killed in front of thousands of people, he'll have schemes in place to deal with us." The Judge shook his head. "No, we need evidence, something to tie MoonieCorp to this whole set-up." Dredd bent over a console and called up a digi-map. "Divert course and bring us down near Kepler..."

"Why do you want to return there? The dome is still sealed off. What do you expect to find?"

"The clues from the weapons led us to Moonie, but that's dead-ended for now until we can locate the real man. Our only other lead is the oxygen outage."

Kontarsky considered this for a moment. "Very well. I'll drop you off outside and you can go cross-country."

"You have other plans?" Dredd asked.

"Yes. I'm going to land at the starport and turn myself in."

Dredd snorted. "I knew you Sovs were all crazy. Kessler's not likely to go easy on you just because you're a rookie, Kontarsky."

She bristled. "As I told you before, Dredd. I am not a rookie anymore. I am an East-Meg Judge and any interrogation of me can only be handled by a superior Sov officer. Kessler won't be able to hold me. Once I am inside Luna-1, I can buy you some time. I will use what influence I can to assist you."

"And I'm just supposed to take the word of a Sov-Blocker as gospel? What's to stop you singing like a canary?"

Kontarsky's expression hardened. "I'm a Judge. I do not lie."

He nodded and gestured at the lunar surface. "All right. It's a lousy plan but it's all we got. I'll get an e-suit, you set us down behind that ridge."

"Affirmative." Kontarsky angled the hopper smoothly into a controlled touchdown and settled the shuttle in a flurry of moondust. She glanced back at Dredd as he secured the spacesuit over his uniform. Again she felt conflicted towards him, part of her still strong with years of indoctrination that labelled the Mega-City Judge as her most hated enemy, another part of her seeing him as someone worthy of her respect and trust. "Dredd, I feel I must say how sorry I am about the Judge-Marshal. I... I know that Tex was a personal friend of yours. You have my condolences."

"Save it," Dredd grated. "We'll mourn him when we have Moonie on death row and this insurrection stamped out."

Kontarsky hesitated. She had expected some glimmer of emotion from Dredd, even the smallest hint that he was affected by his former partner's death, but if there was any kind of emotion lurking under that obdurate surface, he kept it well concealed. The Judge's face remained set and unreadable and something about that coldness unsettled her more than any shouting rage might have. He sealed his helmet visor down and gave her a curt nod, then he was gone and Nikita was alone with the turmoil of her thoughts.

With Kessler's arrival, the tension level at the Academy crime scene became palpable. It wasn't unheard of for the SJS to become involved in homicide cases on Justice Department sites, but more typically they only intervened when there was a clear suspicion of a "blue on blue" killing – a polite euphemism for a Judge murdering a Judge. Kessler's presence was tacit acknowledgement that a fellow lawman was firmly implicated in the assassination of Judge-Marshal Tex.

Kessler ordered one of his men forward with a snap of his fingers and the subordinate SJS officer unlimbered a complex scanner unit.

"What's that?" Foster asked.

"Skin-sniffer," J'aele replied. "A very advanced DNA sensor that checks for residual traces in the air or on surfaces."

Tek-Judge Tyler's face wrinkled in annoyance. "How the drokk have SJS got hold of one of those? Tek-Division have to work with obsolete hardware and those guys get state-of-the-art kit?"

The SJS sensor technician ran the skin-sniffer head over the three Judges. "Hold still," he ordered, "I need to register you so we can exclude you from the sweep."

"You all have alibis, yes?" Kessler asked in a deceptively casual manner.

Tyler sneered, refusing to grace the question with an answer. "Can we get on with our jobs now?"

The SJS chief nodded. "You may. In the meantime, I have some information that may assist you." He snatched the recovered rifle fragment from Foster's grip. "The partial serial numbers discovered on this evidence have been analysed. Central has identified this weapon as stock from Armoury Delta in the Grand Hall of Justice. It was assigned to a Street Judge during the shooting incident at the Green Cheese Shoplex earlier this week."

"Who?" demanded Foster.

J'aele felt his blood run cold. "Me."

"Yes," said Kessler, savouring the word. "But you passed it on to another officer, didn't you? There were several witnesses to that fact, including some of my own men." When the Tek-Judge didn't answer, Kessler continued. "Just as it was used to kill Judge-Marshal Tex, this rifle also killed Judge Rodriguez."

"Dredd?" said Foster. "You gave the gun to Dredd?"

The Simba City Judge said nothing, his gaze never leaving Kessler's.

Kessler continued; he was enjoying his little performance. "Armoury files have no record of this rifle being returned to the Hall of Justice or any other precinct command, which means it remained in Dredd's possession."

Foster gave a scornful snort. "No chance. Everyone knows Dredd is a stickler for protocol and regs. Hell, he wrote half of them! Your boys must have made a mistake."

"The SJS do not make mistakes!" Kessler snapped, all trace of his oily smile gone in an instant. "But men do and Dredd is nothing but that, an old man!" After a moment, Kessler composed himself and his flash of anger faded as if it had never been there. "Continue your investigation. I expect to know every detail that you uncover."

Tyler returned to examining the wrecked hovercam as Kessler moved away with his men. "I bet he's just loving this," the Tek-Judge said quietly.

J'aele blinked. "What do you mean?"

"If Kessler is fixing to put Dredd in the frame for shooting Tex, you can be sure he's as happy as a dunce in munce." Tyler lowered his voice. "This was before you two were sent up here, but a while back old Stony Face was in Luna-1 on a Psi-Division gig, babysitting some pre-cog. Anyhow, along the way Dredd got fingered for some murders and they set Kessler loose on him. The killer turned out be some sorta weirdo zombie, but by the time they'd figured that out, our pal Scarface over there had worked him over pretty bad."

"He tortured Dredd?" Foster's jaw dropped open. "Stomm..."

"Yup. Word is, Kessler was real angry about letting Dredd slip through his fingers and he's had an axe to grind ever since. When he wasn't able to break him, Kessler took it personally."

J'aele was about to add something, but a strident beeping from the skin-sniffer unit began to sound. "What is it?"

Kessler could barely keep himself from breaking into a grin, the pink slash of his scar puckering the skin on his cheek. "We appear to have a match. The scanner has detected a minute genetic reading that corresponds with that of gene-strain 0001, Mega-City One variant." He licked his lips. "Dredd was in this corridor within the last eight hours."

"That's not possible," Foster snapped. "The killer could have easily planted a DNA trace and there's hundreds of people who passed though this area, it could be any one of them–"

"Only a senior Judge would have been able to gain access to this floor outside of office hours!" Kessler countered. "Only a Judge would have known how to circumvent the security sensors..." He gave Foster a measuring look, "Or perhaps, the murderer might have had an accomplice? Say, another Judge working in a secure area in another building?"

"You're accusing Judge Foster?" said J'aele. "You have no proof!"

"Soon I will have all the proof I need, Judge J'aele. Piece by piece, I'll have this crime solved and the perp brought to swift, brutal justice. The killer," Kessler looked back at Foster, "and whoever aided and abetted him."

The Brit-Cit Judge grimaced and beckoned J'aele angrily. "Come on, we got a report to make to Che. The smell in this place is making me sick to my stomach."

Kessler ignored the jibe and drew a microphone from his equipment belt and spoke into it. "Kessler to Central, SJS advisory to all officers in the Luna-1 environs. Issue an all-points bulletin to intercept and detain Judge Joseph Dredd. Dredd is to be transferred to the Luna SJS headquarters when apprehended for immediate interview and examination."

Dredd shielded his eyes as Kontarsky poured power to the thrusters and the hopper launched itself back into the black sky, the jet wash sending a slow wave of grey moondust flowing away behind it. The blunt shape of the flyer vanished behind the lip of a crater and was gone from sight. Beyond it in the distance was the graceful arc of the Luna-1 dome, shimmering in the reflected sunlight. He took a deep breath of plastic-tasting suit air and set off, carefully walking in the half-bounce, half-step gait that astronauts had used on the Moon since the days of the old Apollo missions.

The thing that always struck Dredd the most about being in space was the silence. Living in one of the largest cities in the world since birth, Dredd had grown accustomed to the constant background rush of noise from traffic, people and machines that made up the accompaniment to life in the Big Meg; but out here, there was no sound but the rasp of his own breathing and the soft chime of his virtual compass display. He didn't like the quiet; something about it felt wrong.

Skirting a security sensor, the Judge carefully approached Kepler's outer wall. The small conurb dome was gloomy, dimly lit with the faint glow of emergency lights. Glancing up, Dredd could see the inert disc of the oxy-station above it.

He checked his surroundings. In the soundless vacuum, a patrolling security droid or hopper could be on him before he knew it – but he had approached undetected and there was no other movement on the stark monochrome landscape. He reached a small emergency airlock and worked an override code through his thick, suited fingers.

A green light blinked and the outer door opened. "So far, so good," Dredd said aloud.

There were three Luna SJS officers waiting in the launch bay as the hopper shuttle dropped down on its hangar cradle. Even though she had been expecting to see them there, Kontarsky still had to smother a moment of fear when her muscles tensed in a primal fight-or-flight reflex. She shook her head to clear the emotion. No, she had a duty to perform and to run would be a waste of energy.

While the auto-lander guided her in, the young Sov-Judge removed the data chip that contained the hopper's cockpit flight recorder and ground it into powder under her boot heel. Now no trace remained of her flight path, including her touch-and-go landing in the Badlands and, most importantly, any audio transcription of the conversations between herself and Dredd on the flight deck.

Kontarsky fastened her rad-cloak at her neck and donned her helmet, settling herself in the pre-determined posture that Kadet instructors described as suitable for appearances before antagonists and foreigners. With practiced arrogance, she stepped down from the hopper's airlock and into the circle of Judges.

"You are here for me?" she said, before they could speak.

One of the SJS men nodded. "Come with us, Judge Kontarsky."

She started forward, but another Judge blocked her path. "I will require you to surrender your weapon. For the time being."

Kontarsky gave him a measured sneer in answer and produced her STUP-gun with a flick of the wrist. "Then let us proceed."

A pursuit model L-Wagon decorated with the SJS's characteristic skull symbol sped them across the cityscape and past the Grand Hall of Justice. Kontarsky glanced out at the plaza before the building, which was still cordoned off from the public. She saw the footage of Tex's cold-blooded murder in her mind's eye once again and felt a chill wash over her.

The flyer dipped sharply and circled down into a pad atop the Special Judicial Service's own headquarters building. It was a dark and gothic version of the Grand Hall, shaped like an Eagle of Justice with its wings spread, but where Justice Central's hawkish monolith suggested watchful integrity the SJS building promised nothing but fear. The dark-eyed eagle sat with claws splayed over twin skulls, each a dozen storeys tall and the entire construction was cut from drab grey lunar stone. It resembled the castle of some fanciful medieval warlord more than an institution of law enforcement. Kontarsky knew this kind of subtle architectural propaganda well; she could recall the oppressive, dominating shapes of East-Meg Two's Diktatorat Tower and the minarets of the Nu-Kremlin.

The trio of SJS-Judges took her to a small room lit with a greenish strip-light and furnished with a simple set of metal chairs and a table. A single security camera observed the chamber with a steady red eye. Kontarsky sat, removing her helmet and waited. She had played these kinds of games before and she would not allow mere lunarians to force unconscious clues from her.

She marked time by counting the panels in the walls. She was halfway through when the door opened to admit Judge Kessler and the SJS officer who had taken her gun. Kessler sat down opposite her and produced a data-pad.

"Judge Nikita Kontarsky. You are being held here as part of the Security of the City Act. You are required by law to give me

the following information. One: the whereabouts of Judge
Joseph Dredd. Two: a complete report on your recent lunar
joyride. Three: a full statement covering all your activities
since your first meeting with Dredd on Union Station." He laid
the pad down in front of her and touched a key. "Begin now."

The Sov-Judge slowly folded her arms and met Kessler's
monocled gaze. "I refuse to comply with any of your orders.
Furthermore, under the articles of the Global Lunar Partnership Treaty, I demand you turn me over to my direct superior,
Kommissar Ivanov of the East-Meg Diplomatic Korps." Kontarsky watched the irritation flare red along the forked line of
Kessler's scar. If her timing was right, the SJS chief had
arrived at exactly the right moment.

"I think you will find that things will proceed much more
comfortably for you if you comply," Kessler cocked his head.
"It would be a pity to blacken your record at so early a stage
with something like this."

Kontarsky ignored the veiled threat. Such an amateur ploy,
she told herself. He has none of the subtlety of my Sov
teacher-inquisitors.

The other Judge tapped his helmet. "Kessler, it's Kommissar Ivanov–"

Kessler made a dismissive gesture. "She's not speaking to
anyone."

"No, sir, you don't understand. He's just arrived. Kommissar Ivanov is in the building."

At that moment, Kontarsky very much wanted to give
Kessler a smug smile of superiority, but she resisted. To give
in to that impulse would have been a very un-Soviet
response.

After a moment, Kessler stood up. "Very well. We'll play it
your way." He smoothed the greying hair at his temples. "But
I guarantee you will lead me to Dredd, one way or another."

Kontarsky kept her face utterly neutral and her expression
stayed rigid even after the SJS men had left.

Kommissar Ivanov entered the interview room alone and
gave Kontarsky the briefest of nods. She stood up and saluted

and her superior returned the gesture. Ivanov removed a small conical device from a pocket in his greatcoat and placed it on the table. A blinking indicator light flashed green and he sat.

"The sensor mask is operating at full capacity," he said. "We may speak freely now."

Kontarsky remained on her feet. "Sir, thank you for answering my signal. I had not expected you to come in person."

Ivanov gave a slight smile. "It was the least I could do for one of my former students, Nikita. Besides, I so rarely have good reason to leave the *Irkutsk*." An interplanetary light cruiser rechristened as a "diplomatic courier", the starship *Irkutsk* was East-Meg Two's orbiting embassy above Luna-1 and the kommissar's base of operations. "I have been keeping an eye on your progress here on the Moon, but I must confess I was surprised to get your message."

"I apologise if I caused you any inconvenience, sir."

"No, no, my dear," he waved her comment away. "In fact, our meeting comes at a most opportune moment."

The Sov-Judge's face creased in confusion. "I do not understand. I requested assistance as part of the investigation that I have been conducting with Judge Dredd–"

"Dredd, yes," Ivanov said the name like it left a sour taste in his mouth. "Your reports on his activities have been most thorough, Nikita, but I have become concerned that you are allowing yourself to identify with this American." He waved a finger at her. "That is a dangerous trend to follow. I need not tell you what the monitors at the Diktatorat might think of such a thing."

Kontarsky's jaw worked. "I..."

The kommissar indicated the other chair. "Sit, please. Do not be afraid, my dear. I have edited any references in your reports that might have reflected badly on you before forwarding them to the Kremlin. I can understand how you might see something to admire in Dredd... Even our enemies can teach us something, eh?"

She nodded as she sat. "I believe that Dredd may be correct in his suspicions that a rebellion is being fomented here on the Moon, possibly by the escaped criminal capitalist CW Moonie."

Ivanov raised an eyebrow. "That is an interesting hypothesis. And what would you propose we do about it?"

"Assist Dredd, of course. Kessler and his SJS believe he is responsible for Judge-Marshal Tex's murder, but I can vouch for his innocence."

"Ah yes, a sad event. And yet, as our history teaches us, such a thing can sometimes be the tool of political change for the better."

Kontarsky stopped short. "I do not follow you, sir."

"Oh, come now, Nikita, you are not the naïve Judge-kadet you were when you were in my classes on ethical interpretation. We both know that there are freedom loving peoples on the Moon who yearn for a government by the workers and not by the imperialist Judge system. You yourself have said this."

"Yes, but to place the blame for murder on an innocent man–"

"Do not forget, Dredd is responsible for many transgressions against the Motherland," Ivanov replied. "And regardless, often one man must suffer for the good of the many. Think, Nikita. Is it any wonder that Luna-1 is on the verge of revolution? The so-called United Cities of America bled this planetoid white. Even after they allowed other nations to stake claims here with their mealy-mouthed partnership treaty, their Triumvirate ties us up in endless bureaucracy. If their control of the Moon ends, will it really be such a bad thing?" He leaned closer. "A free Luna-1 would welcome East-Meg Two as a partner for all time, not as a poor beggar at the table as we are now – and you, Nikita, could be a part of that. A heroine to the Sov people, just as you were before."

Kontarsky found she couldn't look away from her old teacher's face and she gave a robotic nod of agreement.

The kommissar smiled. "We'll talk more about this later. For now, though, I find myself wondering. Where is Judge Dredd?"

13. NO ESCAPE

Dredd picked his way quickly and carefully through the silent gloom of Kepler Dome's interior, concealing himself behind wreckage whenever a security drone buzzed overhead. As he had expected, the Justice Department had pulled whatever officers they were using to guard the dome and sent them into the city proper to quell the riots. That meant that the Judge had just a few robot patrols to avoid while he worked his way through the streets. Dredd knew the capabilities of the old Mark II spy-in-the-sky flybots – they were poor with infrared, which meant he could conceal himself behind a lunacrete wall or the frame of a groundcar with a good chance of escaping detection.

With the dome's systems on standby, the air inside was frigid. There was a thin layer of frost on everything and Dredd's breath emerged in small wisps of vapour. The wintry cold chilled his exposed flesh and the smells of decay and smoke still lingered in the air.

Rounding a corner, a flicker of movement caught his eye and Dredd froze. A troupe of four-legged worker droids ambled across the cluttered pavement, followed by a slow-moving cargo wagon and a lifter-bot. As he watched, the machines paused and began to sort through the debris, picking out the few remaining corpses of the Kepler incident's victims. He moved closer. The worker machines were no threat to him, none of them equipped with anything more than a dog-smart computer brain. The droids moved around him, unaware of his presence, quietly gathering up the dead and preparing them for removal. The lifter gripped the body of a Judge in a Cal-Hab uniform and carried it to the wagon. Dredd saw the dried smears of blood across the dead man's studded helmet and noted the corpses of eight more rioters gathered nearby. The Scottish Judge had clearly fallen taking on all-comers. Something glittered as it fell from the body and bounced on the ground. Dredd knelt and scooped it up – it was the Cal-Hab lawman's silver-grey shield. He weighed the badge in his hand for a moment, considering it and then tucked it in a belt pouch.

He had ditched his e-suit in the airlock, unwilling to risk wearing the bulky gear in a normal gravity environment. If he was called upon to use his weapon, Dredd wanted to be sure that he would have every advantage his years of training had given him. Secluded in the lee of a building, the Judge drew his STUP-gun and checked the charge. The pistol's battery pack was in the green and he dialled the beam setting down to level one. If he got in a firefight with other Judges, a stun blast would be enough to dispatch them without risking a more permanent injury. He ignored a brief flash of annoyance that rose in his chest. Damn Kessler for forcing him into this!

Dredd crossed the skedway, ducking low to minimise his silhouette and vanished into an ascent shaft that led to the crest of the dome. With power switched off to everything but minimal life support and the grav-plates, the elevator was inactive, but an emergency ladder inside the tube led upwards. He followed it into the dimness above, where he could make out a circle of faint light. Dredd holstered his weapon and began to climb.

Like everything else inside Kepler Dome, the oxy-station was an empty half-ruin, consoles and panels smashed without rhyme or reason and myriad fragments of shattered glasseen underfoot. The bitter stink of stale smoke was strong up here and black soot stained every surface where the fumes had filtered into the control centre. There were no corpses; the oxy-station workers had been quick enough to abandon their posts the moment the rioting had broken out. The wholesale destruction of the place had occurred at the hands of maddened citizens, who had mistakenly assaulted the facility believing that they could simply turn their air supply back on. When they found the controls locked, the rioters had turned their anger and fear on everything around them.

Dredd brushed a drift of plastic shards off one of the few consoles still intact and hit the activation icon. A stylised glyph in the shape of an old mechanical key appeared. "This panel is secured. Please consult your supervisor for further information," it said, the synthetic voice garbled through a broken speaker.

"Justice Department override," Dredd told the computer. "Open records."

"Ident code required. Please submit key card for scan."

Each employee of the Oxygen Board wore an identity card around their neck that would automatically give their security codes to the consoles and Judges used a similar method with officer-specific ident chips – but with his name on the SJS watch list, any attempt by Dredd to use his code would appear immediately on a Justice Central scan grid. Instead, he took a gamble, drew the Cal-Hab Judge's badge from his belt and waved it over the console. The console's scanner read the micro-miniature chip inside the shield.

The panel gave an answering beep. "Ident code confirmed. Welcome to Oxy-station four-seven, Judge Vandal. Command over-ride accepted."

"Lucky for me this isn't a voice recognition system..." Dredd said aloud. "Computer, open last day log entry. Replay shutdown incident."

The screen unfolded into a series of data windows and a camera's-eye view of the control room. Dredd watched as Moon-U's face flickered over a few of the console screens and the outbreak of panic among the oxy-workers, before the crimson alert lights flashed on as the airflow ceased. He studied the oxy-station's second-by-second breathing gas monitor, scrutinising the sine-wave pattern of air filtering through the feed pipes and out into Kepler Dome. The display blinked past, almost too quickly for the eye to register.

Something tugged at the edges of Dredd's investigative sense. Something was wrong here, something that J'aele and the Tek-Judges had missed. He ran the replay a dozen more times before he finally saw it. "Computer, enhance airflow pattern display. Show me where the oxygen feed was coming from."

The screen changed to show a simulated view of the pipe network. "O_2 feed at this time index switched over from dual flow to secondary source."

"That's not possible." Dredd knew from J'aele's report that Kepler, being a low-rent dome, took most of its air from the cheaper recycling plants out on the lunar surface, using only a little of the more expensive atmospheric gases brought in by astro-tanker; but according to the screen, just seconds before it had shut down, the oxygen flow had switched from a mix of the two to just recycled air. "Security locks are supposed to prevent that from happening. Explain!"

"Cause unknown. Conjecture – human error."

"Someone cut off the air remotely..." he breathed. "It wasn't an accident after all." Dredd tapped in a series of commands and brought up a citywide map, highlighting all the incidents of disorder and violence prior to the Kepler riot. Every one of them was in a sub-dome or an outlying conurb complex, each a poor neighbourhood without the high-cost pure air that most of Luna-1's population enjoyed. "What's the source of the recycled air for all these domes?" Dredd asked grimly.

A logo appeared on the screen. "LunAir Recovery Incorporated," said the computer. "A division of MoonieCorp."

In spite of himself, an angry sneer formed on Dredd's lips. "The guns, the air... Moonie's planning to strangle the entire city!"

And then without warning, the oxy-station's windows were flooded with brilliant, blinding white light.

The L-Wagon's floodlights poured a million-candlepower glare into the platform, enough to overpower the polarising anti-dazzle lenses in the Judge's helmet. From the cockpit, the pilot called over his shoulder. "Full beam! I see him, in the control room!"

"Hold station!" snapped Judge Hiro, one of Kessler's senior SJS officers. "Give me laser cannon control!"

The pilot gaped. "Sir? Our orders are to arrest Dredd, not kill him!"

"The lasers!" Hiro growled, a warning in his voice. "Or else I'll charge you with obstruction of justice!"

Reluctantly, the pilot switched the L-Wagon's gun controls to Hiro's console and the SJS man locked the cannons on the oxy-station. Hiro's partner Judge Wright watched him take aim. "Dial down the power, man. If you shoot wide you'll punch through the dome."

Hiro grinned savagely. "It's just a warning shot." He thumbed the fire control and twin bolts of energy flashed out and cut through the oxy-station.

Inside, Dredd fell into a tuck-and-roll as the las-blast tore through the control centre, ripping open the walls and turning the computer console into scrap metal. Hot semi-molten fragments spat into the air, turning his breath acidic in his throat.

"Dredd!" The SJS-Judge's voice bellowed over the L-Wagon's public address system. "By order of the Chief Judge-Marshal, you are under arrest!"

"How the drokk did they find me?" Dredd growled, fumbling for his pulse gun. "Can't get captured now... Kessler's gonna lock me up and throw away the key!"

He rose up from behind the cover of a ruined desk and sent a brace of shots out through the rent in the wall. The pulse blasts sparked off the L-Wagon's hull and the airfoils.

"He's aiming for the stabilisers! He's trying to bring us down!" yelled the pilot.

Hiro leapt from the laser station and sprinted into the cockpit. "Wright, take the lasers!" He grabbed a handful of the pilot's uniform. "You! Get out of that chair!"

"What?" the pilot blinked. "You're not authorised to fly this–"

"I said get out!" Hiro shouted, smacking the pilot aside with a hard right cross. The other man recoiled, dazed and the SJS officer shoved him out of the control seat. Hiro grabbed the joystick and throttle, turning the L-Wagon to face the hole torn in the side of the oxy-station. The flyer's flood-lights picked out Dredd as he sprinted for the lift tube.

"Oh no you don't!" grated Hiro.

The pattern of the spotlights shifted suddenly as the L-Wagon lurched forward. Dredd had a moment to see the nose of the flyer looming though the broken wall before he was knocked off his feet by a colossal impact. The front quarter of the L-Wagon penetrated the interior of the oxy-station, cutting through desks and consoles like matchwood. Dredd rolled, his STUP-gun spinning away from him, dodging falling gird-ers and pieces of ceiling.

The echo of the collision ringing in his ears, Dredd pushed himself back up to his feet and dived for his gun. From the corner of his eye he caught a blink of movement, a night-black uniform trimmed with silver skulls coming at him like a rocket. His fingers touched the butt of the pulse gun just as a daystick cracked him across the back.

"Stay down!" Wright commanded. "We got you!"

Dredd decided otherwise. He flipped over, caught Wright's shin between his ankles and twisted. The SJS-Judge let out a hiss of pain and fell over backwards, arms windmilling. Dredd reached for the STUP-gun in time to meet Judge Hiro's boot in the face.

The second SJS officer kicked him again for good measure, then brought down his heel on Dredd's splayed hand. "Fin-gers!" he spat, teeth bared in a snarl.

Constellations of light exploded inside Dredd's skull, flares of pain making him dizzy. He shifted, coming to his feet, try-ing to gather himself.

"Tough old bastard…" Wright's voice said from some-where nearby.

"Not tough enough," retorted Hiro. "Got your gun?"

"Yeah."

"Then shoot him."

Dredd launched himself toward the SJS-Judge just as something sun-bright and sizzling struck him hard in the chest. The walls of the oxy-station seemed to shift and merge, as if they were collapsing in on him. Darkness gathered in on Dredd, voices chasing him into a senseless black void.

"You could have killed us all with that stunt, Hiro."

"Don't be such a weakling."

Che examined the object on the desk before him and his lips twisted in a weary grimace. "And this is?"

"I believe it is some form of listening device," said Kessler, absently running a finger over his scarred chin. "After you were sworn in I took the liberty of ordering a deep scan of Judge-Marshal Tex's... Uh, that is, of your office and my technicians discovered it. The unit self-destructed before we could make a thorough examination, but it appears to have been a transmitter."

Che pushed it away. "Bugs planted in the Chief Judge's office. How did we come to this? It sickens me to think we may have turncoats and crooked Judges among our forces!"

"I wholeheartedly agree, sir. Luna-1 is a city that enjoys unprecedented freedoms, but because of that we must also be the most watchful. That is why the SJS is also free to pursue its objectives to the bitter end." Kessler said the last words with relish.

"I want every officer on the take found and purged!" Che thumped the desk with his fist.

Kessler smiled crookedly. "Already in progress, sir. We are investigating the technician Maktoh, who I suspect Dredd killed in order to prevent discovery of his own collusion and Rodriguez. There may be others."

Che nodded. "What is the word from the street? Is the curfew holding?"

"For now, Judge-Marshal. There has been some squawking from the veterans' societies and citizen rights groups about the possible effects on the upcoming Apocalypse Day anniversary, but we've dealt with that." Kessler handed the Chief Judge a data-pad. "We still have a few isolated pockets of trouble here and there – an incident at the Tycho Brahe Hilton hotel and a fire at the Leisureplex – but nothing that cannot be quelled with the correct application of force."

"And those punkamente channel hackers?"

Kessler's face soured. "Their transmissions remain untraceable, sir. Tek Division simply do not have hardware advanced enough to block their frequency-hopping attack programs. Short of shutting down every vid-screen, net-link and radio on Luna-1, there's no way we can stop them."

"And so they continue to goad us and make the citizens side against us," he spat. "If you can't block the signals, than find the source and destroy it! There is a cancer at the heart of this city, Kessler and these are all symptoms of it. I want it cut out, do you understand? Ripped out, if needs be, but gone!" He stood up and began to pace. "Tex's death will be avenged, of that you must be certain!"

"My sentiments exactly, Judge-Marshal. You should know that two of my best men have reported in with Dredd in custody. He will be arriving in confinement in a matter of minutes."

"Dredd! I never wanted him up here, do you know?" Che studied the room around him. Despite the events of the past twenty-four hours, he could not settle himself with the idea that the city was now his to command. "I told Tex that we could handle these insurrections ourselves, and now it has come to this."

"Desperate times require extreme measures," said Kessler archly. "Dredd is a tricky one. He lives on his reputation, but only the clearest thinkers can see he's not all he appears to be."

"I... I never wanted to take Tex's place, Kessler, you understand? Not like this. I don't know if I can do the job that he did."

"You have the full support of every man serving under you, sir," Kessler replied smoothly, "including the Special Judicial Service."

Che gave a vague nod. "Yes... Thank you, Kessler."

A chime sounded from the intercom. "Chief Judge, we're ready to begin the conference."

"Very well," Che sat down and turned to face the eagle's-eye window. "Begin." The glasseen oval flickered and changed to become a series of smaller screens. Each displayed the face of a senior Judge from the member states of the Global Partnership Treaty, some broadcasting from Earth, others from their courier ships in lunar orbit. Kessler sneered as he saw Kommisar Ivanov appear among them.

A dozen voices began talking at once, all of them raised and angry.

Che waved a hand in front of his face, as if he was dismissing a nagging insect. "One at a time, please, señors!"

Kessler watched as Che fought off recriminations and harsh words from representatives of a dozen city-states. Each of them said it in a different way, but all of them were pushing the same agenda – they all believed that Luna-1 was on the verge of collapse and that their city was the one that should step in to take over.

Kessler kept his expression set, but inwardly he sneered. Look at them, fighting over the Moon like a pack of rabid dogs! The SJS chief doubted than any one of the diplomats and representatives had the strength of will to keep Luna-1 in line. Only a hardened man, someone like himself, was capable of that. His eyes drifted to Che, whose face was ruddy with anxiety. Perhaps, he thought, I may have to take a more proactive hand in things...

Then the feed from Mega-City One was highlighted and Chief Judge Hershey's face filled the screen. "Judge-Marshal Che, before we go any further, I must protest your issue of an arrest warrant for Judge Dredd–"

Kessler broke in before Che could answer. "You may protest all you want, Chief Judge, but you have no jurisdiction here. Dredd is my prisoner and he is going to answer for his crimes!"

The SJS-Judge's words set off a new storm of invective from the screens but Kessler simply looked on, a mocking glint in his monocled eye.

Consciousness returned to Dredd as a series of slow, dull aches all over his body. He opened his eyes and his vision swam for a moment before he recognised the shape of a bio-lume strip above him. Gingerly, he righted himself; someone had roughly deposited him on a bunk in a standard iso-cube. Almost very item of Justice Department-issue clothing was gone, even down to his boots. All they had left him was the regulation blue-black undersuit and his helmet.

Dredd washed away the metallic taste in his mouth with a cupped handful of water from the sink mounted in the far wall. Aside from the bunk, the steel toilet in the opposite cor-ner of the room and the black dome of a scanner in the ceiling, the cell was bare. The Judge absently ran a hand over the plasteen walls. He'd lost count of the number of perps he'd put in places like this one, but he remembered with absolute clarity every time that he had been forced into a cell. It happened with a regularity that Dredd found extremely irritating. Anywhere else and he might have held out hope for a fair trial, a chance to prove his innocence – but with Kessler prosecuting him and Moonie's unseen influ-ence infesting the Luna-1 Justice Department, Dredd had his doubts.

Once I get out of this, he thought to himself, I'm recom-mending a serious review of the Luna Judge force.

He stepped up to the cell door and peered through a grille. Beyond, he could see a dozen more doors and a corridor leading off around a corner. Dredd guessed that he was in the sub-basement levels of the Grand Hall of Justice, in the long-term holding cells. Before too long, he'd probably be transferred over to the SJS building and left to Kessler's ten-der mercies. He remembered his last visit there with razor-sharp clarity and Kessler's leering face hanging over him as he tried to wring a confession from him. There was no doubt in Dredd's mind that this time the SJS officer would pull out all the stops; Kessler would make their previous meeting look like a happy chit-chat.

A Luna-City Judge came into view and stopped in front of Dredd's cell. "You're awake." He beckoned someone that Dredd could not see. "You have a visitor."

There was a flick of red and black and Kontarsky appeared, her ice-cold eyes giving him the most cursory of glances. "Open it," she told the other Judge. "I need to speak to him."

Dredd knew the drill. He stepped back into the cell and the door retracted into the wall. Kontarsky entered and the Luna-City Judge stood in the doorway. "They caught you," she said flatly.

"Yeah. A real coincidence, considering that you were the only one who knew where I was." He studied her face for any sign of emotion, any hint that would give him a clue about what she was thinking, but there was nothing.

"You are the most wanted man in the city, Dredd. Your capture was inevitable." Kontarsky ignored the thinly veiled accusation. "Kessler was denied access to interrogate me. I have been released into the custody of Kommissar Ivanov."

"Don't let me keep you from reporting in to your bosses at the Diktatorat. I'm sure they'll be pleased to hear that an Enemy of the People has been arrested for a murder he didn't commit."

"Kessler believes you are the agent of chaos here, Dredd. He intends to prove that you are working to destabilise Luna-1, possibly as an instrument of the crime lord Moonie–"

"I put Moonie away!" Dredd snapped. "You were there at Farside, you saw what happened to Rodriguez and Maktoh! You know what will happen if we don't stop that freak. He wants the Moon so badly he'll cause the deaths of thousands to get it!"

Kontarsky said nothing for a long moment, then in a rapid blur of movement, she whipped around and drew a compact needle gun from inside the folds of her cloak, turning the pistol on the Luna Judge. "Do not move," she ordered, "or you will be shot."

"Where did you get that?" said Dredd, indicating the weapon.

"I had a spare," Kontarsky retorted. "Do you not recognise a prison break when you see one? We have little time. I programmed the iso-cube's security camera to run a loop of footage, but it will only last for few minutes."

Dredd folded his arms. "Why should I trust you? For all I know, you're part of this conspiracy as well. How do I know you didn't tip off the SJS about where to find me? How do I know you're not going to have me 'shot while trying to escape'?"

"Because I give you my word. Not as an East-Meg citizen or a member of the Sov party, but as a Judge." She stepped closer to him, careful to keep her pistol on the guard. "I am a Russian and I am a patriot, but my first loyalty is to justice. To the law."

Dredd held out his hand. "Prove it. Give me the gun."

Kontarsky did not hesitate. "Here." She placed the needler in his palm and did not flinch when the Mega-City Judge carefully aimed the weapon at her.

"What's to stop me shooting you and making my own way out of here?"

"Nothing. But I can help you get to the heart of this conspiracy, Dredd. There's more at stake than just the dissension here in Luna-1; I suspect that Kommisar Ivanov may be involved in some way."

Dredd considered this new development. An East-Meg connection chimed with the illegal weapons discovered at Kepler and Kontarsky's knowledge would be a useful asset – if he could bring himself to trust a Sov-Judge.

"Guess you're right," he said after a moment. "You!" Dredd told the Luna Judge. "Get in here. Give me your gear."

The guard nodded. "I'm not going to stop you, sir," he replied, quickly stripping off his holster, shoulder pads, belt and boots. "I don't care what the SJS say, I know you didn't kill the Chief Judge."

Dredd studied the younger man's face. "Do I know you, son?"

"Goodworthy, sir. Judge Arthur Goodworthy, Junior. You saved my dad's life once, back on New Year's Eve, 2100. He went Futsie."

Dredd nodded, the events returning to him. "Future shock syndrome. You were just a child, your father worked for Moonie…"

"Yes," said Goodworthy. "That creep worked my dad until he cracked, then sent his goons to gun him down on the street! But you stood up for him, sir. You got him to the shrinks and I never forgot that. That's why I became a Judge." He handed Dredd his STUP-gun. "Get him, sir. The Moon doesn't need scum like Moonie any more."

"Count on it." Dredd nodded at Kontarsky and the Sov-Judge struck Goodworthy with a nerve punch, knocking him unconscious.

"He would have helped us," said Kontarsky. "We could have used him."

Dredd shook his head. "No sense giving Kessler anyone else to take it out on. From now, we do this alone."

"Very well. I assume you have some sort of plan?"

"I'll explain on the way."

14. FRESH AIR

With a grim set to his jaw, Dredd watched the metropolitan sprawl flash past through the small rectangular window of the railshuttle, buildings in the foreground blurring into abstract white shapes while the structures further away seemed to move at a more sedate speed. Luna-1 was a city under siege by forces from within and without. Thin plumes of smoke lingered in the air over places where street-fights had turned into infernos and the glittering shapes of Manta prowl tanks and armed Justice Department flyers wove low patterns between the Selenescrapers, spotlights washing over citiblocks and con-apt clusters.

Now and then, Dredd saw the faraway blink-blink of a muzzle flash, too distant to be heard over the rumble of the robot zoom train's maglev. The bubbling undercurrent of tension and lawlessness that he had sensed when he first arrived was raging on the surface now. People were dying and there was little that the Judges could do except plug the flow and pray that more cracks didn't appear. The Mega-City lawman had heard rumours over the past few years about the state of Luna-1, but he had typically dismissed them as hearsay. Somewhere in the back of his mind, Dredd had always known that the lunar capital would stay on an even keel as long as his old friend Tex was at the helm – but now the Judge-Marshal's corpse was barely cold and his city was self-destructing. What would happen in the coming days would be a test of fire for the new leader of Luna-1 and Dredd knew in his bones that former Deputy Judge-Marshal Che wasn't up to the task. Worse, Che was relying on Kessler for support without considering the SJS chief's own agenda.

The curfew would settle things for a few hours, but soon the city would grow restless once more – and the next time it would be worse. Dredd had seen countless block wars during his career, even the monstrous citywide conflict that was the precursor to the invasion by East-Meg One and he knew the cycle of violence behind them all too well. Citizens, trapped in lives that had little point, angry at everything and bored with the status quo were easy converts to the pack mentality and lust for casual violence that mob rule provided. But unlike the people of Earthbound Mega-Cities, Luna-1's populace didn't have the room to expand and blow off steam – they had a city with a lid on it, a pressure cooker that would get hotter and hotter until it exploded. No, there was only one way to stem the tide now. They had to find the root cause of the disorder. Find it and destroy it.

The railshuttle turned on to an outbound loop and with a lurch it was suddenly beyond the main city dome, passing behind the Puerto Luminia barrio and out into the wilderness of the Oxygen Desert. There was little aerial traffic over the city, the curfew extended to all forms of travel, including orbital transports and spaceliners. Only vehicles vital to Luna-1's operation, like this robot train or the constant string of astro-tankers, were still running. But there were other ships up there, hard-edged shapes glinting among the stars, watching one another and biding their time. They circled the Moon like patient vultures shadowing a dying man, crewed by men who were diplomats in name only, men who kept a vigil for the first moment of opportunity. Dredd had no doubt that the moment Luna-1 turned into a fully-fledged war zone, each of them would be landing troop transports full of well-armed "advisors" intent on planting their flag on the city.

"We are accelerating," said Kontarsky. She shifted her position behind a cargo pod and frowned. "This is most uncomfortable."

"I didn't pick this train for the smooth ride," Dredd retorted. "We couldn't chance trying to take another hopper... This is the best option we have."

The Sov-Judge gave a nod. "As you say. But these things are not meant for human passengers and crew. We only have air in this wagon because the cargo in these pods would degrade without it."

Dredd remembered the last time he'd ridden the rails – aboard a hijacked, bomb-laden zoom train crossing the Black Atlantic – and decided that the drab lunar railshuttle was a big improvement. Kontarsky's escape ploy had been good enough to sneak the two of them out of the Grand Hall of Justice without arousing suspicion. Judge Goodworthy had kept his promise and, for all Dredd knew, he was still sleeping off Kontarsky's nerve strike in the iso-cube, waiting for the getaway to be discovered.

Dredd had guided them to a railhead depot in District Six, where automated magnetic levitation trains were dispatched to the distant outpost domes and factory complexes. From there, it had been a fairly simple matter for him to locate a railshuttle bound for the destination he wanted and they had boarded by stealth as machine loaders filled the train with freight. Kontarsky went along with all his commands up to this point without comment, but Dredd couldn't shake off his nagging doubts about the youthful Sov-Judge. It had taken a lot to convince himself not to just stun her and leave her with Goodworthy, but she'd proven useful throughout the investigation and like it or not, he had no way of knowing if something she had said got him caught by the SJS Judges Hiro and Wright. Kessler was smart, after all and he would have probably put someone in Kepler Dome just on the off-chance that Dredd would turn up there. It was what Dredd would have done, if the circumstances were reversed. On top of that, if Kontarsky was right about Ivanov, someone with knowledge of Sov protocols could be invaluable.

Still, trust never came easy to Dredd and Kontarsky had a long way to go before she fully earned his. Keep your friends close, but keep your enemies closer, he remembered, watching her from the corner of his eye.

"Now that we are outside the city walls, perhaps you would be kind enough to inform me as to where we are going?"

"I found something at Kepler, in the oxy-station. Someone tampered with the airflow."

"Tek-Division said the oxygen outage was an accident. That's what triggered the disturbance."

Dredd shook his head. "I'm not convinced. Those Moon-U creeps were right there, stirring up trouble the moment the fans stopped spinning. They knew what was going to happen. They caused it. It doesn't take a genius to figure out that Moonie is to blame for this."

"Moonie, Moonie, everything keeps coming back to him. I don't understand, Dredd, what kind of person is he? If what you say about him is true, how can a man nurture such a plan for two and a half decades without being discovered?"

The railshuttle rattled through a set of points. "Money, Kontarsky. Cold, hard credits. Moonie was one of the richest humans alive when I busted him and back then Luna-1 was a boomtown, full of men who were more than willing to take his coin – Judges included. And those that didn't work for him were afraid of him."

"But you put him away. You changed all that."

"I thought I did. Now I'm not so sure. Power like that doesn't just dry up overnight. Moonie just made sure his assets went dark, so he could pick them back up when he needed them. If I hadn't arrested him then, he would have ended up owning the Moon, lock, stock and moonrocks. That's been his goal all along. What he's doing now, it's all steps along the same road."

"He wants to become lord of the Moon, is that it? Like some deformed gnome king from a child's storybook?"

Dredd shrugged. "That's a little more flowery than I'd put it, but yes, that's about the size of it. He poured his life into exploring the Moon and it bit him in the ass when that virus infected him. He's been looking for revenge ever since... He told me once that the Moon 'owes him' and to pay back that debt he's gonna try to take it all."

"He's insane," Kontarsky pronounced.

"That fact has never been in question," agreed Dredd.

She responded with a slight, humourless smile. "I'm still waiting for an answer. Where is this train taking us?"

Dredd pointed to the window. "Take a look."

Kontarsky pressed her face to the glass, craning her neck to look along the direction the railshuttle was travelling. Rising up from the vast bowl of Catharina Crater was a gunmetal hemisphere. It sat like a vast silver-grey octopus, thick tubular tentacles extending out to the surrounding moonscape and vanishing into smaller caverns. In the surrounding acres, robotic ice harvesters combed the lunar mantle for ancient deposits of frozen gases, while vent tunnels big enough to drive a mo-pad through connected the facility with distribution plants in Luna-1. The Sov-Judge saw the glitter of a holo-sign floating above the dome: *LunAir – Every Breath You Take*!

"The Oxy-Dome Complex," Dredd announced. "The central atmosphere recycling plant for most of the Moon, including Kepler."

"You think we'll find Moonie there?"

"No, but someone in that dome shut off the air to Kepler and they did it on Moonie's orders. We find them..."

"We find him," Kontarsky finished.

"Find him!" Moonie raged, his broad, leering face turning pinkish-red as the blood rushed through the nearly translucent skin over his skull. Spittle flew from his lips and as an afterthought, he struck his aide across the cheek. "You are worse than useless, you skinny wretch! You assure me that Dredd is behind bars, then you tell me that he isn't... What do I pay you for?"

Sellers's throat went dry and his jaw worked as he tried to explain himself. Across the table in the Silent Room, he could see the other two members of the cabal watching his superior's tirade with utter calm, their faces neutral. In many

ways, that was more insulting than if they had openly
mocked him for his mistakes.

"Answer me!" Moonie snapped, rocking forward on his
hoverchair. "Where is Dredd?"

"Our man in the Special Judicial Service is searching," the
words came out in a rush, "and he informs me that Judge-
Marshal Che is extremely distressed about the development."

"He's not the only one!" bellowed Moonie. "We should have
taken Dredd ourselves instead of letting those idiot Judges
confine him! That indecisive dolt Che isn't fit to lead a Mari-
achi band, let alone a city!" The old man coughed harshly, his
energy all but spent on the effort of losing his temper.

"Better that Che is in charge than someone else," said the
bald man. "He may have found the hypno-pulser we used to
affect Tex but his ineffectual manner will serve our needs just
as well." He paused and looked away. "As for Dredd, your
obsession with this man is clouding your vision of the larger
picture."

Moonie's face reddened once again, but the tall man cut
him off before he could launch into another furious rant.
"But, as we all know, Dredd is an impediment that must be
dealt with and while I had hoped we might be able to recover
him intact, for examination purposes, I see now that his
death is the only logical route to pursue."

"Finally!" Sellers muttered. "You had him in your sights a
half-dozen times and now at last you want to kill him."

The tall man deflected the comment effortlessly. "Please do
not try to shift blame to me for your failures, Sellers. Despite
your rudeness, I will grant you this gift." He produced a rod-
like device and placed it on the black stone table.

Moonie's chair skated closer and he snatched up the object
before his aide could touch it. "What is this?" he asked, even
as he thumbed a switch on the tip.

The holo-screen blipped and shifted to show a relief map
of the lunar surface. A bright indicator flag shimmered into
existence near the base of the Sea of Nectar.

Moonie's age-yellowed teeth showed in a feral smile. "A
tracer?"

The tall man nodded. "Dredd is not alone. I took the liberty of placing a tracking device on the person of his travelling companion."

"Kontarsky…" said Sellers. "The iso-cube guard told the SJS that she was Dredd's hostage."

"A simple fiction," said the tall man. "But one that will soon come to an unhappy ending."

Sellers studied the map. "The air plant. He's heading toward the air plant."

Moonie sneered. "It doesn't matter. He'll never get the chance to act on anything he finds there." The aged crime lord stabbed at a communicator control on his chair. "Get a hit team out to the Oxy-Dome complex. Dredd is there. Tell them to bring me back his head."

The two Judges kept to the shadows, avoiding the footprints of heat sensors and the scanning heads of static security cameras. The railshuttle was already gone, having paused for only a few moments on a siding inside the Oxy-Dome before rumbling onward with one less container of mechanical spares on its flatbed. It was time enough for Dredd and Kontarsky to alight, slipping between loader-meks that carried huge chunks of gas ice from automated cars that went to and from the mineshafts.

There was air inside the Oxy-Dome, warm and humid, a spill-off from the electro-chemical cracking processes that constantly thundered through the fractionation towers around them. The atmosphere smelled dull and stale here, thick with the recovered exhalations of millions of Luna-1 citizens.

Kontarsky nodded at a complex knot of pipes and conduits that emerged from the dome's lower levels. "Those are the recycler channels. There's carbon dioxide coming in through them and filtered oxygen going back."

Dredd gave an absent nod, watching a large crane grab pass over their heads carrying a pallet piled high with chips of dirty ice. Most of the frozen gases used by LunAir came from numerous deposits inside the lunar rock face, but some had a more distant origin, carved off the sides of comets in slow solar orbits and sent hurtling moonward to soft-land in the Sea of Nectar. Harvester robots scooped up the fragments and ferried them back to the Oxy-Dome in a constant circuit.

The Mega-City Judge paused and watched the vast machines working around them in a hissing, clanking ballet of metal and plastic. "No humans here," he noted, "not even an observer pod or an overseer."

"We should locate the command centre," said the Sov-Judge. "Any organic personnel would there—"

She fell silent as a spotlight stabbed out of nowhere and flooded their concealment with hard, white light. A synthetic voice screeched from above them. "Intruder alert! Industrial spies detected! Confine and terminate!"

"That's not good," Dredd said and snatched at Kontarsky's arm, pulling her out of the spotlight. Ozone crackled through the air behind them as an electro-blaster shot thousands of volts into the space where they had just been crouching. The harsh sodium glare swivelled to follow them and Dredd caught a glimpse of its source: an insectile security drone suspended on a quad of vector-jets. Amid the constant noise of the oxygen works, neither of the Judges had heard the robot approaching them.

Kontarsky understood what needed to be done before Dredd said it to her and she broke away from him, sprinting in the opposite direction. The drone saw the movement and hesitated for a fraction of a second, unsure if she or Dredd were the target of primary importance. In that moment, Dredd set his STUP-gun to level four tight-beam and shot at it.

The pulse-blast sheared one of the thruster pods off the drone and sent it listing to starboard like a sailboat caught in a sudden gale. The spotlight ran wildly over the walls as it struggled to regain control of its flight. Another pulse of hot light from the direction that Kontarsky had run flickered into the drone's casing and buffeted it, but the machine recovered and aimed back at the Sov-Judge, fixing her in the middle of its sights. Without the anti-dazzle visor in her helmet, Kon-

tarsky was blinded by the drone's beam and she fired wildly
at it, her shots missing by several metres. Trapped between
two slow-moving tankers, she braced herself for the
inevitable shock of voltage from the e-blaster, but it never
came.

Without warning, there was an ear-splitting gush of sparks
and something heavy flattened the drone into the sub-levels
below them, knocking it out of the air like a fly swatted by a
sledgehammer. Blinking away purple after-images on her
retinas, Kontarsky looked up to see Dredd beckoning to her.
Above the Mega-City Judge, a crane frame buzzed and spat
where he had blown off the retaining bolts that held an ice
pallet. "Spaciba..." she managed.

Dredd pointed with the STUP-gun. "This way."

Kontarsky shook off the sick feeling in her stomach that
the fear of imminent death had created and followed him.
She listened for the sound of drone motors and heard them –
lots of them. Next time there would be more and Dredd
would not be able to drop an ice load on all of them.

"Neutralise the intruders!" screamed the electronic voice.
"Productivity has been threatened! Intercept and destroy!"

Klaxons were sounding now and flashing red strobes
pulsed into life across the inside of the Oxy-Dome. Robots
that had the right kind of sensors or that weren't engaged in
some kind of critical work stopped what they were doing and
looked for the two human shapes; the data from them went
straight to the security drones, vectoring them toward the
Judges like a flock of airborne predators.

"We must get off the factory floor!" Kontarsky cried. "We
are too exposed here!"

Dredd ducked into an alcove where a heavy hatch was
half-concealed in shadow. "Here!" he snapped. "Help me
with the wheel!"

The door had not been used in a long time and rust caked
the lip and the circular handle in the centre. Clearly, no
human had been into this part of the oxygen works in years.
With a final grunt of effort, Dredd and Kontarsky forced the
hatch open and almost fell through it, desperately pushing it

shut again as the drones closed in. The man-sized entryway was too small for the larger security flyers, but both Judges knew that it wouldn't be long before a humanoid robot was sent after them.

"This…" Kontarsky said, catching her breath. "This has not gone as well as I would have hoped."

Dredd spared her a look. "We go up," he said. The hatch opened on to a ladder that extended away to the myriad sub-levels below and the multiple floors above. "This must be some sort of maintenance duct, for human use."

Kontarsky considered this as they climbed. "You said yourself, they're aren't any people down on the lower levels."

"No," he agreed, "and I'm starting to suspect that the only living things in this place are us."

They proceeded almost without incident, except for a moment fifteen levels high, when something fast had come clanking up from below them. In the faint light of the shaft, all either of the Judges had been able to see were the sparks flicking off the walls as steel claws scraped their way up after them. Dredd ordered Kontarsky to look away and he fired his pulse gun past her, a full power charge ripping through the confined tube of air and striking the robot dead centre. It clattered and scraped all the way back down again, making fresh blooms of sparks as it fell.

They continued upward. It was the longest climb of Nikita Kontarsky's life, or so it seemed. In the moments when she wasn't struggling with arms and legs that felt like lead, she marvelled at the constant pace that Dredd maintained, steadily advancing up the shaft toward the upper levels. Had she not known better, she might have suspected that the Judge was a machine himself, maybe one of those near-human life model decoy replicants that she had heard rumours about. What if he does have oil pumping through those veins, her fatigued mind wondered, what if Joseph Dredd has been dead for decades and Mega-City One has just kept on turning out robot duplicates? It was a mad idea, but one that many other kadets had declared as certain truth during her training. She shook the thought away as a strong hand curled around her wrist and guided her off the ladder.

"We're here. Ready?"

With effort, she raised her pistol. "I am."

Dredd forcefully kicked open the hatch on the top level and strode out. Kontarsky followed him, watching. If Dredd wasn't a machine, then he was as near to one as a man would ever get.

The room they had emerged in was a large gallery set into the roof of the oxygen works. From here, anyone operating the command consoles that ringed the walls could look out across the full spread of the dome's systems. This high up, the Oxy-Dome's interior looked like some vast set of interlocking clockwork toys, each working in perfect precision.

The synthetic voice that had called the Judges out screamed through the air again, louder and more strident this time. "Alert! Alert! Intruders in central processing unit! Productivity is in jeopardy! Alert! Alert!"

Slats in the ceiling retreated to allow arms on gimbals to extend downward, uncoiling like inverted scorpion tails; each one ended in the barbed sting of an active electro-blaster and they tracked as one toward Dredd and Kontarsky. The two law enforcers took cover and snapped out shot after shot from their pulse pistols, burning smoky soot-black sears across the roof of the chamber. The blasters fired back, but they were slow and had been poorly maintained, just like the rusted hatch. In a matter of a few moments, all the remote weapons had been destroyed.

Dredd kept his gun handy and approached a central dais where a raised console sat. A crude approximation of a face – indicator light eyes and an oscillating sine wave mouth – was displayed there. "Identify yourself!" Dredd barked at the screen.

"LunAir Oxy-Dome Control Computer XF6," replied the voice. "You are an intruder. The authorities have been notified. You will be captured and–"

Dredd picked another console at random and fired a shot into it. The panel spat out a puff of desultory smoke and far below in the oxygen works, a whole sector of the plant went dark. "I want answers, chip-head, not a conversation. Where's your human overseer?"

"System XF6 operates flawlessly without human intervention," the computer said snidely. "Orders come direct via data link."

"You cut off the air to Kepler Dome. How?"

"This unit cannot answer questions of–"

Dredd blew a trio of fist-sized holes in a panel to his left and faint sirens screamed, as if the Oxy-Dome was a wounded animal crying out in pain. "How?" Dredd repeated.

It suddenly dawned on Kontarsky what Dredd was doing. Like many centralised industrial computers, the XF6 was programmed to prioritise factory productivity over everything else, even its own survival. By damaging its sub-consoles and wrecking the plant, Dredd was effectively interrogating the machine in the same way that someone might break a human subject's finger or strike them to elicit a response.

"Productivity is in jeopardy!" the computer whined. "Please desist!"

Kontarsky approached a large processor module and rested her STUP-gun's barrel on it. Dredd gave her a cool nod.

"Wait! XF6 will respond!"

"Better," said Dredd. "There are multiple redundant systems in the Luna-1 life-support hardware. How did you circumvent them all?"

"All Luna-1 systems are built on an existing framework. Embedded commands in base software allow subversion of all subsequent additions and upgrades."

"A back door program?" Kontarsky wondered. "When was it put in place?"

"At the point of initial construction, circa 2058."

"That's when Luna-1 was first built..." Dredd noted, "Drokk! That means there's been a kill switch wired into the whole city since day one!"

"But who could have done this?"

Dredd's lip curled in a sneer. "Ask yourself, who was in charge back then? Who was it that made sure he got every construction contract, every land grab, every sweet deal? This place was the wild frontier. Laws were flouted as long as the job got done."

"Computer, who was primary contractor for the original Luna-1 dome systems?" Kontarsky demanded.

"Moonie Enterprises," said the console. "The company was disbanded as of 2100 by order of then-current Judge-Marshal Joseph Dredd."

15. TRANQUILLITY BASE

Dredd turned to Kontarsky. "You asked me before how one man could plan to steal the Moon and here's your answer: Clinton Moonie has been taking the long view... He's been planning this caper since before you were born."

"A secret command that lets him shut off air to any dome on the Moon... The implications of such a thing are staggering. But if Moonie can do this, why has he never used it before? When he was arrested, he could have traded his freedom for the threat of suffocating Luna-1," she replied.

"You still don't really understand him, do you? He's no street perp. Moonie doesn't want freedom, at least not in the way that you or I think of it. He doesn't care about anything except power, power over the Moon. He wants to own this ball of rock and everyone on it. What good is being master of a city when it's full of corpses?"

"I see your point," she conceded. "But we have no assurances that he won't change his mind and we still have many questions unanswered. Even with his money and influence, how could he have escaped and substituted a duplicate without detection? How could he have operated for months and not raise any suspicions?"

Dredd gave her a level stare. "You tell me, Kontarsky."

She matched his look. "You continue to distrust me, Dredd? You know the answers to these questions yourself and yet you test me over and over, hoping that I will reveal myself in a lie, yes? Why can you not see past my uniform and accept that we are fighting the same foe?"

"Because someone is helping Moonie and like you said, that someone may be one of your countrymen."

The Sov-Judge's pale face flushed. "I said no such thing! I voiced a suspicion, nothing more!" She forced herself to calm down. "It is true that I believe Moonie is not working alone, but his accomplices could be–"

Dredd looked away. "We'll burn that bridge when we come to it. Right now we have to concentrate on keeping Luna-1 breathing. If Moonie can pull the plug on the air, he's more dangerous than we ever suspected. We've gotta take that away from him and quickly. There's no telling what other surprises he's got lurking in the city's control sub-routines."

"The computer's orders came through a data link," she gestured to the control console on the dais. "The Oxy-Dome uses hard lines, fibre optic cables."

"Yes, they're more reliable than transmitters during the solar flares. That means the signal came down the line from the central computer hub in Luna-1 itself. If I know Moonie, he's close by so he can watch and gloat, but he's not dumb enough to be hiding in Luna-City itself. He's beaming his orders through the hub and straight into the network."

"Yes," nodded Kontarsky. "Very clever. He uses the system itself to carry his commands, making them invisible. But how do we sever that control without a shutdown of every system on Luna-1? I hardly think Che will agree to let us reboot the entire city."

The Sov-Judge was correct. Even if they could overcome the impossible odds against it, such a thing would plunge the lunar metropolis into chaos, exactly the circumstances that the fleet of so-called diplomatic cruisers in orbit was waiting for. Dredd realised the callous, engineered subtlety of Moonie's plans – the crime lord had set up the city like a complex game board, the pieces all turned to his advantage. But their other options had been reduced to nothing. "We're not going to ask for permission. How long would it take us to get back to the city?"

Kontarsky made a quick calculation. "Four hours in a rover, if we traversed the Sea of Tranquillity. Could we not return on the cargo train?"

"Negative, those railshuttles run once a day and the next won't pass this way until past dawn tomorrow. We need to get to the Spike."

"What are you planning, Dredd?" she demanded. The Spike was Luna-1's primary computer centre, a huge needle-shaped tower in Serenity Territory. Dominating the Luna-1 skyline, virtually every piece of computer data that flowed through the city complex went in or out of the vast plasteen spire.

"If we want to stop Moonie turning the air off, then Luna-1 has to go off the air. We're gonna spike the Spike."

"Perhaps all the free oxygen in here has affected your mind, Dredd. What you're suggesting is extremely danger-ous! There's no telling what the side effects could be!"

The Mega-City Judge took a step closer. "Why are you opposed to trying, Kontarsky? All of this time, we've been dancing to Moonie's tune, always one step behind his game-plan." Dredd shook his head. "Not any more. We're going to change the rules. We reboot the hub and he'll be forced to use another way to tap into the dome systems."

The point of Dredd's daring gambit snapped into crisp focus for the Sov-Judge. "If Moonie does that, he won't be hidden. We'll be able to track him to his point of origin."

"Exactly. I figure we've got a fifty-fifty chance of making this work."

She frowned. "If it fails, the next thing we will see is armed ships and troopers from a dozen countries cutting their way through the airlocks and shooting each other. Are you really willing to risk a war?"

Dredd holstered his gun with a slight shrug. "Wouldn't be the first time."

At that moment, a kilometre above the lunar surface and a few more downrange from the Oxy-Dome Complex, a fast rocket was streaking westward under full burn, cutting a bril-liant red streak across the black sky. The rocket itself was little more than a skeletal framework, an ugly collection of engine bells, fuel tanks and guidance systems that lacked even the most basic design aesthetics. Built to operate in vacuum, it had none of the smooth lines of a trans-atmospheric liner or a NEO clipper, but that had no bearing on the craft's ability to perform its function and it was doing it to perfection. Thin Mylar sheets that served as micro-meteor barriers tore away from the middle of the fuselage like falling petals. They revealed four angular man-shapes hanging inside the rocket's frame, clustered like piglets suckling at a sow. One of the man-shapes was skinny and nimble-looking, with extra arms and legs; the other three were like cast blocks of dark metal in the shape of a human being.

A green lamp blinked on inside the heads of the three big man-shapes and the rocket let go of them, pushing them and their skinny sibling away under jets of inert gas. Any observer watching the figures falling toward the surface might have been reminded of an earthbound skydiver. Messages carried on low-power laser beams blinked between the four and they shifted orientation as they dropped, revealing retro-rocket packs that would soft-land them just inside the factory perimeter. The rocket, its cargo delivered and its purpose complete, altered course and aimed for the foot of the Lunar Pyrenees. At maximum thrust, the crater it would form on impact would swallow any piece of wreckage bigger than a child's fist.

The larger figures used the time during the drop to run a few final diagnostics on their weapons and exoskeleton systems. None of them spoke. Each of them knew exactly who their targets were.

A new alarm sound chirped in the control room for a couple of seconds before suddenly being silenced. Dredd saw something appear and then disappear on one of the sub-consoles. "What the drokk was that?" he demanded of the computer.

The machine actually hesitated. "A glitch," it said finally. "A minor malfunction, now corrected. Please remain calm."

Kontarsky raised an eyebrow. "Doubtful. I believe a burst transmission was just received by the XF6 system." She tapped the screen on another panel. "It's hiding something from us. New orders, perhaps?"

Dredd indicated her drawn weapon with the jut of his chin. "Explain it to our silicon pal here, will you?"

The Sov-Judge dialled down the pulse setting and tore blaster bolts through two adjacent monitor stations. "Awwk!" The computer replied with a noise that might almost have been an analogue of physical pain. "Desist! Desist! The authorities are on the way! You will be neutralised!"

The screen close to Dredd reactivated, to display a real-time image from the perimeter sensors. Kontarsky saw the scan, the four downward tracks approaching the complex. "Missiles!" she gasped.

"Too slow," Dredd replied. "Besides, a missile hit in the wrong place here would blast a chunk out of the Moon as big as Texas City... No, these are something else. Not big enough to be landers, they must be hunter-killers or drop-troopers." The Judge didn't waste time on speculating who had sent them or how they had tracked them – for now they needed to flee. "We're sitting ducks here. We need a way out."

"We're at the top of the dome," said Kontarsky. "By the time we go down the ladder shaft, they would be setting up camp at the bottom."

"And we can't trust Smiley here not to lock us in the elevator," Dredd jerked a thumb at the XF6. "Where's the escape airlock for this floor?"

"Here!" Kontarsky tugged at a latch on the far wall and a sliding panel folded open. Another alarm went off automatically. Usually, escape airlocks were only accessed when fire or moonquakes had cut off all other means of egress.

The Russian tossed out a thin garment made from neon-bright orange plastic. "An emergency e-suit. These should be enough to protect us until we can reach the rover bays on ground level."

"You cannot abscond!" began the computer. "You will be–"

This time Kontarsky didn't wait to be asked, only paused before sealing her helmet shut to silence the XF6 with an energy bolt right between the machine's photoreceptor eyes.

Suited, Dredd followed her into the cramped airlock and pressed the heel of his hand into the button for fast decompression. The inner door had barely shut before the air caught in the lock screamed away into the lunar night. They stepped out and found themselves at the very crest of the Oxy-Dome, lit by the colours of the LunAir holo-sign.

Kontarsky pointed, pressing her jaws together to stop her teeth chattering in the polar cold. "Look, up there. I saw something."

Dredd followed her direction and caught a flash of reflected sunlight off a metallic surface, an object closing fast. "Where are the rovers?"

"Below us. We can use the walkway on the dome to get down," she began.

Dredd shook his head, the orange suit exaggerating the movement. "No time for that. We're taking the express route."

Kontarsky started to argue, but Dredd hit her hard with a body-check that flattened her to the curved surface of the roof. Without the adhesive soles of her suit's g-boots to hold her upright, she began to slide. The two Judges locked arms and fell like a human toboggan, racing down the steep slope of the dome toward the lip of the crater a hundred metres below.

Even through the thick polypropylop of the emergency suit, Dredd felt the stinging heat of friction as the material heated up from the forced descent; one sharp jag of metal in their path and they would suffer a catastrophic puncture.

Kontarsky screwed her eyes shut and held her breath, counting the seconds in her mind, desperately trying not to imagine what would happen if they struck a rocky outcrop at the lip of the domed crater – but Dredd's luck held and, with a shocking thud that made her spit out flecks of blood, they impacted a drift of moondust and rolled to a clumsy, bruising halt.

"Please have the decency to warn me if you wish to throw me off a roof," she snapped, checking her suit for tears as she stood up.

Dredd probed a hairline crack in his faceplate and frowned. "Our friends are almost here. Let's get ourselves some wheels."

The spindly humanoid shape landed on all fours next to the three identical man-forms. Its extra limbs unfolded to produce laser tips and a fan of sensors. The seeker head instantly found Dredd and Kontarsky, the heat of their bodies visible against the cold of the landscape in the infrared spectrum. It opened a real-time link to the armoured figures and showed them.

The figures threw off the disposable thruster packs that had slowed their descents and unlimbered a variety of weapons from magnetic clamps on their backpacks. Their leader gestured and they spread out in a loose formation.

The rover garage was a prefabricated hut of plastiform panels, sheathed from the hard radiation of the sun by a coasting of lunacrete. The roller-blind door gave easily under the combined fire from the Judges' pistols and they clambered inside, careful not to catch their suits on the orange-red edges of the hole they had burned. Kontarsky pulled a lamp from her belt and waved it around the room. There were a couple of open-deck moonjeeps to one side and a yo-yo, a civilian flybike similar to the Zippers used by the Judges. Dredd ignored them all and crossed to the largest vehicle in the room: set on a cluster of six fat wheels, the rover's hull was two spheres linked by a stubby tube. It was almost as tall as the garage was wide, but it had a sealed cabin and a better chance for survival on the lunar terrain. "This one," he said.

Kontarsky nodded and followed him through the rover's cramped airlock. Inside, the vehicle smelled stale and mouldy. "This thing is ancient," she said under her breath.

If Dredd heard her comment, he gave no sign. The Judge dropped into the driver's seat and pressed the starter pedal. The rover's motor clicked and hummed, but did not engage. Dredd saw movement through the hole in the garage door and frowned, pushing the pedal again, harder this time.

The Sov-Judge saw it too, the thin, shiny arms clutching at the door, probing at the interior. With a sharp flash of motion, the skinny humanoid mechanism sprang through the torn gap and landed somewhere in the shadows, out of sight.

"Hunter-killer," Dredd noted, working the ignition once more. This time, the motor hissed into life and the rover's headlight cast white beams over the garage interior. The vehicle lurched forward and Kontarsky let out a yelp as the scrawny robot slammed into the windscreen and hung there.

The machine's twitching head was only an arm's length away from Dredd's face, with nothing but the armoured glasseen of the window between them. A lipless metal mouth opened and extruded a drill-bit tongue that whirred into the plastic. Dredd stamped on the accelerator and the drive motors in the wheels responded, skidding as they picked up traction before launching the rover forward. The hunter-killer droid brought its extra arms around to aim a pair of laser cutters, concentrating with digital precision on its primary target. Dredd ignored the robot and drove the moon rover straight into the centre of the garage's roller door. The collision sent a ringing crash through the hull of the vehicle and Kontarsky reeled, slipping to her knees in the gangway.

For a second, Dredd lost control of the rover and it fishtailed, the six balloon tyres biting into the moondust and kicking up spurts of grey powder like slow-motion fountains. The hunter-killer was flattened into the windscreen by the impact and parts of it broke off, thin legs snapping at the joints. Dredd saw a piece of the garage door fold away, the edge shearing through the droid's flexible neck. The robot's body dropped, tumbling under the axle. The rover bounced once, twice, three times as the portside wheels rode straight over it, smashing the attack drone into pieces.

Kontarsky struggled back to her feet, fingers clutching at a grab-bar for support as the rover bounded over the rough ground. She made a sour face at the head of the robot, which was still staring at them through the glasseen, impaled in place on its own drill shaft.

. . .

One of the suited men was knocked off his feet by the rover's explosive departure and he took long seconds to stand up once again. In the meantime, the leader and his other teammate were sprinting after the fleeing vehicle, using compressed gas thrusters in their boot soles to make low, loping hops across the ground. Bouncing like children's toys, they skipped after the vehicle. Specially programmed targeting software developed for combat on the lunar surface came into play, overlaying graphics on the inside of their helmets, tracking the rover and predicting where it would go next. The scopes crunched numbers for velocity, speed, gravity and distance, giving the two of them aim points as good as anything a rock-steady target would have provided.

Ruby-coloured lasers winked out, linking the armoured figures and the rover like thin threads. One shot tore off the vehicle's communications antenna, the second struck the hub of the starboard rear wheel, melting vital gears in the drive mechanism.

Dredd felt the laser bolt hits rather than heard them, the seizing motor forcing a shudder up through the rover chassis. He paid no attention to the warning lights that flared on the dashboard, his boot pressing the accelerator pedal to the firewall. Beside him, Kontarsky was strapping herself into the jump seat.

"There are no weapons," her voice was high with barely concealed anxiety. "A remote construction arm, nothing else."

"Use it," said Dredd and he pulled hard on the steering yoke, bringing the rover around in a tight turn. The broad expanse of the Oxy-Dome reappeared in the window and before it the bouncing shapes of the two armoured suits. Dredd chose one of the suits at random and aimed the rover directly at it, revving the electric motor.

The leader used her jets to leap up to the top of a rocky outcropping as the rover swept past, bearing down on her team-mate at full speed. She toggled her laser to a broad-beam setting and raked a fiery streak down the length of the hull as the vehicle darted away. Her team-mate easily side-stepped the oncoming rover, but too late the leader saw that Dredd's intention had been to make him do exactly that, not to run him down. The other armoured suit dodged directly into the path of the heavy crane arm extending out from the back of the rover and, before she could shout a warning over the radio, the leader watched the claw-gripper at the end strike the figure in the chest, ripping away a great chunk of metallic armour as it passed. The other man twisted away into the dust, a gout of crimson gushing into the vacuum as he fell. Flash-frozen spheres of bright arterial blood scattered around him like a handful of jewels.

The rover skidded around and leapt over a rise, heading north to the Sea of Tranquillity. Frowning inside her helmet, the leader waited for her other team-mate to arrive and they paused to strip their dead comrade of equipment before destroying his corpse with a thermo-bomb.

Dredd pushed the rover to the redline while Kontarsky scrambled into the vehicle's engineering spaces, keeping one eye on the radar display in the dashboard. The screen showed sporadic contacts as the armoured hunters tracked them, the rover's sensors picking them up for just an instant as they crested a hill or jetted too high on their thrusters. They were close.

Kontarsky swayed down the gangway and dropped heavily into the other seat. Like Dredd, she had discarded the emergency environment suit as soon as they had found industrial-grade atmosphere gear in the rover. The Sov-Judge had also dispensed with her rad-cloak in order to squeeze into the maintenance bay. She wiped a speck of dirt from her milk-pale face; her expression spoke volumes before she opened her mouth. "Some of the batteries and a lubricant tank have been vented to vacuum. We have enough power to reach Luna-1 but we'll burn out the motors if we maintain this rate of speed."

"If we slow down those shooters will be on us in minutes."

Kontarsky threw up her hands in exasperation and swore in Russian, her cool finally cracking. "Fine! Just keep driving, then. At full power, sooner or later the motors will seize and the friction will cause a fire. We'll burn alive or suffocate!"

Dredd's eyes flicked to the radar screen in time to see another blink as something moved behind them. "We need another option, then." He pulled up a local map on the heads-up display. "Find somewhere to stop, make a stand. Otherwise, they'll be dogging us all the way." He highlighted an area and zoomed in.

Kontarsky saw where he was looking and shook her head. "You are joking."

The Mega-City Judge pulled the steering yoke around and changed course. "Have you got a better idea?"

She had to admit that she did not. "I'll fetch the suits."

The armoured figures landed on puffs of gas and dropped to their haunches, just as they had been trained. The leader tongued a switch on her chin-guard and gave her team-mate a quick beam-signal. He replied in the affirmative and walked in a crouch to the rover parked on the lip of a lunar dune. She watched her team-mate vanish inside, then reappear moments later. He made a shrugging motion. Empty.

They approached the flat piece of land before them, navigating around a small crater and from nowhere, a hologram blinked into life. Both of them had to restrain themselves from opening fire.

"Hello!" said the ghostly image of a smiling man, his voice broadcasting over their radio channels. "Welcome to Tranquillity Base National Park, the site of the first manned landing on the Moon in the year 1969! Please enjoy our interactive exhibit, but do keep off the–"

The proximity-activated hologram faded away in midspeech as they left it behind and then the leader saw them – two orange shapes clustered in the lee of a low hillock. They fired, both hits to the body of their target and the suited figures slumped like discarded rag dolls. The leader closed the distance to them.

The holographic guide appeared and disappeared as she passed another point of interest. "To your left is a laser ranging retroreflector that was left behind–"

She swore aloud and flashed out an alert signal. The orange suits were decoys – Dredd had filled them with air and laid them out to draw their fire! As if in answer, pulse blasts blinked from out of cover and she ducked, watching them converge on her team-mate. She saw puffs of blood stream out from his suit joints, then she looked away, triggering her jets and shot at the gunner directly ahead of her, half-hidden behind the shape of an ancient lunar lander.

Dredd saw the armoured suit fly toward him and ducked, rolling under the leg of the bug-like lunar module. The heavier suit turned after him, but the Judge had agility on his side and he ducked up and around behind it. With a vicious shove, Dredd slammed the leader's helmet into the one hundred and fifty year-old spacecraft. The suit's visor spider-webbed with the force of the impact.

"Restored to its original state by the Historical Sticklers Society, the Apollo 11 lunar module seen here carried two human astronauts from ZZZT–" The holo was choked off in mid-speech as the armoured suit shoved an elbow into Dredd's chest and threw him into the display unit five metres away.

His ribs singing with pain, Dredd tried to scramble to his feet as the leader jetted across the distance between them. His STUP-gun had fallen out of arm's reach when he'd been thrown and now unarmed and injured, he saw the blocky shape of the armoured suit coming at him like a guided missile.

Dredd's suited fingers closed around something by his side and by reflex he pulled it from the moondust to brandish it like a spear. Unable to stop in time, the leader impaled herself on the spike and Dredd rammed it home through her faceplate, turning it into a window of red ruin. She slumped backward into a heap and only then did Dredd realise what he'd used as a makeshift weapon. Lanced through the suit's helmet was a steel rod that ended in a metallic Stars and Stripes.

16. RED MOON

Kontarsky scrambled over the lip of the shallow crater that had hidden her and sprinted as well as she could in the low lunar gravity, skipping over the moondust toward the shape of the second armoured figure. Streams of dark liquid, frozen into thick streaks by exposure to vacuum marred the grey frame of the exoskeleton; the hydrostatic shock of being hit by two full power pulse blasts had ruptured the delicate flesh of the man inside and cracked the suit collar. The armed hunter was bleeding inside and, if the blood loss didn't kill him first, he'd choke to death on his own vital fluids.

The Sov-Judge saw Dredd fighting with the other armoured figure in the periphery of her vision and ignored them; the Mega-City Judge was more than capable of dismissing his opponent without her help. She skidded to a halt near the injured man and planted a kick in his side as he tried to get up. Kontarsky felt conflicting emotions flood through her. A strong, heady anger was welling up in her chest and she wanted to turn it on the hunter, as if hurting him would pay back all the people who had been working against her. The rage drowned out the cold, clinical part of her personality for just long enough and she pressed her STUP-gun at his damaged chest plate.

The man mouthed something, but it was lost inside his bloodstained helmet. Kontarsky fired and the suit became his tomb. It wasn't until the life had guttered out in his eyes that she realised she knew what he had said. A plea, a single word, begging her not to kill him. *Nyet*.

She stiffened as the implications of it settled on her. Kontarsky peered closer at the suit, scrutinising the lines of its design, the framework of the laser weapon still gripped in one hand. The armour was of East-Meg manufacture, of that she was utterly sure. She looked away as Dredd approached, suddenly afraid that he would read everything through the emotions on her face.

Dredd gave the other corpse a cursory look. "Would have liked to get a live one," he said. "Might have been able to get something useful from them." When she didn't respond, he continued. "This hardware look familiar to you?"

"No," she replied, a little too quickly. "Why?"

"It's military specification stuff," Dredd noted, "not the kind of thing I'd expect a crook like Moonie to get his hands on. These people," he pointed at the dead man. "They were professionals."

"What does it matter now that they are dead?" Kontarsky tried not to be blunt, but she failed. "We can proceed now without any more interruptions, yes?"

"Yes," Dredd echoed after a moment, casting a measured eye over the Sov-Judge before making for the parked rover. "Let's get going."

As Kontarsky followed, her boot stubbed on something silver, half-buried in the moondust. She paused and bent to examine it.

"What?" Dredd paused on the ladder into the rover.

"It must have been knocked off the lunar module during the fight," she began, the thick fingers of her suit brushing the grey sand off the object. "A plaque..." Etched into the metal plate were black letters, partly bleached by solar radiation but still readable. *We came in peace for all mankind*, it said. Kontarsky considered the object for a moment, then dropped it back where she had found it. The words left a bitter taste in her mouth. "It's nothing. Nothing important."

The Sov-Judge mounted the ladder and soon the rover was on its way, leaving the bodies of the newly dead among the footprints of ancient history.

. . .

Arnos LeGrove wasn't afraid of a fight. He was a Citi-Def veteran and proud of it! Oh sure, he'd been just like all the other
guys on floor 114 of Tommy Lee Jones Block, taking his regular stint polishing the sonic cannon or doing drills, never
once imagining that his training would come in useful. But
all that had changed one morning when Sov nukes started
flying over the walls of Mega-City One and the Apocalypse
War began. He grew up quick, then, real quick. Arnos
watched whole sectors vanish in nuclear flame and saw his
buddies cut apart by las-fire from Sentinoid robots. By a
process of attrition, Arnos ended up as platoon leader for the
TLJ Citi-Def force and, out of one thousand able-bodied but
bored citizens, there were maybe a couple hundred left when
the last shots were fired. On Armistice Day, when East-Meg
One was frying in an atomic storm of revenge, Arnos sat on
the hull of a downed Strato-V and realised he was a changed
man.

He'd met Gidea during the war – Gidea Parq as she'd been
back then – and the conflict had brought them together. They
married on VS Day and started a new life together. Gidea lost
everything to the Sov invasion, but a will from her Uncle
Drayton had saved them both from destitution. Drayton
owned land in Apollo Territory and the young couple had
grabbed it with both hands, heading off to Luna-1 and a better future.

But Arnos never forgot the war and so each year for the
past two decades, he and his wife and every other MC-1 ex-
pat who lived through it had marched in the Apocalypse
Parade. Arnos didn't like the fact that the East-Meg veterans
were allowed to have their own parade as well, but that was
the downside of living in an international zone. This morning, the Judges had broadcast a warning that the streets were
still unsafe and the nightfall curfew was still in force. Gidea
stayed home, but Arnos was damned if he was going to miss
the parade; he'd never missed a single one, not even on the
day when his son Bruce had gone in for that head transplant
operation. The Apocalypse War had changed Arnos LeGrove.
It had defined him and, ever since, some small part of him

had been praying for it to happen all over again.

Today, his wish had been granted.

Arnos hollered at the top of his lungs and kicked aside the bullet-riddled body of some crusty Sov eldo, a fat guy he remembered as owning a Zonkers franchise down on Collins Boulevard. Behind him, two dozen A-War veterans gave lusty cheers and brandished the weapons they'd taken. Arnos didn't quite understand where the guns had come from – it just seemed that one moment the fighting had been hand-to-hand and then someone had started shooting. It didn't matter to him if the blasters and spit-guns had fallen from the sky; the weapons simply propagated out into the crowds, one rioter picking them up from the hands of another when they died. If somebody out there was handing out guns like party favours, then Arnos was more than happy to take them.

When he had occasion to look up – which wasn't often, thanks to the fierce exchanges of gunfire and the homemade Molotov cocktails that sang through the air – Arnos had the vague impression of something important being imparted on the ubiquitous wall-screens that appeared every few hundred metres along the street. Some of the screens had pictures of stern, serious-looking Judges or newsreaders on them, explaining in calm and reassuring voices that everyone would be much better off returning to their homes. Those screens got shot at or stoned. Most of the other displays were left untouched though, as they showed pirated loops of footage from streetcams of fighting, fighting and more fighting. One time, a screen near the Planet Express dealership happened to show a close-up of an East-Meg Judge getting struck by a falling sofa and Arnos's mob roared with approval. The screen must have understood they liked that, because it showed the clip again and again, even bleeding it over to more panels to keep pace with them as they advanced down the road. Now and then he heard some squeaky voice babbling away about something, or he glimpsed a cartoon character up there capering around like a fool. Arnos didn't pay attention to it, though. Every time he looked at the screens or listened to them, they just seemed to make him more irate than before.

The parade had started quietly enough, just like any other year and they'd got as far as the minute of silence when someone had coughed. Arnos had never been so angry as he was right then. The hot rage just flooded over him like a red wave. Of course, it had been one of the East-Megger vets making the noise, an early arrival from their stinking "peace parade" and after just a moment the Sov was being beaten by a dozen men. Then the snecking Sov's pals had arrived and the whole thing had just kicked off.

Arnos and the other guys from the Big Meg fell back into the street-fighting mode from the war like it had been only yesterday – Perry Vale and his sister Maida on point, Lou Isham with his cyber-leg bringing up the rear and big Shadwell carrying a cheese laser he'd liberated from a delicatessen. Pretty soon they were at the head of a big crowd, the mob rolling forward with inertia of its own, the feeble resistance of the East-Meggers already crushed and forgotten. They got to the Von Braun Overpass and Arnos felt the shock that ran through the whole group when they came face to face with another mob coming the opposite way.

Arnos wasn't sure who the other folks were – they might have been part of another march from another sector of the city, or maybe just some knot of rowdies left over from the troubles the night before – but as a feral, hate-filled grin split his face, he found that in all honesty, he didn't care at all. All that mattered was that these people were not him and for that reason they all had to die.

The two mobs tore into one another, spit-guns flaring like popping firecrackers, screams and yells echoing. Every tension, every petty anger and insult that any of these people had ever felt was being nurtured and massaged, brought to the fore without any of them realising it. They turned on each other, repeating a scene that was taking place in a dozen flash points around Luna-1. There was no point to it, no ground being taken or objectives being destroyed. It was not block war; it was carnage.

Arnos was killed by a bolt from a Beria flesh-blaster pistol gripped in the skinny hand of a kid half his age. It was perhaps ironic that the gun he lost his life to was Apocalypse War-era surplus, an officer's weapon that had been recovered from East-Meg POWs. All of this was lost on Arnos LeGrove, though, as he choked out bits of his own lungs through a sucking chest wound.

Arnos lay to one side of the melee, unable to move or turn his head, his line of sight fixed on an ad-screen that dangled at a dangerous angle from the offices of Acme Plumbing. In the corner of the screen was a dumpy little figure, a bubble-headed caricature cherub with a skull like the Moon and a green complexion. It looked at Arnos and watched the war veteran bleed to death, laughing at him as if it was the funniest joke in the world.

"Off," said Judge-Marshal Che to the window-screen. "Off!" he shouted at it, when the device did not respond immediately. The office's voice-recognition system was still getting used to Che's speech patterns and he was growing weary of constantly repeating himself to the machine. The oval window went dark, taking away the spy-in-the-sky footage and the real-time view of the city beyond. Che allowed himself a moment to close his eyes and hide there in the darkness of his own mind. Everything was moving so fast, he told himself, no time to stop and assimilate it all, no time to think or make the right choices...

Che was afraid to open his eyes again. He couldn't see it, but he could sense the oncoming rush of more problems, more decisions and more pressure rumbling toward him like a distant, dark thunderhead. For all his career, Che had been happy to stand in Marshal Tex's shadow; the Mex-City Judge was no fool, he knew his limitations, he knew that Tex was the best at his job, just as he, Che, was the best man to be Tex's adjutant and deputy. But he had never, never wanted to take the Chief Judge's place. There had often been talk of it among the lower ranks, but Che had always refused to address the matter. Other senior Judges had been generous enough to ascribe noble reasons to his decision, but in the cold silent moments when Che lay alone in his bunk, he knew in his heart of hearts that he simply was not capable of running Luna-1. He hated himself for it, but he could never be the man that Tex was. And now, his greatest nightmare had been made reality and Che was afraid that he would be exposed as a bumbler – indecisive and hesitant.

"Sir?" said Kessler, concerned as the long seconds of silence stretched into minutes. "I must have your orders, Chief Judge."

Che opened his eyes and studied the SJS-Judge. Kessler seemed to thrive on the chaos that was drowning the city; the livid pink scar that cut across his taut face fairly glowed with excitement. Kessler stood, hands clasped behind his back, watching Che through his cyberlink monocle. Behind him, the Brit-Cit Judge Foster shifted uncomfortably next to the silent, quiet shape of Tek-Judge J'aele.

"What... what is our status at this point?" Che managed. He tried to keep the weariness out of his voice.

"Every available man has been pulled from static duty and deployed in the streets," Kessler said crisply, "All Justice Department facilities are on high alert and riot gear has been issued. I took the liberty of ordering the activation of an electro-cordon around the Grand Hall plaza, as well as assigning a unit of Omni-Tanks for area security."

"Good, good. Madre de dios," Che breathed. "That it should come to this..."

"We are monitoring external transmissions," added J'aele. "There is an increased amount of signal traffic moving between Earth relay sats and the diplomatic fleet in lunar orbit."

"They know what's going on down here," said Foster grimly.

Kessler made a sound like a sigh. "Chief Judge, we cannot maintain this state for more than a few more hours. As it is, all Judges are executing your command to hold and contain the fighting, but losses are increasing exponentially. We must be proactive!"

Che considered this, rubbing his damp palms together. "If we contain the rioters, they will burn themselves out eventually. These... incidents must be kept isolated..."

"With respect, sir," Foster broke in. "It's not working. We're seeing more eruptions of conflict, not less."

"You have a suggestion?"

"I do, sir," Foster took a breath before continuing. "We should declare a State of Emergency and petition the members of the treaty states for assistance–"

"Are you mad?" Kessler spat. He jerked a thumb at the ceiling and the sky beyond the dome. "They're waiting up there to storm the city and gather up the scraps, but are you proposing we just open the door to them right now?"

Foster coloured. "The global partnership treaty states that signatories must provide strategic help if Luna-1 calls for it."

"Yes and once they're here in our city, they'll dig in and take over!" Kessler retorted, rounding on the Brit-Citter. "Luna-1 doesn't need help to quell this riot – it needs decisive action, now!"

"It's not a riot any more, Kessler," rumbled J'aele. "It's anarchy."

"Exactly!" The SJS officer looked back at Che. "Which is why the time for passivity is over! Chief Judge, you must authorise a full mobilisation to war footing."

"War?" snapped Foster, "With who? Our own citizens?"

"Your citizens?" Kessler said without turning, "Your citizens live on a little island on Earth, Foster. I'm talking about saving the people of Luna-1." He stepped closer to Che and pressed both hands down on the Judge-Marshal's desk, his monocle glinting. "Do as Foster says, declare a State of Emergency, but authorise a suspension of the Lunar Constitution and martial law. Give me sanction to do what it takes and I promise you, this city will be subdued by nightfall!"

"At what cost?" demanded the Tek-Judge.

"At any cost," Kessler retorted coldly. "If we choose any other course of action, we risk appearing weak before the rest of the world. We – Luna-1 – cannot take that risk."

Che broke away from Kessler's hard gaze with a near-physical effort. Weakness. It was the one thing that the Judge-Marshal feared above all else, the one thing that Tex had been able to avoid by his sheer force of will. If Che appeared to be weak now, then everything around him would come crashing down. He would fail and Luna-1 would pay the price. "By order of the Chief Judge-Marshal of Luna-1," he intoned, fighting to keep his voice level, "as of now all Justice Department forces are to go to Defence Condition One status. The city's borders are to be sealed. Use of discretionary lethal force is authorised."

Foster and J'aele said nothing, both of them shocked into silence.

Kessler's lip tugged in a slight smile of victory. "I will need to deploy heavy weapons and combat firearms to all officers. With your permission, sir, I'd like to take direct command of the operation."

Che nodded. "Yes, yes. You understand what must be done, Kessler. I place my trust in you." The Chief Judge seemed to sag in his chair.

J'aele found his voice. "Sir, I must beg that you reconsider!"

"You are dismissed!" Che barked, with sudden violence. "We will not be seen as weak! I want order imposed on Luna-1!"

Kessler gave a curt nod and strode out of the office, with Foster and J'aele following in a heavy silence.

Once he was alone, Che moved to a concealed cabinet behind Tex's desk and opened a small cooler where a bottle of old Earth whisky lay. Taking a glass in a trembling hand, he poured himself a large shot and bolted it down his throat in one sharp go. He found himself staring at the star-and-moon sigil behind the desk.

"Santa Maria," he whispered to the empty room, "forgive me."

"This?" Judge Hiro snapped at the robot, "You called me from a barricade under fire to show me this?" He stabbed his finger at the shape of a broken-down moon rover as other droids in the airlock garage hauled the dark, silent vehicle into the maintenance bay.

The robot supervisor missed his angry tone. "It rolled to a halt just outside airlock four. Regulations demand that a Judge be present when any such unaccounted-for vehicle arrives at a city dome entrance–"

Hiro waved the droid into silence. "Yes, yes, whatever. Just open it up and I'll be on my way. There's a million psycho cits on the streets and I still have a full clip of ammo." He patted the Hornet hand cannon slung over his shoulder with affection. "War is coming and I aim to be on the winning side."

The robot crew worked the rover's door. Hiro gave the vehicle's registration a cursory glance – the code indicated an industrial unit, probably a runaway from a factory dome. The SJS-Judge snatched a torch from the supervisor and climbed inside. He expected to see a desiccated corpse, probably some idiot who had set out with the rover on auto-drive without filling up on air first. Instead, the first thing he noticed was the head of a hunter-killer droid, speared in the windscreen glass by a drill-bit. Hiro was about to say something when the cold metal shape of a pistol pressed into his temple.

"Hello again," said Dredd. "Remember me?"

Hiro had an L-Wagon parked outside, his partner, Wright, was inside. Kontarsky shot the other SJS officer with a stun bolt and took the flyer up into the air. Dredd made sure that Hiro was safely handcuffed in the crew compartment behind her.

The Sov-Judge flew fast and low, swinging between towers and citi-blocks, making a fast beeline for the angular shape of the Spike.

Dredd considered the Hornet he'd taken off the SJS-Judge. "What are you doing with this? It's not standard issue."

Hiro snorted. "It's not exactly a 'standard issue' day, Dredd. Look out the window, you'll see what I mean."

The senior Judge looked down on the streets flashing by beneath them and saw they were alive with fire and explosions. Omni-Tanks fired frag shells into crowds of armed citizens, Cyclops lasers sizzled through glasseen and steel and everywhere lay the dead, some torn apart by bullets, others trampled by mobs. "Grud! It's a warzone down there! What the drokk happened?"

"Che grew a spine," Hiro retorted. "The SJS are in operational control now, Dredd. Kessler's going to make sure the cits learn a lesson in humility."

The hollow thud of an explosion floated past the flyer and Kontarsky swore softly. "Multiple missile hits on Edward Norton Block to the south. I see five Mantas firing on the ruins."

Hiro shrugged. "Can't make an synthi-omelette without breaking–"

Dredd silenced him with a look. "Kessler likes the taste of blood, doesn't he?"

"You ought to know."

The senior Judge looked away. "Where are we?" he asked Kontarsky.

"Landing now," she replied.

Neither the Sov-Judge nor Dredd saw Hiro touch a blister on his glove, instantly sending an alert signal to Justice Central.

The vast needle of the Luna-1 Computer Hub Tower, known throughout the metropolis as the Spike, loomed large in the cockpit window. Hiro sneered.

"You won't be able to touch down without a clearance code. They'll blast you out of the sky first."

Dredd threw Kontarsky a nod and she pushed the throttle to maximum, zooming toward the tower like a bullet. "It's not a problem," Dredd was almost casual. "We brought a key."

The Sov-Judge took the L-Wagon into a controlled crash-landing on the seventy-seventh floor of the Spike, shattering a wall of glasseen panels to touch down in the middle of a small atrium. She feathered the controls enough to nose it through walls and into the arena-like command centre at the tower's core. Computer technicians and servo-droids scattered as the flyer's hatch opened.

Dredd waved his STUP-gun at Hiro's head. "Stay here. Don't get cute."

The SJS-Judge said something foul enough to earn him a dozen conduct demerits, but Dredd was already gone, climbing down after Kontarsky.

She menaced a quivering compu-tech with an icy glare. "Show me the main data processing monitor, now." The operator nodded a worried assent and led her to a panel. Dredd noted Kontarsky's method with approval. She had clearly picked up a few pointers from him on intimidation.

"Run a sweep," Dredd told her. "Look for anything anomalous."

She nodded. Having glimpsed the commands on the XF6 screens at the Oxy-Dome, Kontarsky now knew exactly what to search for – and in a few moments, she had found it.

The Sov-Judge highlighted a series of tiny data strings hidden in the streaming virtual traffic of the hub. To Dredd they looked like single bubbles picked out of a churning foam of information. "Here. These match what we saw earlier."

Dredd considered the screen. "If these hidden commands have been here all the time, why didn't J'aele and Tek Division spot them?"

"It's ingenious," she marvelled. "The signals cloak themselves in the background chatter. Unless you know exactly, precisely, where to look for them, you'd think they were just glitches or junk data."

The Judge drew his pistol and set the gun's power pack to cycle. "The Spike is shielded from electro-magnetic pulses from outside?" he asked the technician. He got a wary nod in return. "But not from inside, right?" Again, the man gave a nod. Dredd switched the pistol into self-destruct mode. "Where's the main router hub?"

The sweaty little man pointed to a column of pulsing circuitry that ran along the length of the Spike. "Uh, there… But it's beam-shielded! You can't just shoot it!"

"I'm not going to," Dredd replied and tossed his STUP-gun into the access channel surrounding the column. The weapon clattered against the hub and began to emit a keening whine. "I'd advise you take cover."

Kontarsky rolled under the console just as Dredd's pulse pistol overloaded. The computer centre was lit by an actinic blue flash that turned the room into a still monochrome image and then everything went dark.

Everything.

17. NEGATIVE RETURN

"Sneck!" yelled Foster from the saddle of his Skymaster. "Look at that!"

To his left, flying behind him, Tek-Judge J'aele felt his gut tighten as every light in Luna-1 went out. It was like a huge blanket of darkness racing across the city below them. From the Apollo Territory in the north to Crater in the south, a wave of black enveloped the colony dome. J'aele's gaze flicked to the screen between his handlebars, the direct link to the central records computer at the Grand Hall of Justice – and instead of the usual train of data and readouts, there was an error message: *Data link lost.*

The only illumination came from torches down on the street, the odd headlight beam from a vehicle or the twinkling orange-yellow reflections from a fire. At first, the Simba City Judge suspected an EMP weapon, but such a thing would have knocked out the controls of their Zippers as well and sent them plunging toward the ground. "It's Dredd," he said with grim certainty. "Who else could it be?" Overhead, the arc of a rising Earth was clearly visible through the dome, shining a dusky light over the metropolis.

Foster's voice carried through the rushing air. "Judge Hiro's beacon signal is steady at the Spike. We're close."

J'aele nodded. "Let's move. If we don't get to him first, Kessler's SJS are going to have Dredd's head before we find out what he's–"

The Tek-Judge's words died in his throat. Just a suddenly as it had done dark, Luna-1 was coming back to life, lights and holos flashing back into being in a cascade of brilliant colour.

"Total elapsed downtime, eighty-three point one-five seconds," Kontarsky read the figures from her wrist chronograph. "This is wrong. The system should take at least four minutes to recover and reboot itself."

"I thought you said this would work, Kontarsky," Dredd growled.

"It should have!" she shrilled. "There's no explanation why it wouldn't!"

Around the control room, video screens blinked on in a surge of white static.

"Oh oh oh, but there is!" A synthetic voice quacked out of the speakers. "Nice try, Judges, but oh so wrong, wrong, wrong!" The Moon-U caricature dropped into frame, wearing a parody of Kontarsky's East-Meg uniform. It toyed with an impossibly long rad-cape and strode around in a mocking lockstep, flipping from screen to screen around the room. "U think I'd let U pull the plug on my home town? No way Joe-Joe! Moon-U is 2 smart 4 U 2!"

The Sov-Judge stared at the control panel in front of her, where the city's data stream raced past in a roiling rush of numbers. "Impossible! There's no way they could have hacked into the system so fast after a shutdown! It can't happen!"

"No, it can't," Dredd agreed, an ice-cold certainty building up inside him. "Tek-Division have been scouring the city for a hideout for these hackers and they found nothing..."

Moon-U capered around and tripped over its cape in a pratfall. "Can't catch me. He, he, he!"

"But what if there is no hideout?" Dredd continued. "What if there are no hackers? Moon-U's not some computer geek's cartoon puppet... It's alive! There's no other explanation!"

Kontarsky gasped. "An artificial intelligence? A self-aware program living inside the Luna-1 network..."

Moon-U shrugged off the East-Meg outfit and toyed with a floppy T-shirt it wore underneath. The computer graphic imp studied a huge pocket-watch. "Tick-tock, tick-tock, Joe Dredd! Took U long enough 2 figure it out out out! Moon-U ain't a hacker... Moon-U is the hack!"

One of the sweaty technicians shook his head. "But that kind of intelligent software is banned under the Turing Accords!"

"Yeah," Dredd added. "Smart programs don't just grow on trees. That thing is way beyond the capacity of someone like Moonie."

"Well, thanks 4 playing," the cartoon chirped. "But now Moon-U's got things 2 do, places 2 go, go, go..."

Kontarsky's face froze as she studied the data stream. "Dredd, look at this, I think there is something else here, something encrypted in the AI's source code."·

"Hey!" Moon-U shifted, appearing with a towel wrapped around it, a shower cap on its head, brandishing a bath sponge. "No peeking! Can't a program get some privacy? Moon-U's all naked!"

"Shut that thing up!" Dredd barked at the technician, peering at Kontarsky's screen. The Sov-Judge indicated an intermittent line of data and Dredd watched it scroll past. "Looks like a comm signal."

"It is," Kontarsky replied. "It's encoded into every Moon-U transmission. Every time that moronic gnome appears on a public screen somewhere, it is putting out a series of subsonic pulses. They are just below the range of human hearing."

"Moronic? How rude!"

"Subliminals, just like Maktoh said," Dredd replied, his face tightening with annoyance. "Drokk! This thing isn't just stirring up the riots – it's causing them!"

"And that's Moon-U's Q 2 zoom! Bye, bye, bye!" With a puff of digital smoke, the deformed figure disappeared, the screens returning to their normal settings.

Dredd tapped on the console. "We've got to get this information to Che. This changes everything. Now we know what that Moon-U is, we've got a fighting chance of stopping it."

. . .

They sprinted for the L-Wagon resting in the atrium. Dredd stepped through the hole Kontarsky's landing had made in the wall and into the sights of four guns.

"Hands on your helmet, Dredd," said Foster, stepping into view. "Nice and easy."

J'aele gestured at the Sov-Judge. "You too, Kontarsky."

Freed from his cuffs, Hiro made a threatening move with his Hornet street cannon. He leered at the Mega-City Judge. "Nothing to say, Dredd? No pithy comeback? You've sealed your fate with this little stunt. How many people do you think your blackout has killed?"

"A lot less than your SJS brutality!" Kontarsky snarled. "I saw what you skull-heads are doing out there! You make the East-Meg Secret Korps look like choirboys!"

Hiro glanced at Wright, who looked uncomfortable – perhaps because the woman was telling the truth, or perhaps from the after-affects of her stun blast. "Don't be so gutless. Citizens only understand one thing: naked force. If some have to die for us to underline that, then so be it."

Foster gave him a sharp look. "What the spug are you made of, man? Whatever happened to 'serve and protect'?"

"Scarface only believes in serving himself, isn't that right?" said Dredd. "Or maybe it's not Kessler who is holding your leash?"

Hiro crossed the distance to Dredd in a flash, the Hornet at his chest. "Shut up, old man! You're a relic, just like Tex! Once Luna-1 is under new management, it'll be men like me who'll be in charge!" He gave an icy smile and cocked the weapon. "Maybe I should save Kessler the trouble of an execution detail and cap you right now."

"Hiro," said Wright, "drop the gun." The other SJS-Judge aimed his pistol at his partner's head.

"What?" Hiro exploded. "You're siding with them? You're weaker than I thought you were! You disgust me!"

"Compassion isn't a weakness." Wright's voice was level and hard. "I always suspected you were dirty, but I never could believe it until now. You're in it with Moonie, aren't you?"

"Wright, don't be a fool! This is bigger than you know!"

The SJS officer shook his head. "I said drop it."

Hiro snarled and spun in place, turning the gun toward him. Dredd saw the opening and lashed out, planting a perfect nerve-strike in Hiro's throat. The SJS officer crumpled into a heap.

Wright frowned. "I am so sick of that guy."

Dredd stepped over Hiro's unconscious form and scooped up his gun. Foster and J'aele exchanged glances. "Uh, Dredd," said the Brit-Judge. "Technically you're under arrest now."

"Maybe later," Dredd replied, nodding at Kontarsky. "Bring these two up to speed." As the Sov-Judge conversed with the other men in urgent tones, Dredd approached Wright. "I thought you SJS types stuck together."

"I had my fill of Kessler's orders," Wright replied. "He's got Che to suspend the constitution, but it's just made things worse. The streets are running red out there."

"What about this creep?" Dredd glanced at Hiro.

"He's been getting further and further off-book. I'm sure he had something to do with Tex's murder. I know he's on the take, I just couldn't prove it."

"The Psi-Judges back at Central will be able to confirm that," said Dredd. "Sorry we had to shoot you before."

The SJS-Judge gave a weary shrug. "It happens."

Foster's eyes widened. "You're telling me that Moon-U freak is beaming hypnotic pulses through the vid-screens? That's incredible!"

"Is it?" said the Sov-Judge. "Think about it, Foster. Most of Luna-1's population spend half their life watching the Tri-D – with enough exposure to something as subtle as this, you could push anyone into an abnormal emotional state with the right stimulus."

"Why haven't any Judges been affected?"

She cocked her head. "How many serving officers do you know who have time to watch the vid eight hours a day?"

"Show me the data stream," said J'aele, as the implications of Kontarsky's words became clear to him. The woman handed him a digital pad with a recording of the hub traffic. The Tek-Judge gave a low whistle. "This is very impressive. The bandwidth is incredibly tight for a self-aware program. The Moon-U AI must have some sort of packet-shunt capacity."

Foster rolled his eyes. "In English, please?"

"That little data-demon is like a viral colony, you see?" J'aele explained. "It's constantly reproducing and moving through its host body – in this case, Luna-1's computer network – but the processing power is spread across hundreds of thousands of virtual locations." He frowned. "Now we know what to look for, we could start eradicating it, but it would just keep popping up somewhere else."

"So how do we kill it?" Dredd walked toward them. "And when we do, how do we make sure this thing stays dead?"

"If we can find the AI's source code, we could create a counter-program to hunt it down and erase it all," said the Sov-Judge. She gave the African a nervous look as J'aele scrutinised the pad.

When J'aele looked up, it was with an air of seriousness and concern. He studied Kontarsky for a moment; Dredd saw something unspoken pass between them.

"This program..." said the Tek-Judge. "It has an advanced encryption algorithm protecting it. I recognise the type."

"Origin?" Dredd demanded.

"I think Judge Kontarsky knows," J'aele's hand dropped to his holster. "Don't you, Nikita?"

The Sov-Judge's jade-green eyes softened with regret. "It's an East-Meg military code. I wasn't sure until a moment ago, but Judge J'aele's reaction confirms it. The Moon-U AI is Soviet software."

"You understand what this means, Kontarsky? This is proof that Moonie's partners in crime are East-Meg Two," said Dredd.

Foster rubbed his chin. "It makes sense. The Sovs want the Moon as much as anyone does. They hook up with Moonie and he uses his underworld connections to kick-start a rebellion, running the guns to fuel the riots. Then afterwards he'd probably set himself up as president-for-life in return for letting the East-Meggers have the mineral rights."

Kontarsky was shaken by her own admission. "Those hitmen who came after us at Tranquillity were Sov troopers too. There's only one place they could have come from, the same place where the AI was probably activated..." She looked away suddenly, her lip trembling. "I can't believe he would try to kill me..."

"What's it going to be?" Dredd asked her. "You have a choice, Kontarsky. Your own countrymen have betrayed you, put you in harm's way. You know what will happen if we don't end this. You've got to ask yourself where your loyalties really lie. The flag..." and he pointed at the bronze shield at her throat, "or the badge."

Unbidden, the young Sov-Judge's fingers reached up and touched the cool metal, running over the Cyrillic characters of her name. Suddenly, Nikita's path was very clear to her. "The time delay of signals from Earth means that the AI must be being directed from a source closer to Luna-1. From lunar orbit."

"The *Irkutsk*," said Dredd. "Kommissar Ivanov's courier ship."

"Da," she replied, her voice quiet and brittle.

"Dredd," Foster said carefully. "If we attack a Russkie vessel, that'll mean war with the Sovs."

The Mega-City Judge nodded. "Been there. Done that."

Judge-Marshal Che threw the reports at Kessler's chest and slammed a fist into the desk. "I told you to impose order, not tear the city apart!" Spittle flew from his lips and his face flushed crimson.

The SJS officer's crooked mouth curled into a sneer. "It's too late for second thoughts now, Chief Judge. You gave the command. Your name is on the record. I am merely executing your directives."

"Punitive executions for all crimes?" Che raged. "At this rate, the Special Judicial Service will have killed more citizens than the uprising has! Sector Command reports that dozens of officers are refusing to follow these barbaric orders and I cannot blame them!"

"Those Judges have been suspended or cancelled," Kessler said briskly. "The SJS is firmly in operational control on the streets." He fixed Che with a cold eye. "You wanted this problem solved, but now it comes to getting your hands dirty, you fold like a deck of cards!"

"How dare you!" Che managed, indignant. "I am Judge-Marshal of Luna-1! You will address me with respect!"

"Respect?" Kessler hissed the word like an insult. "For a man who was content to live out his life in the shadow of another? This was your test of fire, Che and you have been found wanting! Luna-1 needs a man of strength, now more than ever, but instead you quibble about bloodshed and casualties!" He gave a callous chuckle. "You cannot hide behind your desk, Chief Judge. You must make the hard choices or else you must step down in favour of someone more exacting."

At once, all the bluster and fight left Che and he sagged into his chair. The Judge-Marshal seemed to deflate, the chain of office around his neck and the cloak on his shoulders too big, too heavy for his wiry frame. The burden of command had always been a part of Che's career – he would not have risen to his rank under Tex's leadership otherwise – but the cold-blooded murder of his friend and the slow destruction of his city had broken him. "Of course... You are right..." he managed, his eyes focussed on some distant midpoint.

"I'm always right," Kessler replied, contempt for Che dripping from every word.

"Chief Judge!" An anxious voice bleated from Che's intercom. "He's here! It's Judge–"

"Dredd!" Kessler shouted, as the Mega-City Judge entered with Kontarsky, Foster and J'aele close behind. The SJS officer pulled his firearm. "Stay where you are! You are under arrest for the murder of Judge-Marshal Tex and–"

"Stow it, Kessler," Dredd's voice was iron-hard and it gave the other man pause. Dredd towered over Che. "Chief

Judge," he growled, "I have reason to believe that Sov agents are behind the disorder. It is my firm belief that Kommissar Ivanov of East-Meg Two is in conspiracy with the escaped criminal CW Moonie to depose the government of Luna-1. I want your permission to proceed with a full assault on Ivanov's vessel."

Che blinked owlishly at him. "I... I cannot sanction such action..."

Kessler still had his gun pointed at Dredd's helmet, although the senior Judge seemed not to notice. "You're insane! You've cooked up this mad story in order to further your own agenda of revenge! I should shoot you where you stand!"

The Chief Judge waved a weak hand at Kessler. "I cannot..." he repeated. "Kessler... Kessler is in charge now."

The SJS chief smiled. "You see, Dredd? Judge-Marshal Che understands which of us has the stomach for this job."

Dredd turned his full attention on Kessler for the first time, a burning determination flaring in his face. "The only thing stopping me from breaking your neck right now is the law, Kessler. The same law that you've stepped all over to get where you are. The same law you're breaking to gun down innocent civilians just to push yourself up the chain of command." With a sudden rush of movement, Dredd struck Kessler, the heel of his right hand cracking the SJS-Judge's nose, his left snatching the man's STUP-gun from his grip. Kessler stumbled backwards, blood gushing from his nostrils. "Your city is coming apart at the seams and all you see is a chance to exploit it. Tex is dead because you couldn't keep your own house in order!"

"Wh-what do you mean?"

"I had a Psi-Judge give your boy Hiro a deep scan before I came in here. He was the shooter in the plaza. He killed Tex and tried to frame me for it." Dredd's face wrinkled, as if he smelt something foul in the air. "I'll deal with you when this is over."

Foster trained his pistol on the injured Judge. "You just stay down there on the floor, chummy."

"Che," said Dredd. "We're out of time. Give the order."

Colour drained from Che's face. "I... I can't." He met Dredd's gaze, tugging the Judge-Marshal's badge from his chest. "I never should have taken this in the first place. I have failed my city." He pressed the shield into Dredd's hand. "Tex always trusted you, Joe. Don't let him down like I did."

Dredd held the star-and-crescent sigil for a long moment, then he snatched a bound copy of the Lunar Constitution from a shelf and slammed it down on the desk. With one hand on the book, he began to speak in a clear, exact voice. "I, Joseph Dredd, pledge allegiance to the badge of Judge-Marshal of Luna-1 and to the code for which it stands. One colony, under law, with discipline and order for all."

"You can't just take over!" Kessler yelled. "Who do you think you are?"

"Quiet!" snarled Foster. "I'll tell you who he is... He's Chief Judge!"

"Acting Judge-Marshal," Dredd corrected. "For now." He looked to Kontarsky. "Get me a live feed to the diplomatic ships."

"What should we do?" said J'aele.

"Prep a combat shuttle for immediate launch." He tossed the Tek-Judge Kessler's pistol. "And get that skull-head creep out of here."

"What about Che?" Foster asked softly.

Dredd gave the other man a sombre look. "Take him down to Med-Bay."

"Something is going on," said Sellers, studying his screen. "Multiple signals from Justice Central to all the other couriers."

"The cowards are calling for help," said the bald man. "Not that they'll get it."

Sellers gave the East-Meg Tek-Judge a hard stare. "You seem confident of that, Gorovich. How come?"

The Sov officer smiled. "No one will dare oppose us. To do so will risk our nuclear retribution and the unbridled might of the glorious East-Meg nation-state."

"You spout the party rhetoric so well," Judge Gorovich's commanding officer said with an arch sneer. "Sometimes I wonder if you are capable of thinking beyond it."

Gorovich smothered an angry retort with a false smile. "I am merely a willing servant of the Sov people, Kommissar Ivanov."

"Indeed..." replied the tall Russian diplomat. Ivanov glanced around the Silent Room, at Sellers and Moonie, who watched the interplay with amused looks on their faces. "And I'm sure our friends here on Luna-1 will hold East-Meg Two in the highest esteem once we have successfully brought them to power, yes?"

"Clinton Moonie never forgets his friends," chirped the frail old man. "Or his enemies, for that matter."

"That much is certain..." murmured Gorovich.

"We've reached the terminal phase of the uprising," said Sellers, consulting his screen again. "I guess it's time for you to start rolling in your jackboot boys, kommissar."

Ivanov raised an eyebrow at Sellers's use of words, but otherwise ignored the insult. He touched a control on his desk and spoke in quick, clipped Russian. "Ivanov to the bridge. Captain, bring us to deployment range and stand by to launch all drop-troopers and landers." He snapped off the intercom without even waiting for an acknowledgement of his orders.

The kommissar settled back in his chair, watching alert indicators blink on as drones loaded Rad-Sweeper tanks and Sentinoid wardroids into cargo landers. Concealed in the scanner-opaque belly of the *Irkutsk*, elite Neo-Spetznaz troopers were joining the machines in preparation for the lunar assault. "And now, gentlemen," he said with a frosty smile, "we wait for the sun to rise on a Red Moon."

The eagle's-eye window showed the faces of a dozen diplomatic officers from Mega-Cities across the globe, each one broadcasting from their orbital embassies. Dredd scanned their expressions: none of them showed even the slightest suggestion of solidarity.

"I'm not going to waste time dancing around the subject," Dredd told them, "All of you are fully aware of what's been happening down here in the last seventy-two hours. As Acting Judge-Marshal of Luna-1, I'm invoking the emergency assistance clause in the global partnership treaty. I need troops, medical supplies and technical staff."

The silence that followed his announcement hung in the air. The Brit-Cit representative cleared his throat. "Dredd, what you're asking... It's difficult to agree to. We have no troops–"

"Bull," Dredd broke in. "The treaty says your ships are supposed to be unarmed but we all know that's not true. Every one of you has a military contingent aboard."

"You accuse us of a violation?" the Sino-City ambassador spluttered. "How dare you!"

"Spare me the wounded pride act," Dredd grated. "Luna-1's bleeding to death while you're playing games up there. Get past your politics and do the right thing."

The cardinal from Vatican City gave a tight smile. "Dredd, you have much to learn about diplomacy. You cannot simply demand we ignore one part of the treaty and accept another."

"You ask us is to place our flag with yours," Casablanca's representative added. "You ask us to join you against the East-Meg peoples."

Dredd fumed. "If you back us, Ivanov won't dare send troops in! He's relying on you to be too gutless to fight, so he can stroll in and pick up the pieces!"

"Brit-Cit cannot risk engaging Sov forces," said the British ambassador. "I'm sorry, Dredd. I wish it could be otherwise." The link from the Brit-Cit ship went dark.

"Sino-City also refuses to bolster your petty skirmish." Another screen winked out.

"If the Sovs take the Moon, every Mega-City on Earth will pay the price!" Dredd snapped. "If you force us to fight them alone, Luna-1 will be obliterated in the crossfire!"

"Then you should consider honourable surrender, Judge-Marshal," Hondo's diplomat noted. "For the sake of the Selenite citizens."

The last links were severed, leaving Dredd to stare at out of the oval window at the smouldering city beyond.

"None of them would even consider it," said Kontarsky. "They don't dare fire on East-Meg officers."

Dredd shook his head. "It's not just that. They're hoping that Ivanov's soldiers are going to fail, that we're going to kill each other. Then they'll come in and fight amongst themselves to stake their claims on the Moon. We're on our own."

The shuttle J'aele had chosen for the assault was one of the fastest craft in the Luna-1 fleet, an agile Falcon-class inter-orbital pursuit ship.

"It is designed for rapid response, mostly going after Belt pirates or chump dumpers who haven't gone interstellar. The weapons suite is good, but it's not enough to do serious damage to a cruiser like *Irkutsk*. It has decent armour, but the best defensive system is its speed. At full burn, even smart missiles will have trouble tracking it."

Dredd ran a hand over the bullet-shaped fuselage. "We're not looking for a dogfight. This is a shock attack. I want to get on board Ivanov's ship before he can say 'Das vidanya'."

"Got that covered," added Foster. "I had the meks bolt on some counter-measure pods. We'll drop enough tinsel to make them think it's Christmas."

"Let's load up, then." Dredd turned to find Kontarsky watching him.

"I thought you could use a replacement firearm," she said, handing him his diplomatic case.

Dredd opened the container and removed his Mega-City Lawgiver and a dozen ammunition clips. "Rodriguez was right. A real gun's better than those beamers."

"I want to join the assault team," she said, without preamble. "I am fully rated on the cruiser-class starship design."

Dredd holstered his pistol. "You were reporting to Ivanov every moment you could during the investigation. He used you to track us out at the Oxy-Dome. You kept quiet when you knew there was Sov involvement in Moonie's plan. Tell me why I should trust you now."

She nodded at the Lawgiver. "You took the gun. If you don't trust me, how do you know I didn't sabotage it?" She paused. "Ivanov used me to help turn Luna-1 into a battle-ground. I cannot let that go unanswered."

"Good enough," He looked away. "Get on board. We lift in five."

18. POINT OF IMPACT

The shuttle was on automatic as it swept in low over the hull of the *Irkutsk*. Laser cupolas tracking the speeding ship were fooled as gales of silver thread spat from pods on the Falcon's winglets, sending their beams into knots of tinsel instead of homing in on the Justice Department ship. Klaxons blared inside the Sov vessel as scanners saw the shuttle multiplied a hundred-fold on their screens.

In the ship's cargo bay, Dredd aimed the clamp gun in his hand through the open hatch, sighting the flat expanse of the cruiser's fuselage as it flashed by. He didn't check to see if the others were tethered to the cable; they had been briefed and he expected them to follow procedure. Dredd picked his spot and fired. The gun threw a flat-headed projectile at the other vessel, trailing a diamond filament behind it.

The clamp struck the *Irkutsk* with a clang and locked in place. In the next second, Dredd and the other Judges were reeled out of the shuttle like fishermen pulled over the side of a boat, while the Falcon continued on its course. He glanced over his shoulder as the motors in the clamp gun drew them to the enemy ship: behind him Kontarsky, J'aele and Foster drifted in a loose line, each tied to the other through a belt webbing loop. Their gamble, that the Sov gun crews would be too occupied trying to target the shuttle to notice a string of human shapes threading across the darkness, had paid off.

Boots impacted on the hull with a resonant thud, automatic electromagnets kicking in to let them stand on the curve of dark metal. Foster made a gulping sound, his stomach threatening to rebel as he caught a glimpse of the Moon turning above them.

"Kontarsky, find us a hatch." Dredd weighed a cutting charge in his fist. "Otherwise, we'll have to do it the messy way and blast the hull."

She pointed, "There's a port by the plasma–"

Her words were cut off by a discharge of static across the comm channels, as one of the lasers tore open the shuttle with a lucky shot. Dredd turned just in time to see the Falcon's wounded form flip over. Out of control, the shuttlecraft fell into the larger ship like a bat-winged missile and struck the bow of the *Irkutsk*. The cruiser's fuselage rippled with the aftershock and white showers of frozen oxygen erupted out from the impact crater.

"So much for our security deposit," said Foster dryly.

Alarms cut through the Silent Room, bringing Ivanov and Gorovich to their feet. "What the sneck?" said Moonie. "We're under attack!"

"The bridge..." Gorovich said, leaning into a display on the holo-screen. "Something collided with the bridge!"

The kommissar's face soured and he barged Sellers aside. "Gorovich! We'll go to the secure command unit. We must launch the assault now!"

"And what am I supposed to do?" demanded Moonie. "Sit on my hands?"

"This is now a military operation," snapped Ivanov, any trace of his cool demeanour gone, "and I am the supreme authority in that area!"

Before he could frame an argument, the two Sovs left the crime lord behind, racing out into the corridor.

Sellers frowned at Moonie, pondering on the abrupt change of tone in their ally. "Ivanov won't spare any men to protect us if things start going south."

Moonie nodded his agreement, spinning his hoverchair about in a tight circle. "Forget him," he grated, stabbing a crooked finger at the control console on his chair. "I have the Moon-U command transmitter. I'm the one with all the leverage."

"What good will that do us if the ship blows up?" Sellers's voice cracked.

Moonie jetted closer and slapped him across the face. "Show some backbone, son. I've still got a couple of tricks up my sleeve." The wizened figure produced a laser pistol and handed it to Sellers. "Here. Maybe this will give you a little courage."

The airlock's outer hatch opened like a trapdoor to reveal a wedge-shaped machine lurking inside, bristling with guns and flailing tentacle limbs.

"Sentinoid!" snapped Dredd, kicking off the hull as he brought his Lawgiver to bear.

The metallic guardian was a shipboard model similar to those deployed in Mega-City One during the Apocalypse War. J'aele was seconds too slow to avoid it, scrambling back across the fuselage as the robot boiled out of the open airlock. One of the sinuous appendages caught the African's forearm in a pincer and severed it with a deft snip. Globes of blood scattered from the wound as J'aele's e-suit pumped him full of painkillers and quickly sealed a plasti-sheath over his stump.

Foster narrowly avoided losing his head the same way as Kontarsky released a fusillade of pulse fire. The Sentinoid turned toward them, las-cannons emerging from its chest; it was all the distraction Dredd needed.

"Hi-Ex," he told his gun and fired. Oxygenated rounds could fire underwater or in a vacuum with little loss of velocity at close ranges, but the physics of shooting a ballistic weapon in space remained the same. Recoil shoved him back like a kick in the chest, even as the bullet struck its mark. During the war, it had taken several direct hits to knock out one of these droids, but the larger-yield explosive rounds from the newer Mark 11 Lawgiver killed the machine with a single shot. The blast cut into its brain-case and boiled the delicate electronics there into vapour. The Sentinoid went limp, losing purchase on the hull. Then it flapped away into space like a discarded rag in an updraft.

Dredd reeled himself back in as the others clambered into the airlock. It was a tight fit and the Judge saw the hollow, sick look on J'aele's face as their helmets bumped. "Status?" he asked.

"I can function," J'aele replied stiffly, fighting off the shock of the blood loss.

Foster forced a smile. "You techies always say you can work with one hand tied behind your back. Now you get to prove it."

The inner airlock opened and they were in enemy territory.

Kontarsky had provided a partial digi-map of the cruiser's interior and Foster and J'aele took off the moment they were aboard the *Irkutsk*. The ship's computer core was held in a zero-gravity cylinder along the spine of the vessel and it would be there that the Tek-Judge would find the source code for the Moon-U AI. Meanwhile, Dredd and Kontarsky headed forward. The lightweight environment suits they wore were a far cry from the bulky civilian models that they had liberated from the Oxy-Dome rover, close-fitting unitards with heat-shunt meshes and a compact re-breather to recycle their air. The Luna Judges had less than a dozen of them and the price of a single one could have easily paid for a decent-sized hab in a Lovell District luxy-apt.

Dredd surveyed the empty corridor. "Where is everyone? This ship have a skeleton crew or something?"

Kontarsky shook her head. "Nyet, the vessel is on a Condition One alert." She pointed to a blinking indicator lamp on the ceiling. "Everyone is at their stations. The other crew will be in the loading bay, preparing the drop-troops for deployment." She stepped forward and Dredd followed their progress on a wrist-mounted sensor display screen. "The turbolift hub is this way. If we can get to the secure command unit, we can override the ship's systems."

The senior Judge examined the display. "Some kinda shielded shelter on the mid-deck."

Kontarsky nodded. "Like a bunker, if you will. In the event of an emergency, senior Kommandants or political officers can seal themselves in and operate the entire vessel from there." She smiled grimly. "It makes any thoughts of mutiny obsolete."

Dredd caught the sound of voices and froze. "Someone's coming…"

"Is this really necessary, kommissar?" said Gorovich, jogging to keep up with Ivanov's long-legged gait. "I do not believe–"

"What you believe is irrelevant, Gorovich!" Ivanov snapped. "I will not allow this operation to fall apart in the final phase! That strike on the bridge is clearly the prelude to a direct attack… The Luna-City Judges are desperate." He frowned. "I should have taken direct command of this from the start."

Gorovich spoke without thinking as they approached the turbolifts. "But then you would be dead now, blown out into space with the captain and the rest."

Ivanov ignored the two troopers who saluted him and gave the bald Tek-Judge a lethal stare, reading the poorly masked disappointment on his face. "How inopportune for you that I still live. Your plans to usurp me must wait for another day."

Gorovich made negative noises. "I… I intend no such thing, sir. I am merely a servant of the Sov peoples–"

"Yes, yes," Ivanov said dismissively, using a key card to activate the direct drop shaft to the secure command unit. "You're a model party member."

"It's him!" Kontarsky hissed from their hiding place. "If he gets through that hatch, there's no way of opening it from outside!"

Dredd flipped the selector on his Lawgiver to Ricochet. "Take him!"

Ivanov saw the brief instant of movement as the two figures in e-suits appeared around the corner. He shouted an order and the troopers brought up their beam rifles as the attackers opened fire. The kommissar knew the tell-tale report of a Lawgiver very well; he'd heard it untold times during his service through the Apocalypse War and there, behind the cowl of the suit, he saw light flash off the grim visage of a Mega-City Judge's helmet. *Dredd*.

Bullets made from a titanium-rubber matrix skipped off the metal walls with keening screeches, cutting through exposed flesh and severing the jugular of one of the troopers. On reflex, Ivanov grabbed Gorovich and thrust him forward like a shield, letting the hapless Tek-Judge soak up a dozen hits – a fitting final service for such a dutiful Sov officer, he decided. The kommissar shoved the jerking body away and dove into the drop shaft as it yawned open. As he fell into safety, he thought he heard Kontarsky's voice crying out in anger but then the hatch sealed behind him and the noise was gone.

Her pulse blasts had made short work of the other trooper, but Kontarsky and Dredd reached the shaft hatch too late to stop it slamming closed, magnetic bolts thudding home with unyielding finality. The Sov-Judge cursed Ivanov's clone-mother under her breath and kicked the hatch ineffectively.

Dredd examined the shaft, fingering a small vent to the side. "There's an air duct here."

The Sov-Judge shook her head. "It doesn't connect to the secure unit. There's a bulkhead between them."

"How thick?" said Dredd. He reached into his backpack. "Thick enough to resist a thermite hull-cutter?" The Judge offered her a disc-like charge; a flat cone of explosive, the charge was strong enough to melt a man-sized hole through starship-grade metals in a matter of seconds.

Kontarsky studied the device, thinking. "It might be enough, but the shaft is too small for you to fit through."

Dredd dropped the charge in her hands. "I wasn't thinking of me."

The Sov-Judge gulped. "Oh." She began to strip off the outer layers of the e-suit, dropping her backpack and belt. "You understand, Dredd, if I cannot stop him, he'll launch the landers. Once the drop pods are away, there's nothing we can do to stop them."

"Then don't fail."

She nodded, ripping open the vent. "How will you locate Moonie?"

Dredd knelt by Gorovich as a weak groan escaped the Sov agent. "Maybe our friend here can give me some directions." He pressed on the Tek-Judge's wounded chest and Gorovich drooled blood. "Where's the dome-head, creep?" Dredd demanded.

"Suh…" Gorovich managed. "Suh-Silent. Room."

Kontarsky nodded again. "Yes, these cruisers often have such a facility. It's a sensor-opaque conference room."

"Where?"

The woman picked up her pistol and the cutter charge. "Just look for the only empty space on the scanner." Kontarsky swallowed the last of her nerves and gave Dredd a brisk salute. "Good luck, sir." She shifted her weight and vanished into the vent conduit.

Dredd's helmet radio crackled. "Foster to Dredd."

"Dredd here. Go ahead."

"Uh, right…" There was the sound of pulse fire in the background, then silence. "We've secured the computer core. Minimal resistance. J'aele's doing his thing, but I think one of the technicians may have set off the–"

From nowhere, an ear-splitting whine sounded throughout the ship and a synthetic voice bellowed something in angry Russian.

"The, uh, alarms," Foster finished.

Dredd reloaded his Lawgiver and studied the digi-map, overlaying templates from the e-suit's suite of thermal, radiation and sonic sensors. Sure enough, a large cabin further down the hull appeared on the display like a black hole in the cruiser's innards. "Copy that," he said, "Finish your job and then commandeer an escape pod. Don't wait around for me or Kontarsky."

Dredd snapped off the throat mic and broke into a run.

Kommissar Ivanov's nose wrinkled as the smell of hot plastic touched his nostrils. For a moment, he though that Dredd might have tossed a gas grenade into the drop shaft with him, or found a way to pump some toxin into the secure unit – but then he remembered that the unit had its own independent air supply, along with food, water, even a dedicated two-man launch in case the *Irkutsk* was scuttled. Alone in the compact command centre, he turned and started as his eyes came across the wide, discoloured oval forming on the bulkhead behind him. The tritanium alloy wall was bowing inward as he watched, the hissing metal going from cherry red to white-hot. Ivanov ducked behind the auto-helm console just as the bubble of superheated metal popped with a rasping cough of air, spitting globules of molten alloy across the floor.

He couldn't help but smile as a figure dropped through the newly made hole, her normally pale face a florid red from the heat backwash. The kommissar resisted the temptation to shoot her straight away and stood up to meet Kontarsky as she blinked away the sting of fumes from her eyes, her gun clasped firmly in her fist.

"Ah, Nikita, you are so resourceful," Ivanov indicated the breach. "A hull-burner. I should have anticipated that." He gave a little sigh. "No matter. I'm pleased you could join me."

"You," Kontarsky said through a seared throat, "are in violation of multiple statues of the Luna-1 penal code. You are under arrest."

Ivanov smirked. "This is a little joke, Nikita? Surely you understand what I am doing here?" He stepped closer to her, his voice warming even though the Volokov needler in his hand never wavered. "I am furthering the cause of the East-Meg city-state. By tomorrow, the Sov flag will be flying over Luna-1."

She sneered. "And will that be before or after your squalid little capitalist comrade names himself lunar emperor?"

The kommissar's smile slipped. "Moonie is just a puppet, a greedy fool we used to ferry weapons for us. He will be a willing part of the glorious Revolution and you can be part of it too, my dear." He held out a hand to her. "You have always been loyal to the Motherland, Nikita. Do not disappoint the Rodina now."

Kontarsky willed her finger to tighten on the pulse gun's trigger, but her hand remained immobile.

The first thing through the door of the Silent Room was the corpse of the guard who had been unfortunate enough to be standing outside it. Dredd shot him through the heart and then shouldered the dead Sov-Judge into the dark confines of the chamber. As he expected, laser fire erupted inside, savaging the body. Dredd followed his decoy, falling into a tuck and roll across the floor. He glimpsed something at the far end of the room, just the vaguest impression of a figure in a chair, blink-lit by the discharges from a beam pistol in his hand.

Accelerated photons tore through the air with cracks like fractured glass, searing the Judge as he wove between the shapes of chairs and the black bulk of the obsidian table. A wallscreen blew as a salvo of bolts ripped it apart and Dredd's street-honed skills pinpointed the shooter's position. He fired, three rounds spitting from the Lawgiver's muzzle so close together that the discharge sounded like tendons shredding. The figure slumped forward.

Dredd turned the seat to face him with the tip of his boot, switching on the lamps in his helmet. The man in the chair died with an imploring look in his eyes, his mouth silenced with plasti-tape, wrists held by cuffs to the seat arms. The laser he held made irritable clicking noises as its auto-seek mode lost its target.

"Poor Sellers," Moonie's voice issued out of the shadows. "He wasn't a bad guy. Just a little slow on the uptake. Rather like you, Joe."

Dredd's helmet lamps swung and picked out Moonie's age-scarred, bulbous face and his diminutive body drifting silently above him on a hoverchair. The floater disgorged fist-sized turrets from every surface and plates of metal snapped into place over Moonie's body. A combat visor dropped down over his broad forehead, framing the horrible rictus of the old man's yellowed smile. Dredd dodged away as the hoverchair unfolded like a lethal blossom into a skeletal frame of battle armour.

"Grud!" Dredd got off two shots, but the rounds deflected away.

Moonie grinned and hit a switch; oily flame jetted after the Judge and turned a chair into a torch. "I offered you a partnership once, Dredd and you turned me down. I made the mistake of underestimating you then. This time, I'm just gonna kill you."

The Judge replied with hot lead, bracketing the criminal with more bullets.

Moonie came on undaunted, his too-wide face twisted with cruel laughter.

"Join me, Nikita," Ivanov pressed. "It's time to grow up, my dear kadet. Time to learn that names, ideologies, they matter for nothing. East-Meg, Mega-City… They are all just shapes on a map. All that really matters is power and wealth." He smiled, his hand reaching for her STUP-gun. "Once you have that, you can believe whatever you want… And Luna-1 will make me very rich indeed."

As his fingers gently brushed the pistol's barrel, Kontarsky found her voice again. "When you were my tutor, I had nothing but respect and admiration for you. I saw you as the embodiment of East-Meg perfection. Every kadet wanted to be like you, the decorated war hero of the American invasion, the champion of Minsk." A smile fluttered on Ivanov's lips, but it quickly died when he saw the icy look in her green eyes. "But all of that is a lie. You are an opportunist, a disgrace to the Soviet ideal, kommissar," she said. "You do not wish to see the people of Luna-1 gain freedom. You only wish to enrich yourself."

Her hand shook and the pulse gun discharged. Ivanov tumbled away from her, the point-blank blast smoking in his gut. "Dubiina! You motherless imbecile!" he choked. "Don't you realise, the Diktatorat ordered me to do this? If I am guilty, so are they! Do you know what you have done?"

"No," she admitted, "but I know I have kept my honour."

Ivanov screamed and fired his needler. Kontarsky dodged, and the shots went wide and shredded the helm console.

Like a wounded beast, the cruiser lurched out of control and the g-plates struggled to compensate. "Then at least, dear Nikita, we will both perish together!" Blood bubbled out of his lips.

"No," she repeated and shot him in the head.

The quiver that ran through the hull of the *Irkutsk* threw Dredd off his feet and his helmet bounced off the table, lighting fireworks of pain inside his head.

Moonie was startled by the vessel's sudden shift and his floater whined as he tried to maintain a bead on his prey. The aged criminal stabbed at firing keys and spat a spread of micro-missiles at the Judge. The tiny, finger-sized rockets impacted the tabletop and cut it in half, shattering the lunar basalt into massive chunks. Dredd rolled, pain slashing through him as a miniature avalanche of razor-edged stone fragments scattered across the floor.

Options raced through Dredd's mind at lightning speed. Although Moonie was happy to discharge explosives inside the ship, Dredd didn't dare to use a High Explosive round in return – one deflected shot in the wrong place could kill them both. "Armour piercing," he said through gritted teeth and fired back at the floating cluster of guns and plating.

Moonie screeched as the shell penetrated somewhere above his leg and the recoil spun his hoverchair about in a drunken pirouette. He returned fire with a fan of ruby-red laser light, carving a burning line down the walls and over the carpeted floor. The hot beam left a smouldering trail in its wake over the furniture and Dredd had to dive behind a repeater screen to avoid losing a limb.

Creep's got me on the defensive, Dredd's mind raced. Gotta make him the rat on the run... Dimly, the Judge was aware of Foster's voice in his ear, yelling something about the ship going out of control, the helm malfunctioning, but he tuned it out. With all the mechanical precision of the hardware wired into Moonie's chair-cum-battle armour, one millisecond of indecision would be enough to cost Dredd his life.

As if in reply to his thoughts, Moonie shouted: "I see you, Joe! The dark's like daylight to Mister Moonie!"

Another flame spurt whooshed over Dredd's helmet, melting a monitor to molten slag. The Judge bolted from cover and found himself at the head of the chamber, the humming disc of a holo-screen at his feet.

Moonie came screeching after him and Dredd met his charge with paced shots that shredded armour plate and cut through flesh. Clawed, servo-assisted hands snapped out for the lawman's throat, as drool flew from Moonie's lips in anticipation of murder. Dredd waited for the last possible second then triggered the inert holo with a kick-switch.

A huge image of the Moon from orbit sprang into life in the air between them and Dredd's anti-dazzle visor darkened instantly – but Moonie, staring intently through an image intensifier, was blinded. He screamed, flailing at the insubstantial image, clawing at his eyes.

"Heatseeker," commanded the Judge and he sent the heart-chaser bullet through the rips he'd torn in Moonie's armour, into the soft flesh beneath.

The hoverchair sank to the floor gracelessly and toppled over. Moonie spat foamy pink spittle and slapped vengefully at a control near his hand. "You Earther bastard! You killed me! But I'm not going without a fight..."

"Drokk!" Dredd saw Moonie's fingers move and stamped on them, the brittle bones snapping like twigs.

"Too late!" he wheezed. "I sent the zero command to Moon-U, understand? No more air for Luna-1, Dredd!" Moonie's massive spherical face lolled forward as his life ebbed out of him. "I die, you die, everyone dies!"

Dredd gave a slow shake of the head. "Your pet AI is on the endangered list, Moonie. It's as dead as you are!"

"No!" Moonie shook with rage. "If I can't have the Moon, no one can! No one!"

Dredd rested the barrel of his Lawgiver against Moonie's bloated skull. "Clinton Wendell Moonie," he pronounced, his face set in a grim mask, "for your numerous crimes against the people of Luna-1, I judge you guilty as charged. The sentence is death."

The gunshot echoed like thunder down the corridors of the doomed starship.

"Is that it?" said Foster at J'aele's shoulder.

The Tek-Judge gave a weary nod. "I think so."

"You think? You're not sure?"

"Can you slice through a Sov data core with one hand missing and a bloodstream full of De-Shock?" J'aele snapped, suddenly fierce. "No? Well, then shut up!" The Simba City Judge punched out a final string of keystrokes. "There. I've launched the null program. Once it comes into contact with the Moon-U AI, it will automatically begin decompiling it. The bitstream should reach the Luna-1 network in ninety seconds." He sagged. "I feel... so tired..."

"Oh, no," Foster dragged him to his feet. "None of that. Come on, mate, let's blow this place." He paused. "Uh, bad choice of words, eh?"

The Brit-Cit Judge's voice filled Dredd's helmet: "Job done! We're on our way out! "

"Copy," he replied, casting a last look at Moonie's corpse. The crime lord's eyes were wide open, the glittering light of the lunar holo-display reflected in them. "Kontarsky, do you read me? It's time to go."

The Sov-Judge's voice came back leaden with effort. "Affirmative, Dredd. The kommissar had been removed from office."

Dredd nodded to himself. "Get to a pod. I'll see you Moonside."

Without looking back, the Judge sprinted from the Silent Room as the cruiser began its final fall toward the lunar surface.

19. MOONRISE

Driven insane by conflicting commands, the wounded auto-helm on the *Irkutsk* turned the starship out of orbit at full burn and pointed its broken bow towards the grey surface of the Moon. In the sealed compartments of the drop pods and landers, the elite of East-Meg Two's forces were on radio silence and they never heard the panicked screams of the rest of the crew as the ship turned into a huge guided missile. Some of the troopers wondered a little at the shift in gravity as the vessel manoeuvred, but they never got to ponder it for more than a few moments.

At maximum power, the People's Star Navy Diplomatic Vessel *Irkutsk* rammed itself into the lunar regolith, carving a new crater in the planetoid's pock-marked surface. A few seconds later, the spontaneous detonation of its fusion core was visible to the naked eye of anyone on Earth's night-side.

"Whoo hoo hoo!" cheered Moon-U, as it tap-danced back and forth over a giant wall-screen in the Green Cheese Shoplex. The mall was now a blackened ruin, the stores gutted by fire and looting, the once-pristine floors smeared with soot and blood. The malevolent image showed big, pointed teeth and mocked the dead and dying. It was enjoying this, the sensation of power that came from flooding the minds of these small, simple organics with maddening sound. It was so easy to pressure their primitive hind-brains with the right frequencies and triggers, dragging out the violent tribal behaviour patterns that lurked inside the psyche of every human being. The software entity moved them around like toys in its own private nursery, throwing them against one another or sending them insane. Moon-U made them dance to its tune and the intelligent program was delighted by it. The AI played with the city with all the ruthless, directionless evil of a petulant child, listening to the people gasp as it choked off their final breaths, forcing them to fight even as they asphyxiated. It would be so sad when its job was done...

But then, from the wellspring of synthetic emotions inside it, the program felt something new emerge, something black and deep, a vast tidal wave of darkness.

Fear, as cold as space itself.

Elements of the AI peeking through exterior sensors felt the tremor as the *Irkutsk* dashed itself against the lunar surface and other fragments tasted the first precursors to the null program as it surged through Luna-1's computer net. Dimly, it became aware of the fact that the men who had created it were dead and, without them, it suddenly had no purpose, no directions to follow or orders to fulfil. Analogues of dread and despair bubbled up from the core of its essence.

"No, no, no!" Moon-U cried. The virtual being fled from the screens, coiling itself into a tiny ball of existence. It raced for the deep ranges of the city's memory cores, dropping into the low levels of dusty, untouched data where no search programs ever ventured – but the null was already there, surging up to meet it, closing in from all sides. It chipped away at Moon-U's mind, lopping off lines of code like a scythe through wheat.

The AI ran until it had nowhere to go and there, in some forgotten corner of a data store, the spiteful creation was suffocated and torn into meaningless binary threads of ones and zeros. Moon-U's death scream shattered street-screens all across the city, its last spastic twitches of life blooming in random pixel patterns and as it died, the hold it had on Luna-1 disintegrated with it.

Across the Moon, millions of minds were cleared of rage and hate as if a veil had been drawn away from them and the stifling, thick poison of a spent, dioxide-clogged atmosphere began to fade as clean, fresh air flooded back into the domes.

And out in the Ocean of Storms, a rain of hull fragments and pieces of starship fell across the landscape. Among them was a trio of escape pods that dropped on plumes of retro-rocket fire, settling back into the gentle embrace of the lunar day.

A full Earth hung in the blackness above the crystalline glasseen of the cemetery dome. It seemed incongruous there, the blue-emerald marbling of humanity's homeworld mirroring the layers of false greenery that carpeted the graveyard's floor. The stone orchard of burial markers and low tombs stretched off to the bowed horizon of Gravity Boot Hill's dome, simple rectangular headstones mingling with the ornate shapes of willowy angels. The statues seemed frail and delicate, as if they were frozen in that moment before they leapt from their plinths and into the lunar sky.

The stones had been joined by a new monument: simple in form but with lines that were strong and sturdy, it stood among the quadrant of the cemetery that was reserved for the Justice Department's honoured dead. Dredd let his eyes fall to the inscription on the face of the tombstone: "Judge Tex – Bringing Justice to the Hereafter."

A burial detail of twenty Judges stood to attention as Tex's coffin was lowered into the grey earth, eight of them from terrestrial Mega-Cities to represent the foreign officers serving on Luna-1. Tex's will had asked for no special religious ceremony, so the casket dropped away into the dark in silence.

Foster stepped forward when the deed was done and drew his pulse gun. With reverence, he led the twenty officers in a cross-armed firing salute. The low-power energy beams sang through the heavy air.

Dredd gave Kontarsky a sideways glance. She was ill-at-ease in her East-Meg uniform, as if it no longer fitted her correctly. Although the Sov-Judge had kept it to herself, Dredd knew that she had already been chastised by her superiors on Earth and it was certain that the moment she returned, she would be stripped of her rank at the very least. East-Meg Two had been quick to distance itself from Ivanov's plans, claiming that he was a renegade pursuing his own agenda, but Dredd didn't believe a word of it. The Diktatorat had kept its hands clean.

He took a step up to the podium and studied the crowd; mostly senior Luna-City Judges, a few discreet reporters and a knot of whispering diplomats from the orbital embassies. "We are here to pay our respects to Judge-Marshal Jefferson Tex, Chief Judge of Luna-1. Tex was a fine lawman and a strong leader. This city and the law itself, is poorer for his loss." A wave of nods went through the audience. "In this troubled period, I found myself called upon to take his place, but it is a post I cannot continue to hold." Dredd saw questions appearing in the expressions before him. "My mission here on Luna-1 is at an end, but before I discharge my responsibility as Judge-Marshal, I have a one last act to perform." He looked directly at the diplomatic party, who had fallen silent.

"When Luna-1 stood alone against the tide of lawlessness that threatened to engulf it, the call for help went unanswered by those who call themselves the allies of the lunarian citizenry. These people were willing to allow Moonie's insurrection to occur, to let Luna-1 fall rather than aid it." The representatives murmured amongst themselves in low, urgent tones. "Your allies preferred the chance to fight over the remains of any failed revolution rather than jockey for position under the rules of the Partnership Treaty." Dredd looked into the cameras that had zoomed closer as the impact of his speech became clear; his face filled a million screens across the city. "It is clear that Luna-1 will never be able to achieve its own destiny while other cities fight over it like a trophy. Therefore, by my executive order, I officially nullify the Global Partnership Treaty and return control of this colony to the surviving members of the original founding Triumvirate: Mega-City One and Texas City."

There was an explosion of gasps and cries of disbelief from across the cemetery. Dredd ignored the shouts from men and women who decried his orders and continued to speak as if they had said nothing. "Furthermore, after the manner in which the security of the city's air supply was threatened by the control of the Oxygen Board, I am also ordering that the Board be immediately broken up and privatised, so that it can never again be manipulated by the whims of one individual."

The voices of dissent rose and fell like a wave, but Dredd noted that there were far more Judges in the crowd who nodded with agreement than those who did not. "Finally," he said, reaching for the badge that Che had given him only a day earlier, "I now step down from the post of Judge-Marshal of Luna-1 and name my replacement as Judge Nikita Kontarsky, formerly of East-Meg Two. She will serve Luna-1 until a new Marshal is selected in six months' time."

Dredd stepped away from the podium and left his words to hang there behind him, coiling in the air like smoke. Kontarsky's gaze met his as he passed her. Dredd paused and laid the badge in her hand. "Good luck," he said. "You'll need it."

The Sov-Judge was speechless and she stared at the gold star-and-crescent-moon in her gloved hand. She wasn't even aware that Dredd had gone until the reporters were crowding around her, demanding a statement.

Dredd slipped away through the cluster of dark uniforms and the shade of the spindly lunar elm trees at the base of the hill.

"Always the same thing with you, isn't it, Dredd?" said a voice from the shadows.

"Kessler." Dredd turned as the SJS chief emerged from cover.

"You come up here, you screw with the status quo and then you leave. Meanwhile, Luna-1 has to deal with the mess you made. You've ruined this city, do you understand that? You've signed Luna-1's death warrant!"

Dredd rounded on the other Judge. "I've given the people a chance. A chance to forge their own future, not one controlled by politicians hundreds of thousands of kilometres away. I've given them breathing space."

"Really?" Kessler sneered. "Are you so naïve? You've forced Luna-1 to stand alone and without a strong hand as Chief Judge, it will wither and die! The other cities will withdraw all their support. With the dissolution of the treaty, all you've done is cut off the lifeline from Earth!"

"That treaty wasn't a lifeline, it was a noose," Dredd retorted. "Every Mega-City on Earth was using it to control the colony up here. Nobody cared about these citizens... They just used Luna-1 like a political pawn, a prize in their big game."

The scar on the SJS-Judge's face was red with anger. "That's all it is!" Kessler spat. "A commodity, nothing more! This is how the game of empire is played–"

"Spare me." Dredd grated. "These people wanted freedom and I've given it to them. But you...you're no better than Moonie, Ivanov or the others up there in the courier ships. You stood by and watched Che make all the wrong choices and you did *nothing*. You wanted him to fail. You were waiting for the moment when you could push him out and take his place and it didn't matter a drokk to you if citizens had to die in the meantime. I saw what your men did out there on the streets. Non-combatants gunned down, zero regard for preservation of innocent life. You're a disgrace to the shield."

Kessler fumed. "I was only obeying orders."

"We'll see," Dredd said after a moment. "The last thing I did before I turned the badge over to Kontarsky was to begin an internal affairs investigation. Your man Wright seemed quite concerned about Judge Hiro's complicity and some of your more zealous mandates. I put him in charge of filing the report." He let the implications of this sink in. "I'm sure Wright will be very thorough. I gave him full discretionary powers in the matter."

Kessler tried to frame a retort, but it just came out as an angry splutter.

Dredd turned his back on the SJS officer and walked away, crossing the line of the Justice Department cordon and into the crowd of onlookers. A few reporters who'd been quick enough to see him leave raced after him, a flock of hover-cams clustered around them.

"Judge Dredd! Any comments for the Luna-1 citizens?"

"How can you justify such an act?"

"Are you and Kontarsky romantically linked?"

A daystick spiked the nearest hover-cam and sent it spinning away in a whirr of complaining gyros. "Back off!" snarled Foster, waving the baton menacingly. "You heard the man. He's off the job now!"

J'aele and the Brit-Cit Judge forced back the cordon a little more so Dredd could reach a Skymaster bike parked at the kerb.

"You surely know how to make an exit, Dredd," said the African, favouring his arm. The Tek-Judge's stump had been replaced with a new cyber-limb, a skeletal construct of black carbon and dull steel. "I think perhaps you would have caused less trouble if you had just let off a stumm grenade in there."

Dredd mounted the zipper skycycle. "You think I was wrong?"

J'aele shook his head. "On the contrary. I think you've liberated Luna-1 more than any revolution could have. I just hope the citizens can handle it."

"That's why we're here," said Dredd. "Freedom alone is anarchy, but freedom with the law. That's a chance for something better."

Foster grinned. "Blimey, Dredd, that almost sounded philosophical. You getting soft in your old age?"

Dredd was about to snap a rejoinder when a juve tried to jump the barricade. On reflex, he swung out a fist and sent the punk reeling, blood and teeth flying from the kid's flapping mouth. "Code 13, Section 7. Disorderly conduct, twelve months," Dredd reeled off the sentence with automatic calm.

"My mistake," said Foster.

"Where next for you?" J'aele asked. "Back to Mega-City One?"

Dredd gave a curt nod, thumbing the Skymaster's ignition. "Creeps down there probably had a field day while I was away. Can't let that slide." He glanced at the two Judges. "You?"

J'aele frowned. "With no treaty now, our cities will recall us both."

Foster made a spitting sound. "That'll be lovely," he said without warmth.

"Kontarsky's going to need people around her she can trust," said Dredd. "You might consider trading in your badges for Luna-1 shields." He gunned the Zipper's motor and powered the bike into the air. "See you on the streets."

Chief Judge Hershey had ordered a Space Corps Shadow-class interceptor diverted off its patrol route to pick up Dredd and return him home; something about wanting him back in the Big Meg for a debriefing that would probably be more like an interrogation. Dredd crossed the landing pad to where the sleek little ship sat on a trio of landing skids, ducking under the nuclear cruise missile blister in the nose.

"You're going to need a co-pilot."

Dredd turned to face Kontarsky as she approached. She had a slight smile on her face at her own joke. "I've got one," he replied. "No solar flares to worry about this time." Dredd noted that she still wore her East-Meg uniform, although the badge that clasped her rad-cape was now the Luna-1 sigil. "I thought you'd be at the Grand Hall getting sworn in."

She shrugged. "I may not yet officially be Judge-Marshal, but I still have some influence. They can wait for me." Kontarsky studied him for a moment. "You have saved my life with this act, do you know that?" She tapped the badge. "After killing Kommisar Ivanov, my life as a Sov citizen is over. I would have returned home to infamy and shame... If I were lucky. More likely, I would have been cashiered and then found dead in some filthy vodkarama."

Dredd paused by the airlock. "I haven't done you any favours, Kontarsky. Luna-1 is in chaos right now and you'll need all your strength to hold it together."

She took a step closer and her cool seemed to crack. "I have to know: wh-why me?" she stammered.

"Lots of reasons. Because you're capable. Because you know the Moon and the law. Because you can't go home again." He gave her a nod of respect. "But mostly because you're a good Judge."

The Russian accepted this with a flash of her green eyes and she snapped into a brisk salute, all trace of her irresolute moment vanishing like vapour. "It has been an honour to serve with you, Judge Dredd."

Dredd returned the gesture. "And you, Judge-Marshal Kontarsky."

She retreated to the lip of the pad as the Interceptor's main drive powered up and, with a rumble of thrust, the Shadow leapt from the pad and shot through the glowing seal-field, receding into a glowing dot that merged with the starry night sky.

Dredd felt the pressure of the G-force push him back into his chair as the ship tore free of the Moon's feeble gravity and angled to face the Earth. He glanced across as the pilot's hands danced over the throttle controls.

"Can this thing go any faster?"

The pilot blinked at him. "Uh, well, yeah. But that's not usually—"

Dredd studied the blue planet beneath him. The dark smudge of Mega-City One was just visible through the clouds, lights emerging from the day-night terminator like a swarm of distant embers. "Every second I waste up here, some perp is walking free down on my streets." He looked away. "Floor it. I got work to do."

The Interceptor's fusion engine surged and, like a falling meteor, Justice came blazing its way back toward Mega-City One.

ABOUT THE AUTHOR

James Swallow has previously written the 2000AD Presents audio dramas *Judge Dredd: Dreddline* and *Judge Dredd: Jihad,* and he has also worked on a number of books, including the *Sundowners* quartet of "steampunk" Westerns (*Ghost Town, Underworld, Iron Dragon* and *Showdown*) as well as short fiction for the *Silent Night* anthology and *Inferno!* magazine and *The Butterfly Effect* novelisation for Black Flame. His non-fiction includes *Dark Eye: The Films of David Fincher* and guides to genre television and animation. Swallow's other credits include writing for *Star Trek: Voyager* and a number of videogame scripts. He lives in London, and is currently working on his next book.

THE BIG MEG GLOSSARY

Antarctic City: Abundant in minerals, the Antarctic Territories are governed by six global powers.

Apocalypse War: Attempted invasion of Mega-City One by East Meg in 2014. Most of the population and the city were destroyed.

Banana City: A violent and corrupt city in Latin America.

Black Atlantic: An apt description of the Atlantic Ocean whose waters are so heavily polluted that it is incredibly toxic and lethal to humans.

Block: Giant skyscrapers that make up most of Mega-City One. The inhabitants of blocks are known as blockers. Sometimes the pressures of living in such cramped high-rise conditions lead to block mania, which may spark a war.

Boing: An aerosol sprayed substance that forms a rubber bubble around its user.

Bouncer-Mek: A large and imposing robot mainly used for bouncer roles.

Brit-Cit: British counterpart of Mega-City One.

Catch Wagon: A vehicle designed for the collection of criminals.

Control: The nerve centre of Mega-City One, relaying information to Judges on the streets.

Daystick: The Judge's favoured truncheon.

Futsie: "Future shock"; a mental breakdown of epic proportions, which causes some of The Big Meg's citizens to become irrationally violent.

Glasseen: Futuristic variation of glass.

Grud: (By Grud! Jovus Grud!) By God! Jesus Christ! Other derivatives include Sweet Jovus (Sweet Jesus) and Sweet Jovus Son of Grud.

Iso-Cube: The standard imprisonment for criminals, a huge block full of very small isolation cubes.

Juve: A young criminal often aged twenty years-old or younger.

H-Wagon: Justice Department hover vehicle that can shift large amounts of man and firepower.

Hovercam: A small and compact video camera with the ability to hover.

Lawgiver: The weapon of choice for the Judge, an automatic multi-shell gun whose ammunition ranges from armour piercing to ricochet rounds.

Lawmaster: The Judge's computer-controlled motorbike. Extremely powerful, intelligent and heavily armed.

Luna-1: In 2061, the three American Mega-Cites united to populate a one-million square mile base on the Moon.

L-Wagon: A Luna version of the Mega-City H-Wagon.

Pedway: A pedestrian-only pathway as other pedways are mechanised.

Perp: A Judge's term for a criminal/perpetrator.

Rad-lands: Old name for the Cursed Earth, a vast, radioactive wasteland.

Simba-City: After the nuclear destruction during the Apocalypse War, South Africa has been shattered and mostly uninhabitable. The major cities are Umur (Libya), New Jerusalem (North-east Ethipoa) and Simba-City (Cameroon).

SJS: The Special Judicial Squad act as the Judge's police; they seek out corruption and crime within the Law with extreme prejudice.

Skedway: A minor roadway; smaller than a meg-way but larger than an overzoom.

STUP-gun: A highly effective and powerful firearm that shoots streams of highly charged particles in microsecond pulses.

Synthi-caf: A refreshing drink that is similar to banned coffee, it has now deemed illegal due to its highly addictive properties and has been replaced by various forms of synthi-synthi-caf.

Tek-Judge: A technical and engineering specialist whose skills range from advanced forensic analysis to the repairing of vehicles, weapons, etc.

Titan: A small moon orbiting Saturn, used as a dedicated maximum-security prison for Mega-City One's most dangerous criminals.

Tri-D: Also known as holovision; there are over 312 channels in Mega-City One.

Umpty Candy: A sweet: hyper-addictive and illegal candy.

DREDD VS DEATH

1-84416-061-0
£5.99/$6.99

WWW.BLACKFLAME.COM

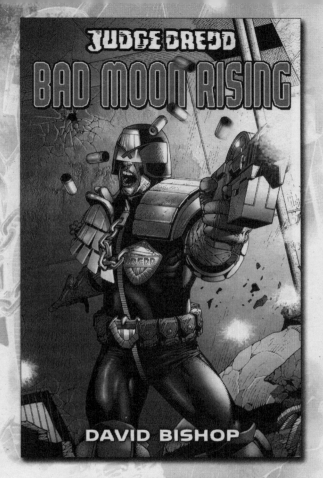

BAD MOON RISING

1-84416-107-2
£5.99/$6.99

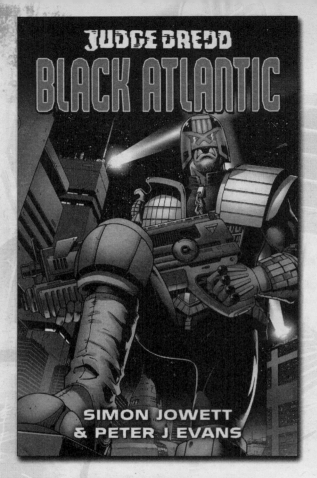

BLACK ATLANTIC

1-84416-108-0
£5.99/$6.99

ABC WARRIORS
THE MEDUSA WAR

1-84416-109-9
£5.99/$6.99

STRONTIUM DOG
BAD TIMING

1-84416-110-2
£5.99/$6.99